ONE ON ONE—TO THE DEATH

Mandalian tossed the lance aside as he stepped down from the roan, pulled the huge bowie knife from its scabbard, and advanced toward the Cree, who stood facing him with weapon in hand.

"Now we're down to a man's game," Mandalian said, closing warily on the Indian, his legs spread apart, while shifting the knife from hand to hand.

The Cree sank into a crouch and began circling Mandalian. *"Aiiieeeee!"* he screamed, lunging forward with a thrust of his knife . . .

EASY COMPANY

EASY COMPANY
AND THE BLOODY FLAG

JOHN WESLEY HOWARD

A JOVE BOOK

EASY COMPANY AND THE BLOODY FLAG

First Jove edition published January 1982

First printing

Printed in the United States of America

Jove books are published by Jove Publications, Inc.,
200 Madison Avenue, New York, NY 10016

Also in the EASY COMPANY series from Jove

EASY COMPANY AND THE SUICIDE BOYS
EASY COMPANY AND THE MEDICINE GUN
EASY COMPANY AND THE GREEN ARROWS
EASY COMPANY AND THE WHITE MAN'S PATH
EASY COMPANY AND THE LONGHORNS
EASY COMPANY AND THE BIG MEDICINE
EASY COMPANY IN THE BLACK HILLS
EASY COMPANY ON THE BITTER TRAIL
EASY COMPANY IN COLTER'S HELL
EASY COMPANY AND THE HEADLINE HUNTER
EASY COMPANY AND THE ENGINEERS

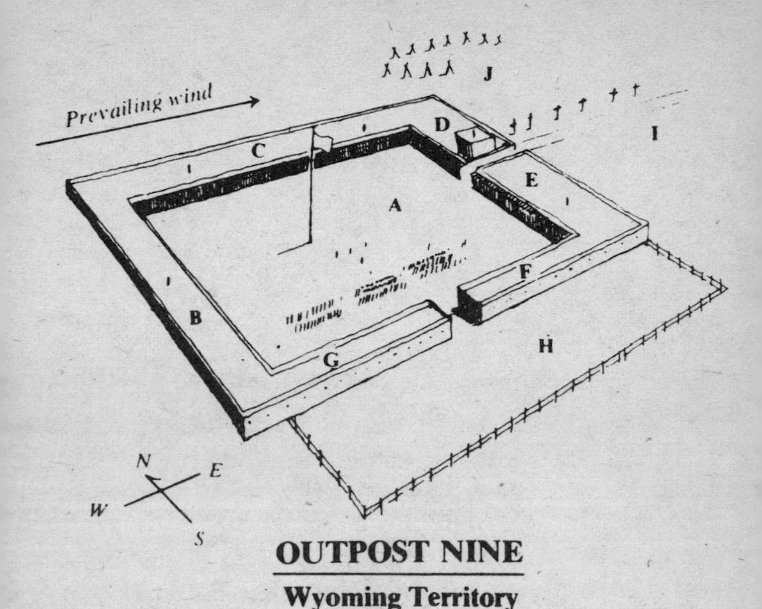

OUTPOST NINE

Wyoming Territory

KEY

A. Parade and flagstaff

B. Officers' quarters ("officers' country")

C. Enlisted men's quarters: barracks, day room, and mess

D. Kitchen, quartermaster supplies, ordnance shop, guardhouse

E. Suttler's store and other shops, tack room, and smithy

F. Stables

G. Quarters for dependents and guests; communal kitchen

H. Paddock

I. Road and telegraph line to regimental headquarters

J. Indian camp occupied by transient "friendlies"

OUTPOST NUMBER NINE

(DETAIL)

Outpost Number Nine is a typical High Plains military outpost of the days following the Battle of the Little Big Horn, and is the home of Easy Company. It is not a "fort"; an official fort is the headquarters of a regiment. However, it resembles a fort in its construction.

The birdseye view shows the general layout and orientation of Outpost Number Nine; features are explained in the Key.

The detail shows a cross-section through the outpost's double walls, which ingeniously combine the functions of fortification and shelter.

The walls are constructed of sod, dug from the prairie on which Outpost Number Nine stands, and are sturdy enough to withstand an assault by anything less than artillery. The roof is of log beams covered by planking, tarpaper, and a top layer of sod. It also provides a parapet from which the outpost's defenders can fire down on an attacking force.

one

There was a faint whisper of breeze filtering through the timber surrounding him, and the tall fir and spruce trees blocked out much of the sunlight, creating an atmosphere of late-afternoon darkness. Where the sun's rays did filter through, they splashed upon the forest floor and warmed the thick carpet of needles spread like a yellow blanket upon the ground. He could hear the distant gurgling sounds of a swiftly moving stream, and occasionally he caught the glint of sunlight on water when a branch far above shifted on the restless wind. Were it not for the mound of stones at his feet, he would have felt a sense of peace and tranquility known only to those completely at home in the forest.

Windy Mandalian had once run traplines in the stream just beyond the glen, and the man lying at his feet, beneath the pile of stones, had once been his partner. That was before the outbreak of the Indian Wars and Windy's call to service as an army scout. As he stood there in nature's silence, leaning against the trunk of a huge spruce, motionless with the exception of a chaw of cut-plug working slowly in his cheek, he could very well have passed as a member of one of the Indian tribes he had fought so long.

With his tall, wiry frame encased in fringed buckskin, and the rugged features of his face accented by the dominance of an aquiline nose, he appeared to be as much a creature of the forest as the white-tailed doe that was now timidly entering the glen from the downwind direction and leading her fawn to water. Nothing escaped Windy's perceptions, and his eyes shifted to the spotted fawn standing in a patch of sunlight, its long ears ever in motion and its shiny black nose twitching to search out some alien scent. Long, spindly legs were tensed for a bounding leap the instant a danger signal sounded in its brain. Then the doe moved forward once more, and the pair of deer walked silently toward the stream.

The grizzled scout smiled inwardly in response to their fruitless precautions, which was what they would have been, had he chosen differently. He was renowned for his deadly accuracy with the big Sharps now cradled in the crook of his left arm, and there was no questioning his skill with either the heavy revolver sagging from one hip or the broad-bladed bowie knife sheathed against the other. He shifted his weight, spat, and glanced down again at the final resting place of his old friend, and his mind went back to the afternoon when he had found Scotty Griffin. It was six years to the day since he had placed the last stone on the shallow grave, and this was his sixth pilgrimage to the burial site just north of Wyoming Territory and nearly twenty miles beyond the Canadian border.

He and Scotty had enjoyed a successful trapping season, and they would have left the following day, their packhorses loaded down with pelts of beaver, otter, and muskrat. While Windy had retrieved their traps from the north end of the stream, Scotty had worked the southern lines. But when Windy had returned to camp, a sense of uneasiness filled his mind. Griffin, an experienced trapper and woodsman, should have returned earlier, the result of having less ground to cover, but there were no indications that he had returned.

The fire rocks were cold, his bedroll was in place, the pelts lay stacked in preparation for loading onto packsaddles, and the lean-to had not been stripped of its protective boughs, a traditional practice. An hour after setting out on horseback, Windy found the reason why. Scotty Griffin lay dead with an arrow through his chest and another buried deeply into his thigh. Where his wiry, sandy-colored hair had been, there was nothing but a blood-red dome of exposed flesh, still wet and sticky to the touch. From the black-and-blue markings on the arrow shafts, Windy assumed Griffin's killers to be Cree Indians, but in the thick carpet of needles he could find no other markings to confirm his assumption.

The loud, squawking call of a blue jay landing on a limb high above his head brought Windy from his reverie. Leaning his rifle against the tree trunk, he stooped to replace some rocks that had tumbled from the mound during the previous winter. As he gently stacked the moss-covered stones, he thought again of Griffin's two children. A boy and a girl, now eight and six respectively, they were freckle-faced and sandy-haired, just as their father had been. Old Scotty would have been proud of them, Windy thought, replacing the final stone and noticing the depression in the ground where the grave had settled through the years. That subtle indication of time's passage, in combination with the evening shadows now gathering about him, caused Windy to rise quickly, pick up the Sharps, and stride away with steps equally as sure and silent as those of the doe and her fawn.

A sense of urgency had come over him, the sudden need to quit Canada, ride to the Clearwater Indian Agency in northern Wyoming, arrange for the sale of the hides, and have the money given to the guardian of Scotty's children, as he had in each of the past six years.

A short distance away, four horses glanced up from their grazing as the scout approached. Two were pack animals laden with hides dried and cured in the sun, and the third bore a burden of traps and chains, while the fourth—a magnificent, tall roan—had a worn but sturdy saddle upon its back. Windy swiftly pulled the picket stakes from the ground, tied the three pack animals in tandem, and then swung up onto the roan. He would pass one more night at the camp he and Scotty had used for so many years, and set out at dawn the following morning for home. That meant he would have to unpack the hides that night and reload them in the morning, but the cargo was too valuable to be left at the camp unguarded, this close to the end of the season. A full month's work had gone into the trapping, skinning, and tanning, and were the pelts to be lost, there would be no time to set the lines again.

With the Sharps again cradled in his arm, Windy's keen eyes searched the forest ahead of him as he guided his mount through the thick timber in the cool evening twilight. With cunning born of years in the wilderness, Windy had sensed three days earlier that he was being watched, and he had seen the imprint of moccasined feet along the riverbank near several of his traps. When he was nearly two hundred yards from his camp, he noticed the roan pricking its ears and glancing curiously off to the right. Instantly, Windy raised the rifle and swung the muzzle in that direction while peering intently into the gloom. Hearing a muffled grunt seconds later, he pulled the hammer back with his thumb and raised the weapon to his shoulder. After a short pause, a stoop-shouldered figure stepped out from behind a tree, his hands held harmlessly at his sides, and stood staring at Windy.

Windy watched the man over his rifle sight, his finger pressed tightly to the trigger and but a few ounces of pressure away from sending a bullet crashing into the other's chest.

"Who the hell are you?" he asked in a tone that showed no fear. There was something about the elderly Indian that he thought he recognized, but in the failing light he could make no positive identification.

"Have you forgotten your old friend?" came the soft reply in a slightly tremulous voice.

"Not if you *are* an old friend. I'm gonna ask you one more time—who the hell are you?"

"Swift Otter."

The scout searched his mind, and when the name finally registered, a slow smile spread across his face. "If that's really you, you should know my name. Tell me what it is before I lower this old tom-tom here."

"Some call you The Snake, but Swift Otter calls you Windy Mandalian. I have spoken."

"Well, I'll be damned!" Windy exclaimed, lowering the Sharps from his shoulder and easing the hammer forward while the smile became a grin. "Didn't 'spect I'd ever see you again. What the hell are you doing here?"

A finger went to the Indian's lips. "Speak softly, my friend. All who are about you do not come in friendship," he said, soundlessly advancing to lay a hand on the roan's withers and look up at Windy. "We will talk later, but now your life is in danger."

Again, instinct prevailed as Windy's head turned with a slow, searching motion. "At my camp?"

"Yes. They lie in wait."

"How many?"

The Indian held up three fingers.

Windy nodded. "How're they armed?"

"Rifles. Leave your horses here. I can take one with a war arrow. You can have the others."

Windy swung from the saddle, dropped the reins to the ground, and ducked beneath his mount's head to grip Swift Otter's bicep. "Thank you, old friend. Do you know their positions?"

"Yes. They are young, but they are not wise. One is by the big rock—I will kill him. The others are behind the fallen tree with the black hole."

Windy mentally judged the placement of the hollow log to the south of his camp, and the huge boulder to the east. "Good. I'll have farther to go than you. Wait until you hear my first shot before you shoot your arrow."

The old Indian nodded, trotted to the tree, picked up his bow and quiver, then vanished into the forest. A warm sensation spread through his chest as Windy watched the old warrior for several seconds before crouching and stealing away in the other direction with the Sharps held before him. The moon, a silver disk, had risen above the treetops, and he worked his way through the ghostly shadows of the darkened timber for nearly five minutes before dropping to his stomach and inching forward.

At first he could not see them, concealed as they were behind the log, then he saw a slight movement and his eyes focused on the nearest warrior, lying prone with his rifle aimed around the end of the log.

Knowing he would have been dead at that moment, had it not been for Swift Otter, Windy smiled slightly, and silently thanked his old friend. Then his face turned deadly serious and the rifle stock came up to his cheek.

"You fellers waitin' for somebody?" he asked in a voice just loud enough to be heard.

There was a startled rustling in the grass, and moonlight glinted off a rifle barrel being turned swiftly. The Sharps belched flame and the Indian flopped over backward in a violent twist. The second warrior, positioned at the other end of the log, fired at Windy's muzzle blast, but the scout had rolled away while jacking another shell into the chamber. A slug slammed into the ground where he had been seconds before, but the Sharps was at his shoulder again, and his second shot blasted into the orange-yellow burst of flame across from him. There was a sharp, gurgling scream, and Windy fired a third time, then waited while the forest absorbed the crashing explosions and silence settled once more over the camp site. Where before the night creatures had been calling, there was now a silent void.

Windy waited in the darkness, his rifle before him at the ready and prepared to fire at any movement or sound from the approximate position of the far end of the log. None came, and after nearly five minutes the scout cautiously rose and advanced. He glanced once at the first Indian, who was obviously dead, then moved forward to turn the second one over with the barrel of his rifle. The man's head had been nearly blown away, and there was a gaping hole in the side of his chest. Having heard no sound from the direction of the rock, Windy crouched behind the log and aimed his weapon toward the large gray object. After waiting nearly a minute, he heard the *caaahhhooo, caaahhhooo,* sound of a calling night owl, which he answered before rising again. He knew Swift Otter's victim had fallen as surely as had his own.

They met near the ring of fire rocks and gripped each other's forearms firmly. "You saved this old hide, Chief," Windy said earnestly. "Sure as hell you did. I'd be dead right now if it wasn't for you. Thanks."

"As would I, if it had not been for you and your friend seven summers ago."

"Has it been that long?"

Swift Otter nodded as their hands dropped away. "It has." His fingers went up and gingerly traced the four ragged scars running down his cheek and across his chest. "I was no match for the great one."

Windy vividly remembered seeing a lone Cree warrior fighting a grizzly bear, armed with nothing but a knife and courage. He and Scotty Griffin had stumbled upon them by accident; the grizzly had Swift Otter's leg clamped in its viselike jaws, and was shaking him violently, as all grizzlies do when they have their prey set up for the kill. Windy had shot the bear, and he and Griffin had taken the Cree chief to their camp and nursed him back to health.

"I'm glad we came along when we did, Swift Otter. That was a long time ago, and I haven't seen you since. How have you been?"

The Cree shrugged. "For an old one of my many seasons, I can ask no more."

"You're tough as an old wolverine, Chief, and always will be," Windy said with a chuckle. "How did you know I was here?"

Swift Otter nodded toward the log. "I heard them talking of counting coup on the greatest prize of all. I knew it had to be you."

"Well, I'm flattered, but I'd say they were more interested in my pelts."

"No. All of our people, as well as the Arapaho, Lakota, Crow, Blackfoot, and Cheyenne know of you. Those who would make war—and there are many among the young ones—believe that having your scalp hanging from their coup belts would bring them great medicine. They do not care that winning such a prize in this manner would make them more like old women. They would not tell the truth of their victory anyway."

"Then there were others with them?"

"No. Those three were cowards and do not deserve to be called Cree warriors. They will cause no more trouble for my people."

Windy dug out his plug of tobacco, sliced off two chunks with his bowie knife, and handed one to the Indian and nestled the other in his cheek before saying, "Then, in that case, let's build a small fire, make some coffee, and talk."

"It is good. I'll go get your horses and my pony."

"Thanks, Chief. I'll have some coffee ready when you get back."

When the coffee had boiled and each man held a steaming cup in his hands, while sitting crosslegged across from each other beside the small blaze, Windy studied the old chief carefully.

"How are things with your people, Swift Otter? Does the Grandmother in England treat you well?"

"She did, but she does not now."

"How do you mean?"

"There is much trouble in Canada. In the Shining Times we were allowed to do what we wanted to do, as long as we didn't get in the way of white people. Canada has much land, and we were always able to stay by ourselves. But now the young ones will bring the Grandmother's soldiers down on us."

"Why?"

"Because of the métis and the ignorance of the young."

"The métis?" Windy asked with a cocked eyebrow, while blowing the steam from his cup. "They're breeds, aren't they? Half French and half Plains Cree?"

Swift Otter nodded and sipped his coffee, and Windy went on, "I know a little bit about them. If my memory is correct, their leader is a feller named Louis Reil, and he fights under what he calls 'the bloody flag.' Supposed to be a big white cloth smeared with blood or some damned thing. As I understand it, he's supposed to be fighting to set up a separate province for the métis here in Canada."

"He is. And he has promised my people safety and citizenship in his new country if we fight by his side. I have told those of my people who will listen that he will fail and that we will be driven from our homeland. The young hear only what they want to hear, and they have chosen to fight on the side of this Louis Riel."

"Have there been any battles so far?"

Swift Otter nodded sadly. "Many. Small and meaningless, but there is a great one to come."

"When?"

"They tell me nothing of their plans. There is a Cree warrior who calls himself Chief Rides Big Horses, and he is the leader of those who do battle on the side of Riel. Rides Big Horses is no rightful chief, but he drinks firewater and fights like a mountain cat. He cares not for the future of our people, but only for the renown that his accomplishments bring him. He is a taker of women, a killer of children, and a disgrace to the Cree people. I know of no one more vicious and cunning."

Windy scratched the back of his head while saying, "Correct me if I'm wrong, but I thought Riel had run away from Canada. Some say he's hiding out in the United States."

Again, Swift Otter nodded. "He is. The métis chief who will lead them into battle is called Johnny Singletree."

"Johnny Singletree? Never heard of him."

"I know little of him, except that he is faithful to Riel and will fight to the death for the métis cause."

"What happens if this Johnny Singletree and Rides Big Horses aren't successful in winning against the Grandmother's soldiers?"

Swift Otter's gaze held on his cup momentarily, then drifted up to Windy's face. "Then we will have two choices: to be killed, or to leave our homeland."

"And there's nothing that can be done? I'd stay and help if I could, but I've got to get back to the outpost. I told the Blue Sleeve captain I wouldn't be gone more than a month, and I'll barely be able to make that now."

"Thank you, my friend," Swift Otter said with a weak smile. "But there is nothing you could do, even if you could stay.

We can only hope for the best. And now I must go," the Cree said, placing his cup aside and rising with some difficulty, favoring the leg that had been broken in the grizzly's mouth.

Windy stood as well, and they clasped forearms once more across the fire. "Thank you for what you did here tonight, Swift Otter. I'll never forget it."

"It would be best if you did, my friend. We are even now, and who knows what lies beyond the lowering of the moon?"

"Nothing between you and me, that's for damned sure," Windy replied, shrugging off the old Indian's concern while digging an extra plug of tobacco from his saddlebag. "Here, take this with you. I'd offer more, but that's the last of it."

There was a guarded tenderness in Swift Otter's eyes as he accepted the plug. Windy knew that the receiving of gifts was a violation of Swift Otter's training as a Cree warrior.

"You are generous."

"Naw. That shit's so old it dries your mouth out trying to work up a spit."

Swift Otter nodded and turned toward his pony before stopping and turning back. "What has happened to your friend?"

"You mean my partner, Scotty Griffin?" Windy asked. "He's dead. Killed just over there, six years ago."

"Do you know who did this?"

"No. There were two war arrows in him when I found him. Looked like Cree arrows to me, but I can't rightly say your people did it."

Swift Otter watched the scout in silence momentarily, as if making up his mind before saying, "I can."

Windy's eyelids narrowed and his body tensed slightly "You can? How and who, if you can tell me?"

"It might be best if I don't."

"Knowin' who done it means a lot to me, Swift Otter. More'n you could ever realize."

"I know that, and I will tell you," the elderly Cree said while nodding toward Windy's Sharps, leaning against his saddle. "Your friend, the one with the curly hair?"

"Yes?"

"Did he have a rifle like that?"

"Yes he did, and there weren't too many of them around at that time."

"Was he scalped?"

"Yes he was," Windy replied firmly. "What about it?"

"There was a young Cree warrior who returned to our camp six seasons ago. He was boastful and proud. He had a fresh scalp hanging from his coup belt and a rifle in his hand exactly like that one."

Windy caught his breath. "Was the hair on the scalp kind of kinky-like and sandy-colored?"

"It was. I knew it was the scalp of your friend when I saw it."

"Tell me the warrior's name and where he is. I'll go after him right now. Those pelts over there"—he gestured impatiently—"and the army be damned."

Swift Otter shook his head. "Where he is, I do not know."

"Why?"

"Because he has gone to do battle at the side of the métis."

"Then what's his name?" Windy asked through gritted teeth. "I'll catch up with him sooner or later."

"I'm sure you will," Swift Otter said with a tired smile. "His name is Rides Big Horses."

With those words, Swift Otter turned away, swung up onto his pony's back and vanished from the ring of firelight. Windy Mandalian stared into the darkness for long minutes before sinking slowly to the ground and leaning against his saddle. Deep into the night his eyes were locked on the lowering coals, while his hands absently worked a stone across the blade of his bowie knife.

two

Referred to as a "soddy" because of the earth-and-cut-lumber construction of its walls, Outpost Number Nine was located on the High Plains of Wyoming to protect the vital communications link known as the South Pass over the Rocky Mountains. Isolated as it was, it appeared to be the only vestige of the white man's presence on the vast, rolling plains. And bathed now in the golden hue of a setting sun, the outpost's rectangular sod walls made it resemble a single bronze brick on a sea of green grass.

The haunting notes of a bugle call, blown with the lowering of the flag on its pole at the center of the outpost's parade, had barely melted into the prairie silence while uniformed soldiers retreated across the parade to the sanctuary of their barracks. Guards atop the surrounding walls walked their posts, shielding their eyes from the setting sun and squinting toward the open land, always watchful for any sign of hostile presence.

Two officers, each wearing dark blue uniforms accented by light blue piping, walked side by side toward the orderly room to share a brandy and conversation at the close of another day. The soldier on the right was the commanding officer of Outpost Number Nine. Captain Warner Conway was a distinguished-looking man in his mid-forties and graying slightly at the temples. He was old enough to have served in the late War Between the States, in which conflict he had held the rank of lieutenant colonel, only to be reduced in rank, like hundreds of other officers, at the end of the war; he had been overdue for promotion now for quite some time, but there was no visible indication of bitterness about him.

His companion was his executive officer, First Lieutenant Matt Kincaid, who somewhat resembled the captain at a younger age. A graduate of West Point, Class of '69, Kincaid had, to his occasional regret, missed the Civil War, but was now serving his second tour of duty on the frontier, having earlier been commended for bravery in the campaign against the Cheyenne. He was the sort of man who seemed born to wear a uniform, and this, combined with his ruggedly handsome features, turned the heads of many of the local women when he traveled now and then into the nearest town, a half-day's ride from the outpost.

The orderly room was empty when they passed through, and after pouring brandy for the two of them and taking a cigar for himself from the humidor that stood on his desk, the captain sank back in his swivel chair and studied the junior officer who sat across the desk from him.

"You seem rather troubled, Matt. Got something on your mind?"

Kincaid smiled as he brought the brandy glass to his lips. "Nothing much, sir."

"Come on, spill it," Conway said, striking a match and touching it to the tip of his cigar. "With the exception of Windy, the only person either of us has to confide in is in this room right now. If you've got something on your mind, I'd like to hear it."

"Well, you hit it right on the head, Captain."

"I did? Do you mean when I mentioned Windy?"

"Yes, that's it," Kincaid replied, twirling his brandy and regarding the oily smoothness of the amber liquid where it clung to the side of the glass. "He's supposed to have been back today."

"Yes, I know. But as each of us is well aware, if any man can take care of himself, that man is Windy Mandalian." Conway studied his cigar for a moment before speaking again. "To tell you the truth, it strikes me as being a little strange that a man would spend his entire year's leave, one full month, up in Canada trapping, instead of roaring off to civilization and raising hell."

"That's the way he is, Captain. And as they say, one man's pudding is another man's poison. Although he's never said anything about it to me, I think those trapping expeditions are as much a self-imposed obligation as a quest for pleasure."

Conway nodded and retrieved his brandy glass from the desktop. "Trapping was his life before he came to the army, Matt. He's the best damned scout either of us has ever seen, and if getting back to the woods by himself is what he wants, that's fine with me."

"Me too, Captain. But he seems to be caught up in some strange obsession. A commitment so deep that he can neither talk about it nor turn his back to it. That's why I'm a little concerned when he's late getting back."

"So am I, but worrying doesn't change things. Tell you what, I'll bet you a dollar he'll come riding through those front gates before ten o'clock tomorrow morning."

"Thanks, Captain, but no thanks. But I will give you a counter-offer."

"What's that?"

"I'll bet you that same dollar that the sun rises in the east tomorrow morning."

Conway laughed and dusted an ash from his cigar. "You're a real sporting man, Matt. A long-shot gambler." Then his face sobered as he leaned back in his chair once more. "What's the latest on Corporal Peterson?"

"Not good, Captain. That temper of his is going to get him either killed or drummed out of the service."

"That's a damned shame," Conway replied, pursing his lips in thought. "He's a valuable man."

"That he is. As you know, he's one of the best squad leaders we've got, and he's certainly proven himself in battle."

"What seems to be his problem?"

Kincaid finished his brandy and leaned forward to place the glass on the captain's desk. "I'm not sure. He's a very high-strung person, I know that much. He treats the men of his squad well. He's neither overly strict with them nor lacking in discipline. But when he goes over to the sutler's and gets drunk on beer as he did last night, he gets moody, then violent. He didn't tear anything up last night, but he sure as hell would have, if a couple of men from his squad hadn't escorted him back to his quarters."

"Why not put old Pop's place off limits to him?"

"I have, but I'm positive it's not the solution. I talked with Private Slater last night, one of the men who took him back to quarters and he said that Peterson is an extremely jealous man. Every time he gets drunk he accuses everyone, even his best friends, of having an affair with his wife, or at least secretly wanting to."

Conway nodded, drew on his cigar, and studied the matter momentarily. "There's no doubt that Mrs. Peterson's a pretty young lady, and quite shapely, I might add. A lot of these enlisted men get lonely, and they don't have a hell of a lot of exposure to attractive women. I wouldn't be surprised if they do sneak a glance or two at her now and then, and maybe even secretly wish they were in Peterson's place. However, that doesn't mean any of them have overtly attempted to approach her or openly solicited an affair."

"I agree. A man's got to expect that, if he brings his wife to an isolated outpost like this one." Kincaid paused before adding, "How do you handle it, sir, if you don't mind my asking? Flora is an incredibly attractive woman."

"Not at all, Matt, not at all," Conway replied with a smile as he reached for the brandy bottle. "How about another short one?"

"Thanks. Sounds good."

"Have you ever heard the old saying, 'If you want to be happy, make an ugly woman your wife'?"

Kincaid watched the captain pour his glass half-full, add a touch to his own, then replace the cork with a slap of his palm. "Might be a good plan, sir, but it's not a rule I'd want to live by."

"Nor would I," Conway said with an agreeing chuckle. "What's the point in owning a beautiful thoroughbred if you don't want anyone to admire it? Anyway, to answer your question, I don't have any problems to 'handle,' as you put it, when it comes to Flora. I married her because I love her and the fact that she's an attractive lady is just one more added benefit. But, first and foremost, she *is* a lady, and she deports herself *like* a lady. In so doing, any man who might admire her knows damned well he hasn't got an icicle's chance in hell of getting anywhere with her. Beyond that, the basic element of love is trust, and since I love her completely, I also trust her completely. To tell you the truth, I would be more surprised if she weren't the object of admiration than angered by the fact that she is."

Kincaid grinned. "A good philosophy, Captain. Beats the hell out of that ugly-woman theory. Maybe Peterson—"

Kincaid was interrupted by a gentle knocking on the door and a softly spoken query: "Warren? May I talk to you for a moment?"

Recognizing Flora's voice, both officers stood while Conway replied, "Come on in, my dear."

Flora stepped inside, closed the door, and said, "I'm sorry to—" Then, as she saw Kincaid, a warm smile replaced the troubled look on her face and she said, "Oh! Good evening, Matt. I didn't know you were here." She glanced at her husband. "I'm sorry, dear, I didn't know you were busy. I'll talk to you later."

"It's all right, Flora," Conway said, rounding the desk and guiding her to a chair. "Here, have a seat. Matt and I were just discussing the philosophical aspects of marriage."

As Flora sat, she looked at Kincaid with a sly twinkle in her eye. "Do you mean to tell me that our most eligible bachelor is about to give in?"

"Good evening, Mrs. Conway," Kincaid said with a warm smile, while sitting again. "No, I'm afraid not. Not for the moment, anyway. We were concerning ourselves with a present marriage that doesn't seem to be going all that well."

"Oh? Whose would that be? Not mine, I hope."

"No, definitely not yours," Kincaid replied as his eyes took in the beautiful woman across from him.

In her late thirties, Flora Conway was the picture of elegance and charm. Even the long years of following her husband from assignment to assignment had not diminished her natural beauty. Her figure, full-busted and obviously firm, was slim, yet curvacious enough to be the envy of a woman ten years her junior. A train of long black hair hung over her left shoulder, and when she smiled, sparkling white, even teeth flashed in her tanned face.

But Flora was not smiling now as she asked, "Then whose marriage?"

"The Petersons'," Conway said, seated behind his desk once again and taking up his cigar from the tray.

"Strange," Flora replied with a confused look. "The Petersons are the reason I'm here."

"Good, then we can all gossip together," Conway said with a grin.

"I wish it were gossip, Warren, but I'm afraid we might be dealing with the truth. I was told by one of the ladies living next door to the Petersons, as a matter of concern, not gossip," she added quickly, "that they had a terrible argument last night. According to Molly, it wasn't the first and isn't likely to be the last."

"I'm not surprised," Conway said. "As I understand it, Peterson was pretty drunk last night. While we can restrict him from the sutler's, we can hardly tell him not to have an occasional argument with his wife. Seems like it goes with the overall scheme of things."

Flora studied her husband in silence for several seconds before saying in a hushed voice, "Would you be that blasé about it if you knew he had beaten her quite severely?"

"What?" Conway asked, leaning forward with a start. "Do you know that to be a fact?"

"Not exactly, but I do know she has a black eye and a bruised cheek. Today was the day she and I were to roll bandages in her quarters. When I knocked on the door, she opened it just a crack and told me she was sick and asked that I come back tomorrow. Of course I agreed, but the door was open wide enough so there could be no mistaking what I saw."

"Did she mention how it happened?"

"Yes. She knew that I'd seen her face and she mentioned something about having tripped and fallen, and hit her head against the doorjamb. She wasn't very convincing, to say the least."

Conway and Kincaid looked at each other, and the expression on Matt's face was a mixture of surprise and disgust. "If he actually did beat her, Captain, we've got a bigger problem on our hands than we thought."

"Yes, I'm aware of that," Conway replied. "There are many habits I deplore, but wife-beating tops the list. You keep an eye on Peterson, Matt. Keep him sober and let's see what happens. Even though it's no excuse, it could have been the drinking that brought it on. Flora? The next time you have a chance to talk to Mrs. Peterson, try to draw her out a little bit, and maybe we can find out what the problem is. Be tactful, though, because—"

"Dear heart, you might be the finest commanding officer in the entire army," Flora said sweetly, "but I would suggest that I might know a little bit more about tact when speaking with other women about marital problems than you do."

Conway threw his hands up in mock defense. "All right, all right! I wash my hands of it. If I'd wanted to talk to women about their problems, I would have been a preacher in the first place." Then he glanced at Kincaid with a grin. "See how quickly they turn on you, Matt? There's a bit of vixen in every one of them."

Kincaid laughed, stood, and reached for his hat. "Good night, Mrs. Conway, Captain. I think I'll get out of here before the counselors become the counseled. I'd hate to have to call the Petersons in here to settle a dispute between you two."

"Flora generally wins, Matt, but I sneak in one now and then. Don't forget about tomorrow."

"Tomorrow, sir?"

"Yes. That's when . . . let me see . . ." Conway paused to refresh his memory from a stack of papers on his desk. "Yes, here it is—that's when Colonel Higgins and his aide, Major Delaney, are supposed to show up here."

"You mean the ones from Regiment? I knew a pair of senior officers were coming out here, but I didn't know their names."

"Those are their names. Apparently the colonel has requested reassignment from his desk job in Washington to command a regiment in the field. For purposes of 'reorientation,' as he calls it, he asked to be attached on temporary-duty status with Easy Company, since we seem to see the most action around here."

"There's not much room for argument there, sir. Do you happen to know this Colonel Higgins's combat record?"

Again, Conway searched the document. "Doesn't say. But I'll bet you that same dollar he's as green as they come."

"And again, thanks but no thanks." Kincaid grinned. "But am I still open on sunrise tomorrow?" he said enticingly.

"You are dismissed, Lieutenant," Conway said sternly. "Take thy dollar and go."

"To quote one of our venerable Founding Fathers and up the ante by a hundred, sir, 'a dollar saved is a dollar earned.'" Kincaid turned with his hand on the door latch. "I'll check the guard mount on the way to my quarters."

"Do that. And have a peek into Pop's place. If Flora's right, I'm more concerned about Peterson's wife's safety than about his disobeying a direct order."

"I don't think he will be, sir, but I'll check anyway. But Private Malone? That's another story."

"And another problem," Conway said with a weary shake of his head. "Thanks, Matt."

It was nearly nightfall when Windy Mandalian reined in his mount and stepped down to relieve himself. He knew he was no more than a quarter of a mile from Ira Griffin's agency buildings on the Clearwater Reservation, and there he planned to camp for the night. Even though he was already one day behind schedule for his projected return to Outpost Number Nine, he wanted to rest the three weary packhorses lined out behind him with their heads drooping. The take of pelts had been greater than Windy could have hoped for, and the heavily laden horses were badly in need of rest. Besides, Windy liked Griffin and his family, and he looked forward to a drink of whiskey with Ira, perhaps a home-cooked meal prepared by Beth, and sharing a tall tale or two with the six children. Such an evening had become an annual event over the course of the past six years, and one that the grizzled scout looked forward to.

As he led the pack string across the worn earth before the buildings, Windy saw the youngest boy, Tommy, cease winding the crank on the well, stare in disbelief, then run toward the house with one suspender on his overalls flapping behind him.

"Daddy! Daddy! Mr. Mandalian's comin'! Mr. Mandalian's comin'!"

Windy smiled at the shrill excitement in the eight-year-old boy's voice, and remembered the wooden horse he had carved for the youngster during those long nights in Canada, and which was now tucked away in his saddlebags. By the time Windy stepped down in front of the house, the entire family was gathered on the front porch and Ira Griffin was striding toward him with an outstretched hand.

"Good to see you, Windy," Griffin said when their hands clasped together in a powerful grip. "Runnin' a day behind schedule, aren't you?"

"Right year, wrong day, Ira," Windy said as their hands fell away and Griffin clasped an arm around the scout's shoulders. "Seems like them old beaver didn't want to quit comin' to the bait."

Griffin glanced over his shoulder. "Looks like quite a haul, at that. Come on, the family's been worryin' about you. We set our calendar once a year by the time you show up. Now you've got 'em all plumb worried about Christmas comin' on time."

Beth Griffin, a once-pretty woman now aged a bit beyond her years by the hard life of prairie dwellers, moved down one step and offered her hand. She wore a long gingham dress, the front of which was covered by a white apron, and she patted a wisp of gray hair blown free from the coils on top of her head by the blustery wind.

"Good to see you again, Windy. You missed the liver and onions last night, but I hope dumplings and chicken stew will be to your liking."

"Sounds mighty good, ma'am," Windy said, taking off his hat and grasping her hand gently. "Sorry if I caused you some concern, but I ran into some problems up in Canada."

"You're here, safe and sound, that's all that matters," Beth replied, turning to address two little girls. "Shelly, you and Lisa get supper on the table. I'm sure Mr. Mandalian will be ready to eat anytime the table is set."

The two girls curtsied to Windy. Shelly, sixteen, was red-haired and fairly attractive, while Lisa was a tawny-haired fourteen-year-old beauty. Stopping in the doorway, they both turned and said in unison, "It's good to see you, Mr. Mandalian."

"Good to see you young ladies," Windy replied with a stiff half-bow. "You're gettin' purtier every year."

"Joseph?" Griffin said to his eldest son, a tall, strapping lad of eighteen. "You and little Tom there shake Mr. Mandalian's hand, then care for his horses and stack those hides in the shed. Don't bother countin' 'em. Whatever Windy tells me he's got there, he's got."

"Sure, Pa," replied Joseph, stepping forward and shaking Windy's hand. "It's mighty good to see you again, Mr. Mandalian."

"Same to you, Joe. Pick out the finest pelt you can find in the lot, and make a Christmas present for your ma."

The young man beamed. "Thank you, Mr. Mandalian. I'd be right pleased to do that."

Little Tom stepped forward, and Windy stooped down to grasp the tiny fingers. "And you, Tom," he said, tousling the boy's hair with one hand, "if you give that old roan back yonder an extra good ration of grain, I've got a surprise for you."

"What is it, Mr. Mandalian?" the boy asked, eyes widening in anticipation.

"Go on now, son," Griffin said, patting the boy lightly on the rump. "Get to your chores. It ain't polite to ask what somebody brought you."

Young Tom scampered away, leaving only two girls, Lisa's

identical twin, Lorie, fourteen, and Sharon, six, standing on the porch. Griffin focused his attention on them. "Lorie, you take Sharon and fetch some water. Mr. Mandalian is gonna want to wash up before supper."

"You bet I am, girls. And if you'll bring my saddlebags in when you're through, I've got a little surprise for you after we've had supper."

With a squeal of delight, the two girls managed a curtsy before running toward the well with skirts flying. Griffin touched Windy's elbow lightly as he moved toward the steps. "Come on, Windy. Let's have a little drink in the sittin' room while we're waitin' for supper. Damned if it ain't good to see you."

"Same here, Ira," Windy replied, stamping his boots on the porch and slapping the dust from his buckskins before stepping into the house.

When the meal was finished and the dishes had been cleared away, the Griffin children stood a respectful distance away from the table in a half-circle. The younger ones couldn't keep their eyes from straying to the saddlebags lying by the door. After Ira had finished what he was saying and paused to fill his pipe and strike a match, Windy turned to look at the children and pointed toward Tommy.

"Young Tom, would you be so kind as to fetch an old man's saddelbags for him?"

"Yessir, Mr. Mandalian!" the boy said, sprinting toward the door to snatch up the heavy leather bags and half-drag them to the table. "Here ya are, Mr. Mandalian."

"Thank you, little Tom. Much obliged," Windy replied with an air of preoccupation as he untied the leather thongs on one of the flaps. "Let me see what we've got in here," he continued as his hand made an overly long search of the bag's contents. "Yep, here we are, I think I've found something'."

Pulling out a yellow knit handbag with a wooden clasp, he smiled and extended it toward Shelly. "Kinda thought this might go nice with that white Sunday dress you were wearin' last time I saw you, lass."

Shelly gapsed in surprise and clutched the bag to her breast. "Oh, Mr. Mandalian, thank you so much. It's absolutely beautiful!"

"Think nothin' of it, Shelly. So are you," Windy replied, continuing to dig. When his hand came out again, it contained two brightly colored bonnets and twin packages of silk ribbon. He motioned to Lisa and Lorie. "Can't think of any young ladies that would look prettier than you two, decked out in these trimmin's. Now I'll really have a tough time tellin' you apart."

The two girls moved forward with absolute rapture written on their faces. Taking the gifts, they expressed their sincere thanks, and Lisa impulsively hugged Windy's neck with a quick, light squeeze before moving away.

Windy could almost feel little Tom's expectant eyes burning on his face as he rummaged even deeper in the bag, shook his head as if something had been lost, then opened the flap on the other side.

"Ah, here it is," Windy said as his hand withdrew. "Darned if I didn't think there for a minute I might've lost it."

With those words he turned and handed the little boy a small but magnificently crafted, hand-carved wooden horse. Tom's eyes bulged in his face and he couldn't take his gaze off the gift as he moved forward.

"Gee willikers, Mr. Mandalian, it looks just like a real one." Even though his hands hadn't touched the carving, he continued to stare at it while saying to his father, "Look, Pa! Look what Mr. Mandalian brought for me!"

Griffin smiled and pushed the boy forward slightly. "Go ahead, son. Thank Mr. Mandalian, and then accept your gift."

Tommy took it gingerly, holding it as though it might break, and tore his eyes away for a split second to look at Windy. "Thanks, Mr. Mandalian. I'm gonna have one just like this someday."

"I'm right certain you will, little Tom. And when you do, you'll be a buckaroo like nobody's ever seen before."

Sharon was the only child left waiting, and her eyes were big and brimming with tears. Windy looked at her, smiled, and drew her to him.

"Come here, honey. Did you think I'd forget you?"

The little girl nodded and her lower lip quivered.

Windy placed an arm around her and squeezed her gently with one big hand while the other disappeared inside the saddlebag. When it withdrew, it held a rag doll with a polkadot dress, red hair, and shoe-button eyes and nose. Red dots identified its cheeks, and a happy smile curved across its face.

Windy handed the doll across to the little girl while kissing her lightly on top of the head. "I could never forget you, honey. What are you going to name her?"

"Pinky," Sharon said without hesitation. "Her name is Pinky. Do you want to hold her?"

"What do you say to Mr. Mandalian?" Griffin asked the little girl.

"Thank you, Mr. Mandalian."

Windy smiled and squeezed her one more time before releasing her. "You're welcome, Sharon. I think Pinky is a perfect name. But I don't want to hold her right now. She might get lonesome for you."

"I know she would," Sharon replied, cradling the doll in her arm.

"All right, children," Mrs. Griffin said, "take your things and leave Mr. Mandalian alone for a while."

"Hold on a second, Beth, and please excuse my interruptin'. There is one more thing I'd like to have 'em see."

"What on earth could that be, Windy? They've already got more than—"

Windy's hand had dipped into the bag again. When he held up the final gift, Beth Griffin was too stunned to continue speaking, and a tinge of red crept into her cheeks. A black lace shawl lay draped across his palm, and he offered it toward her.

"This is for you, Beth. You've been puttin' up with me droppin' by here for six years now, and I kinda thought you might accept a little token of appreciation from me."

"Oh, Windy, I couldn't. It's . . . it's too . . . beautiful." Impulsively she touched her hair. "I haven't got anything to wear with it. I mean . . ." She glanced furtively at her husband. "Tell him, Ira. That must have cost a fortune, and I just couldn't—"

"Yes you can, honey," Griffin said, reaching out and taking her hand gently. "Windy didn't bring it all the way here just to take it back again. He bought it for you because he wanted to, not because he had to. Take it, it's yours. One thing, though," the agent concluded with a grin. "Next year you'd better have something a little better for him to eat than chicken and dumplin's."

A trickle of tears ran down Beth's cheeks as she took the shawl and held it against her face with something like reverence. "I will, Windy. I will. Thank you so much. It's . . . it's just too . . . beautiful."

"You couldn't be more welcome, Beth. And, beggin' Ira's pardon, chicken and dumplin's are my favorite." Windy accepted a kiss on the cheek before turning to Griffin. "Would there be some chance we could talk outside?"

"Sure, Windy," the agent replied, pushing his chair back with a scrape of wood on wood. "I could use another pipe, and Beth doesn't like me showin' off my bad habits more than once a night to the children. Come on."

Outside, the air was crisp and fresh, and with nightfall the blustery wind had subsided to a gentle breeze. The clear sky revealed a magnificent canopy of stars.

At first, as they walked, there was silence between the two men, as if a spoken word would destroy the magic moment they had shared so recently. With Griffin puffing contentedly on his pipe and Windy nursing a fresh chaw of tobacco in his jaw, they walked silently for several minutes before the agent released his clasped hands from behind his back and placed one on Windy's shoulder.

"You know, my friend, that was a kind thing you did tonight. I can't afford to give those children the fine things you gave them, not to mention the shawl for Beth, and I'd like to thank you from the bottom of my heart and ask God's blessing on you."

"What little bit I do for 'em once a year ain't nothin' compared to what you do for 'em every day, Ira. Especially them two little shavers." Windy glanced across at the agent. "Have you told 'em yet?"

Griffin's hands were clasped behind his back again, and he walked in silence for several steps before speaking around the pipestem clenched in his teeth. "You mean about my not being their real father?"

"Yeah. Last year you mentioned something about telling them before too long."

"I know I did, but it's a hard thing to do. You know Scotty's wife died in childbirth delivering Sharon, and Tommy was only two at the time. Me and Beth took care of 'em that same season while Scotty was off trappin' in Canada with you, and then, after he was killed, I raised 'em and loved 'em like they were my own. I know I'll have to tell 'em about Scotty someday, but it just hurts like hell. They've got brothers and sisters now, not just cousins. I don't want to be the one to take that away from them."

It was Windy's turn to be silent while he worked the chaw in his cheek and spat. Finally, after wiping a hand across his mouth, he said, "I don't know a hell of a lot about this kind of stuff, Ira—about kids and all, I mean, never having had none myself. But it seems to me there's two kinds of fathers: the one who actually has the fun of making 'em, and the one who spends his life lovin' 'em. Way I got it figured, the second one's just as important as the first."

Griffin chuckled softly by Windy's side. "You just might know more about it than you think, Windy. I think you just gave me the words I'll need to tell 'em."

"You must've been hurtin' pretty bad for words, then, Ira," Windy allowed before spitting again.

Knowing Windy wanted to change the subject, Griffin puffed once on his pipe, then asked, "How'd the trip go? Seems like you had pretty good luck."

"Yeah, with the trappin' I did. Should bring a damned good piece of change to help tide them kids over till next year. Got jumped by some Cree, but that came out all right too." Windy paused to scratch the back of his head. "I'll be goin' up a little earlier next year, and maybe stay a little longer."

"Why's that?"

"There's a feller up there that calls himself Rides Big Horses that I want to find. Him and me got some business to settle."

"Oh? What kind of business?"

"I'll tell you that when I get back. Would've found him this time, but a feller named Louis Riel's got some kind of rebellion goin' on up there, and he seems to be part of it. He'll keep till next year, I 'spect."

Having known the scout for so many years, Griffin could tell by the sound of Windy's voice that whoever he was looking for was as good as dead and merely had to go through the formality of actually dying. And he also perceived something else that prompted his next question.

"Is he the man who killed my brother?"

"Yup," Windy said simply, with a glance up at the stars. "If you don't mind, Ira, I think we'd better head on back to the house. I've got to turn in and get an early start in the mornin'. Should make the outpost by sometime before noon the followin' day."

"Sure, Windy. I'll have Beth make up a bed for you, if she hasn't already."

"Thanks just the same, Ira, but I'll just spread my bedroll out here under them twinklers up yonder. If I sleep inside, I snore so loud I even wake myself up."

"Every year the same question, every year the same answer," Griffin said with a chuckle. "You ain't never gonna change, are you, Windy?"

"Nope. I'll be gone before you folks get up in the mornin', so give ever'body my best. One more thing—about that war I was talkin' about, up in Canada?"

"Yes?"

"You're a purty good piece of ground from there, but keep an eye out anyway. Never know what them Plains Cree'll do if somebody gets hot on their ass. They could come spillin' down your way, 'cause they don't know a national boundary from a three-eyed toad."

"Kind of like a trapper I know?" Griffin asked with a smile.

"Kinda like. To my way of thinkin', them critters I trapped probably wandered up there from the States in the first place. 'Night, Ira," Windy said, turning toward the barn. "You're a good man, just like your brother was."

"Thanks, Windy," Griffin replied with deep sincerity. "That's the best damned compliment you could ever give me. See you next year."

"Yup. Next year."

three

Returning from his final position check, Major William R. Steele guided his mount through the tall timber growing in wild profusion on the sides of the steep mountain. Below him lay a long, narrow valley that yielded on the far side to another steep ridge, which was also obscured to the distant observer by a lush stand of timber. The valley, approximately two hundred yards in width at the broadest point, wound through the twin mountain ridges along the general course of a meandering stream. Steele was pleased with himself and satisfied with the positioning of his troops. A tall, thin man with a sallow face punctuated by eyes set deeply in his head and brooding above a long, sharp nose that appeared to have been pinched severely at birth, Steele was something less than handsome in appearance. Physical appearance, however, was the least of his concerns. He was an intense man, driven by the desire to succeed and win at all costs. A total victory here against the Cree and métis would mean recognition from his commanding officers, who were under extreme pressure from the British-dominated MacDonald government to bring an end to the métis uprisings once and for all. In the course of things, recognition from them would mean promotion, and promotion equated to increased authority and power, two things that Steele desperately wanted.

As commanding officer of a battalion of Canadian militia, he had risked his entire career on the confession given by a captured métis soldier. Reluctantly, Steele's superiors had given him permission to lay a trap for the Cree, Rides Big Horses, and métis renegade, Johnny Singletree. Now, with two companies concealed in the treeline across from him, and another two just below where he was presently riding, he felt that his trap was properly set and waited only for the prey to venture forth.

Angling downward, Steele reined in and, stepping awkwardly from his saddle, approached a man tied to a tree with a gag tightly secured about his mouth. He stared at the half-breed contemptuously for long moments while slapping the riding crop in his hand against his leg in a studied, threatening manner.

Without taking his eyes from the métis, he barked in a sharp, commanding tone, "Lance Corporal!"

"Yessir?" the soldier replied, scrambling up the steep incline.

"Remove the mouth cover."

"Yessir!"

While the soldier struggled with the secured knots, Steele crossed his arms and held the crop tucked in his armpit while propping one polished boot on an outcropping of rock.

When the gag fell away, the métis worked his mouth, scoured his yellow teeth with a dry tongue, and attempted to spit, but his parched throat would yield no moisture. His dark eyes searched Steele's face, pleading.

"Mischee," he croaked. *"Mischee."*

Steele's lip curled contemptuously. "Speak English. This is Canada, not some heathen land. You are a subject of the Queen and will speak accordingly."

The métis searched his brain while rolling his head and arching his body against the ropes. And when the tortured eyes wandered to Steele's face again, the captive managed a halting, "Wa . . . wat . . . water."

"That's better. But you'll bloody well get no water until this mission is seen through to a successful conclusion. Now, you have told my interpreter that the combined forces of the Cree and métis will proceed through this valley on their way to lay siege to the garrison quartered at Fort Howton. Is that correct?"

Barely understanding a word of the rapidly spoken, heavily accented British words, the métis realized his best answer to the officer's questions was an affirmative nod, which he gave.

"And furthermore, you have told me that two renegades, Rides Big Horses and Johnny Singletree, will be commanding the operation?"

Another affirmative nod, while a dry tongue darted searchingly across parched lips.

"Very good, and you'd bloody well better be correct. If they arrive in the manner you have suggested, and are killed or taken captive, you will be given water and set free. If neither of those goals is met, however, you will be shot and left here to rot. Is that understood?"

Bewildered, the métis again nodded, and assuming he had been comprehended, Steele slapped the crop against his leg one final time and turned to the soldier.

"Secure the mouth cover and stand guard here. I am going down to join my troops for the engagement."

"Yessir!"

Ten minutes away and approaching the narrow valley at a steady pace, one hundred mounted warriors were riding through a lower meadow adjacent to the upper valley. At the head of the random assemblage rode a standard bearer holding a large white flag smeared with blood and attached to a long pole. Some twenty yards in front of him rode two men who were similar in some ways, but totally disparate in others.

To the left was Johnny Singletree, sired by a French trapper of the Hudson's Bay Company and the son of a full-blooded Cree squaw. He wore the traditional clothing of a Cree warrior: tanned buckskin leggings, loincloth, moccasins, and vest. But his skin, although tanned, was of a light complexion, and the long hair touching his shoulders was nearly blond in color. A tall, lean man, his features were sharp and there was a restless nervousness about him that indicated impatience and quickness of temper. Blue eyes peered out with burning intensity from beneath a black derby hat, and there was not the slightest trace of cordiality about the cold smile that seemed perfectly suited to his face.

The man to the right, Rides Big Horses, was true to his name. His mount was nearly a full hand taller than the other horses, and it walked with head held high, neck arched, and tail partially lifted. The man upon its back was big of stature as well, and his demeanor was not dissimilar to that of his horse. For a full-blooded Cree, he was a large man, possibly six feet in height, thick-chested and bull-necked. His braided hair was jet black and his eyes were the color of ebony. There was a cruel twist to his face, the look of a man who prided himself on the uncompromising attitude of one who would neither give nor ask for mercy.

As their horses climbed toward the upper meadow in the brilliant morning sunshine, Rides Big Horses glanced across at his companion. "I do not think it wise, this idea of splitting our forces. Your métis should be here with my Cree."

"René, our leader, has not asked if you think it wise. It was his decision for the métis to close on the garrison from the north while we attack from the south. It is an important decision, and if we do not win this battle, our struggle will be over and we will be driven from Canada."

"And what then?"

Singletree shrugged his shoulders and said simply, "If we win, we won't have that decision to make."

"Kaaaa!" Rides Big Horses snapped, angered by the métis' dismissal of his question through the use of simple logic. "And where is your Louis Riel, the man who is supposed to give us land for helping you defeat the grandmother's soldiers?"

"In the United States. Somewhere in Wyoming Territory."

"And he can do this from there?" Rides Big Horses asked with haughty disdain.

"Better than he can from here, where he would probably be dead. After we have taken the garrison at Fort Howton, he will return to establish a métis-Cree province."

Rides Big Horses turned to look at the warriors strung out behind him, and nodded his satisfaction. "My people will win this battle for you. When the last scalp is taken, then we will smoke and talk of this province of yours."

"Agreed," Singletree said, the tone of discontent having no effect on the cold smile creasing his face.

They were passing through a narrow neck of land now, and approaching the upper valley. Lush, knee-deep grass swished around their horses' legs, and the stream gurgled in a hushed murmur off to their left. Thick stands of timber breasted the meadow on either side, and the forests were dark in contrast to the sunbathed grassland dotted with yellow flowers. All was silent as the lead riders of the war party confidently approached the center of the valley.

Perhaps it was a nervous young soldier, a finger pressed too tightly to the trigger, or merely an accident for which there was no explanation, but suddenly a single shot rang out from the southern slope. A warrior well toward the rear clasped his hands to his chest and toppled from his rearing pony while the two leaders simultaneously jerked their mounts around.

"Fire!" a voice screamed from somewhere in the darkness on the northern ridge, and there was an instantaneous roar of

weapons fire raining bullets down on the Cree from both sides.

More warriors spilled from their spinning, plunging horses, while others fired at invisible targets in the wild confusion.

"Go back! It's a trap!" Singletree shouted, ducking low to his horse's withers and pressing the mount to a run toward the lower meadow, with Rides Big Horses close behind. "Go back!"

Amazingly, the standard bearer had not been hit, and he managed to turn his pony and flee toward the mouth of the meadow, with the remaining warriors streaking behind him. Even though the battle had lasted no more than two minutes, there were thirty Cree sprawled in the tall grass, with dead horses scattered about them. The firing, which had been so intense and lethal, died as quickly as it had risen, as the retreating Cree rapidly moved out of range.

Major Steele was livid with rage as he watched his prey escape from certain death.

"Who's the bloody son of a bitch who fired that shot?" he screamed at the lieutenant nearest him.

"I have no idea, sir."

"We would have had those bastards!" Steele continued, wild-eyed and quivering with uncontrolled anger. "We would have had them! No one was supposed to fire until the whole goddamned rotten bunch of them was in the center of the valley!"

"I know, sir. Would you like for me to find out, Major?"

Steele turned on the lieutenant in a blazing fury. "You're damned right I do! I want the man's name, and I want him hung on the spot! Do you understand, Lieutenant?"

"I understand, sir," the lieutenant replied in a subdued tone.

"Then get cracking!" Steele snarled as his eyes drifted to the mouth of the valley once more. "I'll get you," he said through gritted teeth. "I'll get you if I have to follow you to the bloody ends of the earth. You cannot hide and I'll not sleep until both of you lie dead at my feet."

Somewhat satisfied with his threat, Steele slapped the riding crop against his leg and climbed up the ridge toward his horse.

"What do you want me to do with him, sir?" the corporal asked, nodding toward the métis tied to the tree.

Steele neither broke stride nor glanced toward the hapless prisoner. "Shoot the son of a bitch," he said, taking up his reins and swinging into the saddle. "Our agreement was total victory. What we have just witnessed was something less than that."

With those words, he jerked his horse's head around viciously and, lashing its flank with his crop, sent the mount plunging headlong down the ridge. Behind him a single shot was fired, and its solitary echo quickly faded from the silent valley.

They had ridden for nearly ten minutes, and now, clear of the lower meadow and safely into the timber once again, Rides Big Horses pulled up on the hackamore in his hand and halted the fleeing warriors strung out behind him. Singletree silently assessed the number of Cree who had survived the ambush and who were presently filing into the clearing. Then he glanced unconcernedly at the Cree chief.

"I'd say we lost thirty, maybe thirty-five."

"You would say that," Rides Big Horses said with great disdain. "And I would say we rode into a trap. A trap that could only have been set if the grandmother's soldiers knew of our plans. All of my warriors were present today. Where are the métis?"

"They were where I told you they would be," Singletree snapped, irritated by the chief's innuendo.

Rides Big Horses would not settle for a simple answer this time. "One of your people must have told them. Where is this André of yours?"

Singletree thought of the métis courier who was to have been sent by René Dawson, commander of the métis forces, and who should have arrived two days before. To Singletree's knowledge, he was a trusted lieutenant and the only man who would have complete knowledge of their intended attack while being in a position to fall into the hands of the Canadian militia.

As was his habit, Singletree shrugged with an exaggerated heave of his shoulders. "I have no idea. Perhaps he fell into enemy hands and was tortured into revealing his knowledge of the campaign."

"And he is the one responsible for the loss of my warriors? A métis who knew that none of his own kind would die?"

Anger instantly hardened the ever-present smile on Singletree's face. "You speak with your back to the wind, my friend," he said evenly. "If you have something to say to me, do not play the game of the fox. But before you speak again, let me ask you—would I have knowingly ridden into a trap with you in full awareness that I surely would be killed?"

Rides Big Horses again evidenced his inability to deal with simple logic. "But you were not killed."

"Were you?"

"No," Rides Big Horses answered, his voice revealing a lack of conviction for his fledgling theory.

Now Singletree was on the attack. "Everyone knows of your thirst for whiskey, your lust for women, and your cunning. Perhaps it was you who turned against your own kind, for the money the grandmother has offered for my life as well as Riel's."

Rides Big Horses' chest swelled and his dark eyes burned with anger. "I would never turn against my own people."

"And I would never turn against my cause. Enough of this foolishness," Singletree said, lifting his hackamore from the horse's neck. "We must go. They will be after us soon. It is my belief that the man who hid in ambush for us is Major Steele. He is like the ferret at the door of a squirrel's den. He will never give up until victory is his or he is killed."

Knowing he had lost the mental duel, Rides Big Horses glanced once toward his warriors before looking at Singletree again and speaking in an attempt to regain his compromised authority.

"From now on, my warriors go where I say."

"Fine. And they will lie dead beside you at the hands of Major Steele."

"I am afraid of no white man."

"No, I suppose not. But four hundred white men's rifles? That is entirely another question."

Remembering the thunderous roar of countless rifles as they fired down from the treeline in the meadow, Rides Big Horses mellowed in his belligerence. "You said we must go; where is it that you would have us go? To help the métis in their attack on Fort Howton?"

"No. That battle is lost. We could never get there in time to be part of a victory. They will attack tonight, thinking we will attack as well, but without going through the valley between the mountains, we could never be there in time. My people will be lucky if they lose no more than you did today, and I don't wish to have my name added to their number. We must leave Canada, find Riel, and start over."

"Leave our homeland?"

"You have no homeland. If you stay here, you will be hunted, hated, and killed like the métis. The Canadians and the British have no love for us, and they know you have helped in our cause. We must leave if we are to survive, find Louis Riel, and let him lead us to glorious victory." Singletree paused and his blue eyes held unwaveringly on the Indian's face. "We must cross the border into the United States, where Steele and his soldiers cannot follow."

"I have never been to the United States," Rides Big Horses replied.

"I know, but I have. The High Plains to the north are wide and sparsely settled. If we move constantly, we can hide there until we find Riel."

"These United States," Rides Big Horses asked, "do they have none of the grandmother's soldiers?"

"No, but they have their own soldiers. If we are seen, they will think we are Cheyenne. Your people and the Cheyenne are very similar; you both speak similar tongues, favor the same war colors, and dress in much the same way. The worst that can happen to us is to be put on one of their reservations temporarily."

"Reservation? I do not know this word," Rides Big Horses said. "We will stay here and live in the land of our fathers."

"That's up to you," the métis said, turning his mount away. "But I'll guarantee you this—once Major Steele catches up with you, you won't be *living* in the land of your fathers."

Singletree was riding away and was nearly thirty yards distant before the Cree called out to him to stop.

Singletree reined in his pony and turned to watch Rides Big Horses urge his mount forward. When the Indian pulled in beside him, the two men watched each other in silence for nearly a minute.

"I'm waiting," Singletree finally said with obvious impatience.

"We will go with you to this new land. We are too few to go against the numbers of the grandmother's soldiers."

"Suit yourself. But if you go with me, I will be in command. I know something of the place where we go. I visited there with Riel when we were trying to enlist the aid of the Cheyenne for our war. First we will go to the Clearwater agency and get the things we need: ammunition, blankets, salt, matches, and whatever else we want. Then we will begin the search for Riel."

A crafty look came into Rides Big Horses' eyes. "And what if they will not give us the things we ask for?"

Singletree shrugged and looked away. "Then we will take them. The agent there is a white man, and he'll think we are Cheyenne and they will get the blame."

"It is good, métis," Rides Big Horses said, nodding his head vigorously. "I hate all white men. But their women?" A huge grin split his normally stony expression. "They are pretty, especially the ones with the strange-colored hair."

"We are not going there to take American women. We are going to find Riel. Keep that in mind."

Rides Big Horses continued to grin. "I will, but that doesn't mean I can't think about other things."

"I suppose not. Let's go."

Matt Kincaid and Warner Conway were passing along the upper wall, conducting a routine inspection, and Matt had knelt down to examine a corner of the sod roof when he felt a tap on his shoulder. "Yes, sir?" he asked, looking up.

"Do you have your watch with you, Matt?" Conway asked, smiling slightly.

Kincaid nodded and pulled the watch from his pocket. He studied the captain curiously as he saw him standing above him with his own timepiece in hand. "It's nine-forty-five. Why, sir?"

Conway offered an agreeing nod. "That's what I have as well. Would you care to have a look toward the north?"

Puzzled, Kincaid stood and looked in the direction indicated by the captain's extended finger. A lone rider leading three unladen packhorses was angling toward them across the prairie at a steady walk. Even at that distance there could be no mistaking who he was. A slow grin eased across Kincaid's face.

"That old bastard," he muttered with a mixture of surprise and relief. "He made it back after all."

Conway glanced at his watch again. "Looks that way. And it looks like he's going to be about five minutes early."

"How can you be a day late and five minutes early at the same time?" Matt asked with a grin.

"Only married men know the answer to that secret, Matt. Come on, let's go down and meet him at the gate."

By the time the two officers had climbed down the ladder and crossed the parade to the front gates, which the guards were now swinging open, Windy was approaching as if he were just returning from a one-day jaunt into town.

"Mornin', Cap'n—Matt," he said with a tilt of his head as his mount entered the post and he pulled it to a stop. "Sorry I'm just a tad late, but I hit a strong headwind comin' back."

Kincaid laughed. "Yeah, sure, Windy. More like a good-looking squaw up in Canada, to my way of thinking. Good to have you back."

The scout swung down while saying, "There ain't no good-lookin' squaws, Matt, up in Canada or anywhere else—which don't matter, 'cause they all look the same in the dark, anyway. Good to be back."

"How'd your trip go, Windy?" Conway asked with a glance at the barren pack string. "Same as usual, looks like."

"Yup, same as usual, Cap'n. My luck was so bad I had to eat fish for a whole damned month. Got to dreamin' about old Dutch's shit on a shingle 'bout the third week out."

"That's not a dream, Windy," Kincaid chuckled. "It's a nightmare. Have any luck at all?" he asked, as he and Conway fell in beside the scout, who was leading the horses toward the stable.

"Naw, same old bullshit. Mosquitoes, flies, ants, and cold nights. Might do my trappin' in Mexico next year."

"Yeah, sure you will," Kincaid rejoined. "And I'll be a brigadier general by spring."

Windy looked at Matt with a deadpan stare. "No shit? Does that come before or after captain?"

Conway sighed and laid a hand on Windy's shoulder. "After, Windy. A long time after. How are things up in Canada? Are they having the same kind of Indian problems to contend with that we have here?"

"Nope. They don't horse around with any of this reservation shit. If the Canadian government wants a piece of ground the Indians are living on, they just say, 'Move your red ass over, pardner, white man comin' through.' Kind of simple when you look at it from the short view."

"Yeah," Kincaid agreed, "but that philosophy wouldn't

work here in a million years. We're supposed to be assimilating the Indians into our culture, not treating them as simple savages to be shoved aside at will."

Windy spat, and a puff of dust rose on the parade. "Workin' just dandy too, ain't it, Matt? How many Indians have you seen walkin' behind a mule and plantin' corn since some wise-acre back in Washington decided they could be turned into gentlemen farmers?"

"About as many as you've got hides on that pack string."

"Damned observant. And that's all you're ever gonna see, too."

Windy led his string into the cool, dank-smelling stable and began stripping saddles away, while Kincaid stepped forward to lend a hand.

"Sounds like there might be a bit of a war brewin' up in Canada, way I hear it," the scout said with a grunt as he lifted heavy leather onto a saddle tree. "Seems the métis and the Cree ain't too tickled with the shake they're gettin' from Queen Victoria and old Sir John MacDonald. Talked with an old friend of mine just before I left, and he said a major battle was brewin'."

Kincaid pulled a packsaddle away and turned it upside down against a wall for the padding to dry. "Sounds to me like you're trying to tell us something in that damnable close-mouthed way of yours, Windy. Do you see any involvement in all this for us?"

"Could be, Matt," Windy replied, pausing long enough to dig the chaw from his cheek with a finger, spit, and then resume his work. "Sounds like the MacDonald government is goin' to try an run 'em out of Canada. If they was run out of Canada, where the hell would they go?"

"South."

"Good guess," the scout said, now removing the bit from his horse's mouth. "And, since you're cookin' purty good, what's south of Canada?"

The two officers looked at each other while Kincaid replied, "The United States."

"Yup. Seems like that's our territory, last time I heard. Could come spillin' across the border, and them Plains Cree don't know nothin' 'bout our rules, or anybody else's rules, for that matter. They're used to runnin' wild and free, and like I said, they've got damned little notion as to what boundaries, reservations, and the like are all about. They're used to takin' what they want, when they want it, and then runnin' like hell. Might be kind of rough on some of those settlers up north who think they're dealing with pacified, re—" He paused to look at Kincaid while draping the bridle over a wall peg. "What's that fancy word them Washington fellers use for Indians who're supposed to have learned how to wipe their ass with a piece of paper, Matt?"

"Reconstructed."

"Damned if that ain't it. Them homesteaders is kinda used to 'reconstructed' Indians and not the kind that blow a hole in your guts and walk away with a handful of hair."

"Are you suggesting that we send a patrol up there, Windy?" Kincaid asked.

"No. Could be a wild-goose chase for all I know, but I've got one of them strange feelin's that I get that tells me otherwise. 'Sides, I've got some people that I'm kinda fond of, up that way, and I'd be mighty perturbed if any harm came to 'em."

"What do you think, Captain?" Kincaid asked, turning to the commanding officer. "Windy has a mighty odd way of being right on target with these 'strange feelings' of his. Do you think we ought to send a platoon up there just as a precaution?"

Conway replied, his brow furrowed in concentration, "We've got a problem. Do you remember that telegram I showed you this morning?"

"You mean the one about the colonel postponing his visit to us for three days?"

"That's the one. We were instructed, no, make that *ordered*, not to take any offensive action until his arrival, and that won't be until Wednesday. 'Offensive action' would mean any troop movements outside the compound unless deemed necessary by defensive necessity. If I knew for sure that some of our people were in jeopardy, I'd say to hell with his order and send a platoon up there, and if Windy deems that to be the case, then so be it." Conway hesitated and looked at the scout. "What do you think, Windy? Do you have enough evidence or information to justify disobeying a direct order?"

Windy scratched his jaw in thought. "In my own mind I do, Cap'n, but it ain't nothin' that could be put into words and hold up in a court-martial. You know me—I live by hunches, the smell of the breeze, the look in a man's eye when I talk to him, that sort of thing. I don't think the big hats at Regiment would put a whole lot of stock in that kind of evidence."

"No they wouldn't. Did you see anything or hear anything tangible that would justify my running with your hunch?"

"Nope. Just what an old Cree chief told me. That and the smell of the wind."

Conway smiled regretfully. "I've learned how to write reports awfully well over the years, Windy, you know that. I've doctored up the truth to make it sound like a lie, and stretched a lie so far that the truth wouldn't even sound good, but there's only so much I can do. I'm afraid 'an old Cree chief' and 'the smell of the wind' are pushing me beyond my capabilities." The captain watched his chief scout closely before speaking again. "Now I'll say it one more time; if you have any hard evidence for us to go on—anything solid at all—we'll have a patrol out those gates within the hour, and Regiment be damned."

Windy shook his head. "I ain't got it, Cap'n. I don't suppose the words 'I've got a feelin' in my bones' would help none in your report, either, but that's what I've got."

"No it wouldn't. I guess we'll just have to wait and see and hope for the best." Conway smiled and tried to brighten his voice. "Windy, I know your first priority right now is a hot bath, but after that, would you mind joining Matt and me for dinner in the officers' mess? From what I hear, creamed chipped beef on toast is the main course today. Flora's baking bread, so I'm going to have to share in that delicacy with someone. Matt has no choice, but you have. Care to join us?"

"Sure he would, Captain," Kincaid said with a resounding slap between the scout's shoulder blades. "That's the only way we can find out if it was a dream or a nightmare."

Windy shielded the look of desperation filling his eyes, while swallowing dryly. "Or a lie, Matt. You wonder why I ain't got much to say most times, and that should be as good an answer as any. This old mouth gets me in trouble ever' time she starts to swing on her hinges. I'll be there at noon, Cap'n, but don't be too surprised if I ain't real hungry. Kinda fond of fish right now, as a matter of fact."

four

The afternoon sun burned a scorching trail across the cloudless sky, and the High Plains seemed to have wilted under the intense heat. Prairie dogs, normally perched on the mounds of their dens, were absent now, seeking shelter from the sun in the coolness of burrows far beneath the surface. Buffalo had retreated from their grazing to dusty wallows, and antelope were bedded down on the lee side of grassy knolls to catch the minimal cooling breeze drifting across the plains. High in the sky, three buzzards soared in effortless flight, but even their predictably motionless existence seemed more listless and devoid of ambition than was normally the case.

Rides Big Horses brushed some beads of perspiration from his upper lip and looked around at the vast emptiness in disgust. "This is a terrible land you've brought us to, métis. There are no trees, no shade, and the sun is hotter than the stones of a cooking fire. We are hungry and thirsty, three moons have risen since we left our homeland, and still we have not found the white man's trading post you promised us."

"Be patient, Cree. We are on the Clearwater Reservation now, and the agency is only a short ride away. Select twenty of your warriors and take them with you to get the supplies we need. Tell the agent you are Cheyenne, and he should give you the things you ask for." Singletree's eyes showed no flicker of emotion as he paused to study the Cree chief. "If he will not give them to you, take them. But first, ask him if he knows of a Canadian named Louis Riel and where he might be found."

"It is good, métis," Rides Big Horses replied, licking his lips unconsciously. "We have not had whiskey in a long time. I miss the taste of the white man's *mischee*."

Singletree nodded, but spoke in a cautionary tone. "And so do I, but the supplies are more important, as is any information he can give us. Get what we need first, before anything else. Especially ammunition."

"Manitou will watch over us," Rides Big Horses said, while watching the half-breed closely. "Tell me, why do you not go to the agency with us? Is there too much danger for a métis?"

"No. The agent is but a man with his children." Singletree swept a hand along the side of his face to indicate his physical features. "But with these eyes and this hair, how could I hope to convince him that I am Cheyenne? No, I must wait here with the others."

Rides Big Horses continued to study the métis, as though trying to convince himself that the words he had heard were true. "We have already ridden into one of your traps, métis. I do not wish to ride into another."

"You speak like a fool, Cree. I would have more to lose than to gain by your death on American soil. Go now, we can't stay here too long."

Finally convinced, the Cree chief waved his hand in the direction of several warriors and they moved forward to join their leader and follow him toward the distant swell, while Singletree slid from his pony to sink to his haunches in the tall grass.

Even though the sun beat down upon the broad of his back, Ira Griffin seemed not to notice it as he studied the repaired hub on the naked end of the wagon axle propped up on a chunk of wood. Satisfied, he glanced over at the young boy standing beside him, and smiled.

"Looks like we've got 'er fixed, young Tom," he said with an affectionate smile. "Don't think I could've made it without your help."

"Want me to get the can of grease now, Pa?"

"Yes, would you? There should be a stick laying there too; we'll dab it on with that."

While the boy ran to get the grease from the shed, Griffin turned his attention to the wheel propped against the wagon, and began wiping its hub clean. Behind him the entire Griffin family were busily tending to their chores. Beth was sweeping off the porch and the twins, Lorie and Lisa, were swatting dust from rugs hung on the clothesline. John was working lard into the hide of the pelt Windy had given him, to soften the skin and make it pliable before curing in the sun. Just inside the kitchen door, Shelly churned butter, and the shaded darkness, contrasting with the sunlit brilliance outside, made her long red hair appear to be auburn in color. Sharon, the youngest, was sprinkling water just ahead of Mrs. Griffin's broom to keep the dust down, and there was a silent contentment about an entire family bent to their day's labor.

"Here, Pa," Tommy said, holding the large can in small hands. "I got the grease. Here's the stick too. Want me to hold the can for you?"

"Sure, Tom. You're a good little helper," Griffin replied, dipping the stick into the can and carefully applying the grease to the axle hub. After making several such transfers, he began to distribute the lubricant evenly, with the smooth strokes of a cook spreading frosting on a cake. Dipping into the can one final time for a last application, he swung the stick toward the hub, but it stopped in midmotion at the sound of his oldest son's voice.

"Pa? Got company comin'!"

Griffin straightened slowly and turned with the stick in hand. About twenty warriors, following a man whom he assumed to be their chief, were approaching slowly from the northeast.

Griffin dropped the stick into the can, picked up a rag hanging from the wheel, and methodically wiped his hands as he watched the Indians draw near.

"That'll be enough grease for now, Tommy," he said without looking at the boy. "You can put the can away, and don't forget to put the lid on."

"I won't, Pa," Tommy replied, running toward the shed once more while glancing at the Indians as he moved.

After tossing the rag aside, Griffin hitched one suspender up and walked across the yard to greet the lead rider, whom he could not recall ever having seen before. As a matter of fact, he was strangely puzzled by the entire band of Indians now sitting stoically on their motionless ponies in the center of the yard. While there was a strong resemblance between them and the Cheyenne with whom he dealt on an almost daily basis, there was something different about them that Griffin couldn't quite identify.

"Hello," Griffin said to the broad-chested warrior seated atop an exceptionally large horse. "Is there something I can help you with?"

The Indian offered no reply as his head slowly turned in a meticulous examination of the premises. The women had ceased their labor and stood watching in silence. Having stepped onto the porch, Shelly was shielding her eyes while they adjusted to the light, and her red hair, outlined against the white paint on the wall behind her, glistened in the strong sunlight like a thousand sparkling rubies. Griffin noticed the warrior's particular attention to his oldest daughter, but he was not unduly alarmed, because all Indians who visited the agency were fascinated by the color of her hair.

As if breaking some powerful magnetic force, the Indian tore his eyes from Shelly and his gaze drifted to the agent standing before him.

"We come here for supplies," Rides Big Horses said in an expressionless tone.

"Are you new to the reservation? I can't recall having seen you before."

Rides Big Horses nodded curtly.

"What tribe are you from?"

"Cheyenne."

"And whose band?"

The question clouded Rides Big Horse's eyes momentarily. "I no understand."

The first hint of concern touched the corners of Griffin's mind, and he studied the Indian more closely. There was an accent to his words that he had heard in no other Cheyenne's voice, and there was an indefinably ominous look about the warrior.

"Who is your chief?"

"I am the chief."

"And your name?"

The Indian hesitated as if making a decision before saying, "Swift Otter."

"An unusual name for these parts," Griffin replied, crossing his arms before his chest. "Since you're new here, Chief, I'll have to see your papers and check your registration numbers."

The clouded look was there again, and there seemed to be an even more stern set to the Indian's jaw. "I no understand."

"You are registered with the Bureau of Indian Affairs, aren't you?"

Rides Big Horses nodded.

"Then where are your papers?"

"We come for supplies, not for talk," Rides Big Horses said curtly.

Griffin smiled in an attempt to hide the concern growing

in his mind. "Certainly. But since I haven't seen your papers and have never met you before, I'll have to sell them to you instead of issuing them as I normally do. Is that acceptable to you, Chief? You do have money?"

"Yes. I have money." Then, remembering Singletree's final admonition, he asked, "Do you know of a man named Louis Riel?"

The name and the question triggered yet another alarm bell in Griffin's brain. He remembered Windy's having said something about a war brewing up in Canada, and that the leader of the rebellious element was a man by the name of Louis Riel. He also remembered Windy's warning about the possibility of Cree Indians spilling across the border if their side was defeated.

Aware of his lengthy pause, Griffin nodded and said, "I've heard of him, but I don't know him."

"Have you seen him?"

"No I haven't."

"Do you know where he is?"

The agent thought the question was slightly ludicrous in light of the fact that he had just stated that he had only heard of the man and had never seen him, and he made a mental calculation as to the Indian's intelligence. He knew from past experience that it was the ignorant ones who were the most dangerous, because they had no concept of what the consequences of their actions would be.

"No, I don't know where he is. Come," Griffin said, turning toward the trading post, deciding that the sooner he got the chief and his warriors off the agency, the better. "We'll get those supplies for you."

Rides Big Horses motioned to three braves, and the four of them simultaneously slid from their horses' backs to follow the agent across the yard. Again the Cree's eyes went to Shelly, who continued to stare at him for several seconds before ducking back into the kitchen. A sly smile touched the corners of Rides Big Horses' mouth, and he continued to watch the vacant doorway until it was lost from view as he stepped inside the building behind Griffin.

The agent moved behind the counter to stand in front of flour and grain barrels, sacks of coffee and sugar, and a tub of molasses. Other supplies were stacked neatly on shelves attached to the wall. Rides Big Horses' eyes swept over the room and stopped on several whiskey bottles stored in a separate place on the opposite side of the room and away from the shelves.

"What can I do for you?" Griffin asked, placing his hands on the counter; he was totally aware of the object of the Indian's attention.

Rides Big Horses' eyes darted to Griffin's face, and the agent thought he could detect a renewed hardness about them. "Ammunition," the Indian grunted.

"What caliber?"

The warrior shrugged and held his rifle up for Griffin to see, while keeping it out of his reach.

"Looks like thirty-caliber," the agent said, reaching behind him to the lower shelf. "Four boxes be all right?"

Rides Big Horses nodded, and Griffin placed the shells on the counter while saying, "Now, what else?"

"Salt, flour, matches, sugar, coffee, and tea."

Again the warning note sounded; he knew the Canadians were especially heavy tea drinkers. "Can't help you with the tea, but I've got the other things you want," he said with a smile as he turned to package the staples in separate bags. "Not many people around these parts are fond of tea."

With the exception of the crunching sound of the scoop going into different barrels, the room was deathly quiet, and Griffin felt a shiver run up his spine as he worked with his back to the Indians. When the order had been filled, he hoisted the sacks onto the counter, reached for a pad and pencil, and looked at the chief again with his hand poised to write.

"Now, before I figure up your bill, will there be anything else?"

There was a sullen look on Rides Big Horses' face as he stared at the agent. Finally he grunted a single word.

"Whiskey."

Griffin tried to smile disarmingly. "Sorry, Chief," he said in a controlled, authoritative tone. "I can't sell you that. It's against BIA regulations."

The Cree was truly puzzled. In Canada the Indians were allowed to drink all they wanted, as long as they didn't cause any trouble for white people. And even though he had no intention of paying for the supplies, it angered him that a white man was refusing to sell him what he wanted most.

"Whiskey," he said again, his voice demanding now, with

a hint of threat in it. "We want whiskey."

Griffin held his hands up in a gesture of helplessness. "I'd sell it to you if I could, Chief, but I'd lose my job if I did. I've got a family to support, and—"

"Whiskey!" Rides Big Horses snarled, lashing out with his rifle barrel and striking the agent across the left temple. Griffin staggered backward and his hand instinctively went to the blood running down the side of his head from a gash torn by the rifle sight. Instantly, Rides Big Horses leaped over the counter and slammed the butt of his rifle against the agent's jaw, sending Griffin crashing into the stacked provisions, which clattered to the floor about him as he fell.

The Cree spun on his heel and stalked to the corner where the whiskey was stored, snatched up a bottle, jerked the cork out with his teeth, and spat it to one side. Tilting the bottle, he drank deeply and the liquor flowed in rivulets from the corners of his mouth to drip onto his chest.

The other warriors crossed the room and drank thirstily from the bottle, while their chief mopped his mouth and chest with one hand before selecting another bottle and repeating his actions.

Hearing the crash of falling tins and bottles inside the trading post, Joseph looked up sharply from the hide he was working on, then dropped it and ran across the yard. He could smell whiskey the instant he stepped into the room, and his eyes snapped toward the broken shelves. Glancing quickly over the counter, he saw his father lying unconscious in a pool of molasses pouring from the tub that had been turned over when he fell.

"Pa!" Joseph cried, rounding the end of the counter. "Are you all—"

The sentence was never completed. Hearing the young man's voice, Rides Big Horses turned, aimed, and fired the rifle with one hand while clutching a whiskey bottle in the other. The slug tore into Joseph's ribcage and he crashed against the counter before sliding slowly to the floor.

"Heya!" Rides Big Horses screamed as the bottle went to his lips again. From the corner of his eye he saw the dazed agent struggle to his hands and knees and crawl toward a rifle propped against the wall. The Cree cautiously set the whiskey down, jacked in another shell, and brought the rifle up a second time. Taking careful aim, he squeezed the trigger just as Grif-

fin's hand touched the stock of his rifle, and the slug slammed into the agent's spine. He slumped forward and lay motionless.

Hearing the shots, the warriors waiting outside leaped from their ponies and raced toward the building to crowd through the door.

Inflamed by whiskey and bloodlust, Rides Big Horses waved the whiskey bottle at his braves. "Get his women and drag them outside! The one with the fire hair is mine!"

The warriors spilled from the trading post with excited yells, and several of them ran toward the house, while others cut off the twins just short of the porch. Inside, Shelly was struggling to get the iron bar across the door when it burst open and the first Indian leaped inside. Beth Griffin raised the heavy double-barreled shotgun in her hands and pulled both triggers at the same time. The powerful recoil knocked her backward to sprawl on the floor, and the violent explosion rattled the windows as the warrior pitched forward, nearly cut in half at the waist by buckshot. But other Indians poured into the room mindless of their dead comrade, and two of them seized Shelly, who bit, scratched, and kicked until she was subdued. Two more grabbed Beth by the hair and dragged her through the blood, across the porch, and into the scorching heat of the yard at the same time that Rides Big Horses stepped from the trading post, whiskey bottle in hand.

The heavy ingestion of alcohol in such a short period of time was already taking its toll, and he lurched as he walked toward the warriors standing over the four women held spread-eagled on the ground. There was a leer on his face as his eyes found Shelly, and he raised the bottle for another deep drink before tossing the empty container aside.

He tugged at the leather thongs holding up his leggings, while twisting his loincloth to one side with the other hand.

Shelly's eyes rolled in horror as she lay there. One brave held her legs spread apart, another pinned her shoulders to the ground, and another held his hand over her mouth; her mother and sisters were being held the same way.

"Hear me, Cree warriors!" Rides Big Horses said with unusual excitement in his voice as he sank to his knees before Shelly. "Take the others and fill them with Cree children! Your chief will take the fire-haired one first!"

Excited grunts and yips filled the air as the warriors fell upon the Griffin women. Seven braves declined, and the one holding little Sharon turned her away to shield her from the ugly scene transpiring in the yard. Another sprinted toward the shed into which he had seen Tommy disappear, and whom he now found trying to cock a rusted old single-shot pistol. After ducking several blows swung by the little boy as tears streamed down his cheeks, the warrior snatched him up and carried him into the sunlight while shielding Tommy's eyes with one hand.

The intense heat, the whiskey, and the aftermath of sexual exertion had a draining effect on Rides Big Horses, which was reflected in his increasingly surly attitude. After readjusting his clothing and snatching a whiskey bottle from the hand of the brave nearest him, he drank, stumbled backward, and then stood glaring at the four women.

"Too old," he said, waggling the bottle toward Beth and glancing at one of the warriors who had been with him in the trading post. "Kill her. The gray scalp is yours."

The Cree lurched forward while drawing his knife, and deftly slit her throat before peeling her scalp away. Running Fox, one of the sober warriors, stepped forward in protest.

"We have done enough! The gods . . ."

Rides Big Horses slammed the bottle across the brave's ear with a vicious, backhanded blow, and the dazed warrior dropped to one knee. The chief was upon him instantly with an enraged, wild look in his eyes, and he kicked the warrior under the chin and sent him sprawling in the dust.

"I am Chief Rides Big Horses!" He bellowed, "I take what I want! I have spoken!" With those words he tilted the bottle again, tossed it away, and jerked his knife from its sheath while advancing on Shelly, who was semiconscious. "You are ugly!" he slurred. "But your hair is a prize fit only for a Cree chief." Delirious with power and propelled by drunken hatred, he sank the blade into Shelly's throat, then carefully, almost gently, pulled her long hair out from beneath her back to trail it in the dust before making the incisions necessary to take her scalp. Then he lurched to his feet and thrust the bloody knife in his right hand toward the sky, while brandishing the train of red hair in the other for all to see.

"*Heeyyaaaaa!* Hear me, Gods! Raven, Turtle, and Otter! Chief Rides Big Horses has done as you commanded! You have given me great medicine and I have used it wisely. The whites will burn in their lodge, and their spirits will never go to the Distant Place!"

Rides Big Horses turned to see the last warriors rising from the twins. While Lorie sobbed uncontrollably and shrieked in horror, Lisa stared up at him with cold eyes, and her beautiful face was contorted in unmasked hatred. It was as though she refused to cry, refused to show any emotion, and her only movement was a subtle tugging at the hemline of her dress to pull the material down over her exposed thighs.

The Cree attempted to focus his blurred vision on the identical twins and closed one eye in an apparent response to the thought that he might be seeing double. With their long blond hair, blue eyes, and the matching ribbons that Windy had given them tied in neat bows, he could not tell one from the other. Having never seen identical twins before, he found them both amusing and fascinating, while centuries-old superstitions crept into his dulled brain.

The last warrior to rise pulled out his knife and knelt to take Lorrie's scalp, but Lisa scrambled to her feet and kicked the surprised Indian viciously in the groin. Doubled over in pain, the warrior lunged at her, but Lisa skipped to one side and Rides Big Horses' hand closed about her arm.

"We will not kill these two," he said sternly to the enraged warrior. "They are a sign, a vision from the gods. This one shall be mine; she has the courage of a Cree, and she is fit to lie by a chief's side. The other one, the one of tears and woman sounds, we will give to the métis chief. He deserves nothing more for a war prize."

Then, with an obvious look of disgust, he looked at the warriors who had not taken part in the rape. "Go to the trading post and get the things we came here for. Take the two dead ones with you, and when you have finished, we will burn their lodges to the ground."

Even though they were disgusted with their chief, the warriors quickly complied with his wishes and dragged Beth and Shelly into the trading post before returning with armloads of supplies, including the remaining whiskey bottles. When the supplies were loaded and his braves were again mounted, Rides Big Horses retrieved the greasy rag that Ira had tossed on the ground, touched a match to a corner, then swaggered to the doorway and tossed the flaming cloth onto the floor, where coal oil had spilled from a lamp overturned in Joseph's death fall. A sheet of fire quickly spread across dry wood, and the building was rapidly engulfed in flame. Lisa had been seated on the chief's horse by another warrior, and now Rides Big Horses swung up behind her and clutched the girl to him roughly with an arm around her waist.

One of the two braves holding Tommy and Sharon looked up at the chief. "What will we do with the little ones?"

He shrugged in total unconcern. "Kill them, take them with you, it is of no importance to me," he said, urging his mount forward to lead the raiding party away at a gallop.

"We cannot leave them here," Running Fox said, hoisting little Tommy gently onto his pony's back. "They will die. They probably will anyway, but we can not leave them here."

The other warrior nodded his agreement and placed Sharon on the blanket spread across his horse's back, before vaulting up behind her. The two braves were well behind the others as they rode away from the yard, and behind them the trading post was engulfed in a towering pillar of flame and smoke. The crackling roar of the fire and the snap of burning timbers were the only sounds to be heard on the empty prairie.

five

"This is the dumbest damned thing I ever saw," Windy said, leaning over to spit before reclining against the wall again, his arms folded and one boot cocked behind him.

"Well, he can speak after all," Kincaid returned with a surprised tone and a grin. "You've been even more quiet than normal these past couple of days, Windy."

"Had less to say the past couple of days."

"For you to have less to say is getting damned close to a vow of silence, my friend." Kincaid's eyes went to the soldiers assembling on the parade, and he noticed that the old veterans of so many campaigns had actually made a halfhearted attempt at shining their boots. "You're absolutely correct, Windy, this whole thing is stupid, but it's also military policy."

"One and the same, most times, seems to me like. If this Colonel Higgins fella wants to inspect your troops, why don't he inspect them in battle where they belong, instead of standin' around like so many toy soliders?"

"I'm in total agreement, and with some officers that's the way it would be. But remember, Higgins has never led troops in battle; the captain checked and found that to be true. So this is his way of doing what he thinks is expected of him, a command inspection."

Windy worked the cut in his cheek and spat again in utter contempt. "More military bullshit. If he ain't never been shot at before, then why in hell's name does he want to come out here and play games with people like yourself and the cap'n, who have?"

Kincaid smiled and spoke with weary patience. "Because it's more military bullshit. That's the way it's done. Obviously the colonel has his sights set on making general before he retires, and it's his belief that commanding a field regiment with a good combat record is a means to that end. You're fortunate, Windy, in that you're not directly involved with any of this nonsense. You can watch it from afar and reject the things you don't like. The captain and I, on the other hand, have to tolerate the vagaries of those who outrank us." He paused to think for a moment, then added, "Well, I guess the only fair thing to do is not to prejudge the old boy and give him his chance. He might turn out all right."

"Yup," Windy replied, continuing to stare straight ahead. "And I might enlist in the army someday, too. His restricting us from patrols just so we'd be here when he damned well decides to show up tells me he's a pompous ass and a man not fit to lead mules to water, let alone troops in battle. Besides that, he's three goddamned days late."

The soldiers were lining up in platoon ranks, but there was a highly visible lack of enthusiasm about their movements. "We'll just have to wait and see, I guess," Kincaid said with a heavy sigh. "Suppose I'd better mosey on over and see if I can't help my men get through this ordeal," he concluded, hunching away from the wall.

Windy matched the move and walked beside Kincaid for a short distance. "You said something about my bein' able to watch this sort of shit from afar, and that's exactly what I aim to do. I'll be out at Tipi Town if you need me."

Just before they parted, Kincaid stopped and studied the scout closely. "Do you still have that worry about your friends up north, Windy? Is that what's behind this dark mood of yours?"

"Yup. Mostly, I guess. If it hadn't been for this Higgins feller, we'd of already been up there and checked things out."

"I know. Just as soon as we get this inspection out of the way and have the colonel and his aide settled in, I'll suggest a patrol up that way."

"Don't suggest it, Matt. Demand it. See you later."

Kincaid watched the tall scout stride through the gates before stepping toward the assembled company.

"Matt? Hold on a moment. I'd like to talk to you."

Hearing his name called by Captain Conway, Kincaid stopped and turned to wait for the commanding officer, who was crossing the parade at a brisk pace.

"Afternoon, Captain," Matt said as Conway set for the inspection."

"I wonder if there's anyone in the entire army who hates

inspections more than I do," Conway replied as he stopped and glanced toward the men of his command.

"There are three platoons of soldiers standing over there who would run you a close second, Captain."

Conway smiled. "I suppose you're right. Damned poor way to treat good men who've got more important things to do. Sometimes I think this business of rank and its privileges is more of a hindrance than a help in getting things done."

"No doubt about it in this case, sir. You said you wanted to talk to me about something?"

"Yes I do. Remember the other day when we were talking about Corporal Peterson and his wife? And Flora said she'd talk to Mrs. Peterson the first chance she got?"

"I remember. Have they talked?"

"Yes, this morning. They finally got together for their little bandage-rolling session. I guess Connie's face had healed up enough so that she wouldn't be embarrassed in Flora's presence. At any rate, she finally opened up to Flora and agreed to tell the truth about what happened, on one condition."

"And what's the condition, sir?" Kincaid asked.

"That we take no disciplinary action against her husband for what he did."

Kincaid hesitated momentarily, considering the woman's conditions. "Sounds like what we're dealing with here is true love, Captain."

"Or total fear."

"Did Peterson beat her up, as we suspected?"

"Yes he did. And it's not the first time. It seems they have a perfect marriage when he's sober, but their life is absolute misery when he's been drinking—which seems to be the case more and more, according to what she told Flora. The woman really did need to talk to someone, apparently, and I'm glad we've intervened to the extent that we have."

"I hear through the grapevine that Peterson is getting out when his hitch is up. I checked, and his enlistment will be up in another month."

"Yes, I know that, and it might be for the better." Conway paused, his brow furrowed in thought. "You know what Peterson's problem is, according to his wife?"

"I haven't the slightest idea, sir. Except that a lot of men just naturally get mean when they're drinking."

"That's true," the captain agreed, "but his problem goes a

little beyond that. It seems he came from an exceptionally large family back in Massachusetts, and he wants to have children of his own. Apparently one of them, either he or Connie, cannot conceive a child, and he's taking it out on her."

"Well, sir," Kincaid said with a wan smile, "everyone knows we do the best we can for our men, but that's one thing we can't help them with."

"I know, but it's really a shame, in a way. People who have more children than they can feed and clothe properly seem to turn them out even if they don't want them, and people who desperately want just one can't seem to connect. One of life's odd little twists, I suppose."

"Speaking of odd little twists, Captain, didn't the colonel's telegram say he would be arriving here around five o'clock?"

Conway glanced toward the assembled company. "Yes it did, and it's past five now. Are the troops ready for inspection?"

"They are. Or at least as ready as they're ever going to get. Why was the colonel's arrival here set back three days, anyway? Windy's more than a little upset about being restricted here the way we are, just to wait for some desk colonel from back East. That uneasy feeling of his seems to be gnawing more at him every day."

"I've noticed that," Conway replied with a concerned look crossing his face, "and I'm in complete agreement and sympathy with him. But dammit, Matt, I'm bound by a direct order, the same as anybody else, unless I have justifiable evidence to override it. I would have moved on anything positive, anything at all, but we've had nothing to go on so far."

"I'm aware of that, Captain, and so is Windy. I'll just be glad when the colonel finally gets his butt here and we can get back to business as usual."

"So will I. But I haven't answered your question as to why the colonel is late." The captain paused and watched Kincaid closely. "Are you sure you want an answer?"

"From that look in your eyes, sir, I probably don't, but I'll risk it anyway. Why?"

"At the last minute he changed his mind and decided to stay over in Washington to attend the wedding of an influential general's niece."

Kincaid winced openly. "And we're bound here because of that?"

"Looks like it. Don't tell Windy unless you have to. He's

in a black enough mood as it is right now." Conway started to turn away, then stopped. "Oh, by the way. In keeping with protocol, Flora is preparing dinner for the colonel and his aide tonight. Certainly you'll be there, say around eight o'clock?"

"I'll be there, sir."

"Invite Windy as well, when you see him."

"I will, but he won't come, you know that as well as I do, Captain."

"I do, but offer the invitation anyway," Conway replied, heading toward the orderly room once more. "I've got a couple more things to do, then I'll come out and join you for the charade."

The sun was settling toward the horizon, and all of Easy Company, with the exception of the guard mount, was assembled on the parade, where they had been for the previous two hours. The lateness of the day, the long wait, and the useless display of military pomp caused a grating feeling of impatience to surge through Kincaid's chest, and he walked out to meet Conway, who was once more crossing the parade.

"Excuse me for saying this, sir, but if that son of a bitch isn't here within five minutes, I'm requesting permission to dismiss the company. We've all waited around long enough for something that shouldn't be happening in the first place, and the troops deserve better treatment than this."

"Permission granted, Matt. I don't care what the hell the consequences are, I've had about enough of this myself. Wait—"

"Lieutenant Kincaid!" a sentry shouted down from the lookout tower above the main gate. "Detachment coming, sir! I make it to be two squads, two officers, and a Gatling, sir!"

"Thank you, Private," Kincaid called back, while glancing at Conway. "Did he say a Gatling, Captain?"

"That's what he said, Matt. What the hell does he want with a Gatling gun?"

"Let me guess, sir. If the troops don't pass inspection, they will be executed on the spot?"

"Sounds no less plausible than any of the rest of the shit we've been exposed to, regarding the colonel," Conway said with a disgusted shake of his head. "Come on, let's join the troops and get this damned thing over with."

As Conway and Kincaid walked toward the assembled

troops, the platoon commanders brought their units to attention with a sharp rattle of brass fittings as the soldiers assumed the correct military posture. Each of the three platoons was arrayed in ranks of three squads, with the squad leaders standing at the right-hand end of each squad. Front and center before each platoon stood its commanding officer—a second lieutenant—accompanied by his platoon sergeant. Directly in front of the second platoon and some three paces forward stood Acting Master Sergeant Ben Cohen, whose appearance epitomized the obvious discomfort of all the other men of Easy Company. He stood with his broad shoulders thrust back and the buttons of his tunic dangerously near the bursting point under the strain of his considerable brawn.

The captain and his executive officer assumed their proper positions at the front of the company. The company colors and the flag of the United States were displayed by two stiff-armed corporals, who held the banners out at a forty-five degree angle from their bodies. When the visiting unit cantered onto the parade, the flags were snapped smartly to a vertical position and the two senior officers offered crisp salutes.

As the colonel stopped before them, he raised his gloved hand to his hatbrim and saluted with exaggerated casualness. Then he crossed his hands over the pommel of his saddle and made an initial, cursory inspection of the troops assembled for his review. The slight twist at the right corner of his mouth indicated that he was not entirely pleased with what he saw. Uniforms and equipment were worn and frayed from continuous use in the field, rifle stocks were scratched, dented, and obviously abused, and the soldiers were themselves a hard-eyed assemblage of men who seemed hardly to reflect the high ideals of the War Department.

Captain Conway stepped one pace forward and stood at attention near the colonel's horse. "Captain Warner Conway, sir, commanding officer, E Company, Outpost Number Nine. On behalf of the men of my command, I'd like to welcome you to Wyoming Territory."

Colonel Higgins stared silently down on Conway for several seconds before saying, "Stand at ease, Captain. Put your troops at parade rest."

"Sergeant Cohen!" Kincaid said while staring straight ahead. "Put the company at parade rest."

"Yessir! Company! P'rraaade *rest*!" Cohen barked, and rifles went forward at a forty-five degree angle, as did the flags once again, while left fists snapped to the small of the men's backs as they stepped legs apart.

Higgins nodded his satisfaction while leaning forward to brace his left foot in the stirrup and swing down from the saddle. He was a round-shouldered man with a visible paunch bulging above his waistline. Gray hair and long sideburns accented his florid face, and a severely clipped mustache gave his fleshy jowls the appearance of a bulldog whose face was sagging forward and was about to envelope his mouth. It was with some apparent difficulty that he managed to lift his bulk from the saddle, but Colonel Arthur Higgins's pudgy legs finally alighted on the hard-packed parade of Outpost Number Nine.

To his left and slightly behind him, Major Bradford Delaney also leaned forward preparatory to stepping down. He was a tall, lean individual, and there was the concentrated look about him of a man comfortable with facts and figures. His narrow face was drawn to a pointed chin, and an overly large Adam's apple bulged beneath the skin of his throat, as though he had swallowed a sharp cone that had not passed to his stomach. There was more than a hint of severity to his countenance; it could well have been that a smile might have damaged his face irreparably, so stern was the sharp outline of his overly long, dagger-tipped nose and thin, tightly compressed lips. At best, he appeared to be a man entirely devoid of humor, and at worst, a man for whom any display of levity would be a cardinal sin.

The adjutant stepped quickly forward to make the introductions as Colonel Higgins rounded the head of his horse. "Captain Conway," he said in a fairly high, flat voice, "I present to you Colonel Arthur Higgins, former chief of staff of the Tactical Deployment Council of the War Department. I am Major Bradford Delaney, the colonel's adjutant."

Offering his hand as he stepped forward, Conway felt the soft, mushy grip offered by the colonel and then accepted Delaney's hand, which he noted was surprisingly firm as it closed about his own.

"It is a pleasure to meet both of you, gentlemen," Conway said, sweeping his hand backward to indicate Matt. "May I introduce First Lieutenant Matt Kincaid, my executive officer."

Kincaid stepped forward and gripped each man's hand in turn while offering formal greetings, but it seemed as though the colonel had already dismissed him as his eyes focused not on Kincaid, but instead on the ranks.

"If you don't mind my saying so, Captain," Higgins said in a supercilious tone, "the men of your command are a rather scruffy-looking lot, to say the least."

Conway's chest tightened, but he managed to control his inclination to anger. "Theirs is a miserable job in a scruffy environment, Colonel. Considering the circumstances, I'm quite proud of them and their accomplishments."

Higgins arched an eyebrow while pulling the glove off his right hand and slapping it against his left palm. "Proud, Captain? Perhaps you've been away from a proper military installation for too great a time." Then he smiled with all the warmth of an executioner. "Shall we inspect?"

As the colonel and his aide moved down the line before the first rank of troops, Conway and Kincaid fell in behind. There was no doubting that the men had heard the colonel's undisguised remarks, and they seemed to stand taller, straighter, and prouder than before as a direct result. Kincaid could feel the swell of pride rise collectively within the company, as well as the almost tangible tide of resentment aimed at this deskbound, lard-assed martinet.

Oblivious to any emotions other than his own, Higgins prowled up and down the ranks, occasionally stopping to inspect a torn belt loop or a holster with the flap cut away for rapid access when survival hung in the balance. Nearly five minutes passed before Higgins suspended his scrutiny of the troops without even bothering to inspect the third platoon.

"I think I've seen quite enough, Captain," he said peremptorily. "Somehow I had expected a more acceptable display of military—"

Conway had heard as much as he intended to listen to. "Pardon my interruption, sir, but wasn't there a specific reason why Easy Company was chosen for your 'reorientation' period?"

A flush crept onto the colonel's cheeks and he cleared his throat while trying to judge the hard edge in Conway's tone. "Well . . . ah . . . yes, of course. You have one of the finest combat records of any unit west of the Mississippi, and for that reason you were selected as the unit I should accompany in the field."

"That's well and good, sir, but you seem to be overlooking

the fact that the reputations of the type you just mentioned are *earned*. You have just inspected one of the finest, most courageous groups of fighting men in the entire United States Army." Conway knew he was courting disaster, speaking as loudly as he was and challenging a colonel before a company of enlisted men, but at no expense would he tolerate criticism of any kind of soldiers whom he knew risked their lives daily with less complaint than the colonel might address to a hangnail.

"You might see some irregularities in dress and outfitting," Conway continued, the heat rising in his face, "but when it comes to laying your life on the line, those things don't mean a tinker's damn in hell. Those are fighting men, sir, and if they look a little rough to you, it is precisely because they *are* fighting men. I had assumed, however incorrectly, that that is what army service is all about."

Kincaid instinctively perceived that Conway had been driven to the limits of self-restraint, and knowing that the captain was not a man to be pushed by anyone when he knew his judgment to be correct, he stepped quickly forward.

"Pardon me, Colonel. Perhaps you would like to inspect the stables or the mess hall? There is much more to Outpost Number Nine that you haven't seen, and since the hour is growing late, perhaps we should press on." Matt glanced over his shoulder toward Delaney, and thought he detected a slight understanding smile on the adjutant's lips. "Don't you agree, Major?"

"Yes, of course I do, Lieutenant," Delaney replied with a sweep of his hand across his waist. "Colonel, if you so desire, I'm sure Lieutenant Kincaid would be kind enough to show us the way."

Higgins waved a pudgy hand in a desultory manner. "That won't be necessary, Major. I've seen enough. I'm tired, hungry, and filthy. If my quarters have been prepared, I would like to retire to freshen up."

"Certainly, sir," Kincaid said quickly, with a glance at Conway, who was obviously struggling to regain his composure. "If I may direct you to your quarters, it would be my pleasure. As I understand it, you are invited to dine with Captain Conway and his wife this evening. Is that not correct, Captain?"

The captain's gratitude for Kincaid's timely take-charge attitude was amply displayed through the appreciative look in his eyes. "Yes, of course, Colonel. It will be a pleasure that my wife and I have been anticipating. The major is invited as well, as is Lieutenant Kincaid. I'll have an orderly call for you at eight o'clock."

Delaney looked at Matt, and there was an altered tone of respect in his voice, a tone that indicated he was secretly pleased with the way Conway had stood up to the colonel, and the professional manner in which Kincaid had salvaged the situation for his commanding officer.

"Lieutenant, the escort detachment will be returning to Regiment in the morning, but for tonight they'll need quarters and facilities for their mounts. Would you be so kind as to arrange that for me?"

"Certainly, Major," Kincaid replied, turning back to the ranks. "Sergeant Olsen? See that the colonel's escort detachment and their mounts are properly cared for."

"Yessir!"

"Sergeant Cohen?"

"Yessir?"

"Dismiss the company and have the first and second prepared for combat patrol first thing in the morning."

"Yessir."

As Kincaid led the colonel and the major toward the bachelor officers' quarters, he heard the booming voice of Cohen rolling across the parade.

"Company, disss*missed*!"

The portly senior officer waddled behind Kincaid, and the adjutant followed them both at a respectful distance. Inwardly, Matt smiled at the ridiculousness of the entire situation, and when he glanced toward the main gates, he saw a tall man wearing fringed buckskins shake his head and hunch away from the post to walk alone toward the tipi ring located a short distance away.

It was five minutes before eight, and the lamps spilled forth a mellow, whitish-yellow light in the quarters of Captain and Mrs. Warner Conway. The odors of freshly baked bread, simmering pot roast, and baked potatoes permeated the air, accented by the gentle aroma of Conway's cigar. Flora was resplendent in an off-yellow dress with her black hair neatly coiffured in a series of long, springlike curls trailing down her back. The white apron secured tightly around her narrow waist emphasized the outward thrust of her bosom, and her cheeks were slightly pink from the heat of the stove as she stooped with a potholder to test the progress of her biscuits.

Inside the sitting area, Conway brushed an ash from his cigar and raised his brandy glass towawd Kincaid as if offering a toast. "Matt, I can't thank you enough for stepping in the way you did today. I'd had just about all I could endure from Higgins even before he arrived here, but when he started laying the heavy criticism on our people, that was taking a step beyond anything I feel I have to tolerate."

"I understand that, sir. No thanks necessary, I felt that I was only doing my job."

"Your job!" Conway scoffed. "It was my job not to lose my temper, but I did anyway. I couldn't take some stuffed shirt, who has detained us from our designated mission, riding in like the great white savior while turning his nose up at the troops whose combat record brought him here in the first place!"

"Success does have its drawbacks, Captain. How long is the colonel intending to stay?"

"Christ only knows. Until he feels he has been successfully 'reoriented,' whatever in hell that means to a person who never was 'oriented' in the first place. Then, I guess, he assumes command of a regiment somewhere."

"And when that day comes, Captain," Matt observed, swirling the brandy glass and studying its contents, "it will be a sad occasion for all concerned. But the future will take care of itself, I suppose. Right now our main concern is with the present. Your dinner guests should be arriving shortly, and we're going to have to endure for a couple of hours."

"And endure we will, Matt," Conway responded with a slight twinkle in his eye. "I slipped up this afternoon, but that won't happen again. The only way to deal with a superior officer like Higgins is to implant ideas and logical decisions in his brain in such a manner that he feels they were his ideas all along. We've both learned through long, hard years of experience that you can lead a lame horse a lot farther than you can drag a dead one."

Kincaid chuckled and started to respond, but Flora, poking her head around the doorjamb, prevented his reply.

"Excuse me, gentlemen, but I forgot to ask—Matt? Is Windy going to join us for dinner? We have more than enough, and I hope you passed along the invitation."

"Yes I did, Mrs. Conway," Kincaid replied. "But he declined with thanks. It seems that even the quality of your marvelous dinners was not sufficient enticement to lure him into the colonel's company."

Flora smiled and cocked her head in a coquettish manner. "You'd better watch yourself, Lieutenant Kincaid. You'll use sugar-coated words like that to the wrong woman someday, and there will be a ring on your finger before you know it."

"I'm sure he'll be more cautious with his tongue in situations such as that, my dear," Conway said with a laugh. "And if he isn't, then shame on him."

"And what is *that* supposed to mean?" Flora responded with affected anger, planting her fists on her hips.

"Only that the trap is baited for an abbreviated dinner, love," Conway said with a teasing smile. "It's leg irons and chains after that."

"Hah!" Flora rejoined with a haughty toss of her head, while retreating to the kitchen.

Kincaid offered an easy smile while raising his glass to his lips. "You're a lucky man, Captain. There are few who—"

The sound of knuckles rapping on the door interrupted Kincaid's statement, and he placed his glass on an end table while rising. "It sounds as though your dinner guests have arrived, sir. Shall I show them in?"

"Yes, Matt. Please do. I'll join Flora." When Kincaid opened the door, the orderly stood to one side and said, "Colonel Higgins and Major Delaney, sir."

"Thank you, Corporal. Gentlemen? Won't you please come in?"

Both men wore fresh uniforms, and their boots and brass had obviously enjoyed a recent polishing. There was an air of something nearing cordiality about the colonel, and Kincaid wondered briefly if it was the result of having no enlisted men in the vicinity to impress.

"Good evening, Lieutenant," Higgins said, stepping into the captain's quarters while removing his hat from freshly slicked-back hair. "It was kind of your commanding officer to invite us."

"I'm sure it's his pleasure, sir," Kincaid replied, endeavoring to keep the hint of irony from being too obvious in his voice. "Good evening, Major Delaney."

"Thanks, and the same to you, Lieutenant," Delaney said

in a friendly tone. "I haven't enjoyed a home-cooked meal in a long time."

Kincaid closed the door while saying, "Then you are in for a pleasant surprise, Major. Mrs. Conway is an excellent cook."

As Matt guided them across the room, it was obvious that the colonel was amazed by Flora's beauty. Surprise was plain on his face and he unconsciously traced a pudgy finger across the lower edges of his mustache before tearing his eyes away from her and accepting the outstretched hand of Captain Conway.

"Good of you to come, Colonel," Conway said, while touching Flora's elbow lightly. "I'd like for you to meet my wife, Flora. Flora, this is Colonel Higgins and his adjutant, Major Delaney."

Flora extended her hand daintily while the colonel swept into a deep bow and grasped her fingers at the same time.

"It's a pleasure to meet you, Colonel," Flora offered in a demure tone. "My husband has told me a great deal about you, and I am most fascinated. I'm anxious to learn more."

"The pleasure is mine, my dear," Higgins replied, making no attempt to hide the delight he found in Flora's words. "Mine has been but a humble and dedicated life given to the service of this great country of ours."

"A noble purpose indeed," Flora said with an easy smile while she removed her fingers from the colonel's hand with considerable effort and turned to Delaney. "It's nice to make your acquaintance, Major. Thank you for honoring our invitation to dinner."

Delaney took Flora's hand in a courteous manner and gripped her fingers briefly before releasing them. "My thanks for the thought, Mrs. Conway. I have no idea what you've prepared, but judging by the delectable aroma in this room, I have no fear of disappointment."

"You're very kind," Flora responded. Then she turned to her husband and said, "Warner, won't you please show these gentlemen to the sitting room? Perhaps they would like a glass of brandy while I finish preparing dinner."

"Of course, my dear. Gentlemen?" Conway said, gesturing toward the adjoining room. "Please have a seat and I'll pour the drinks."

After hanging up the visiting officers' hats, Kincaid resumed his seat and accepted a refill from the bottle offered by Conway after glasses had been filled and served to Higgins and Delaney.

"To your health, gentlemen," the captain said, taking up his own glass and extending it. "And to a pleasant stay at Outpost Number Nine."

"Hear, hear," Higgins mumbled, swilling down half the drink with a bob of his double chin, then mopping his mouth with the back of a hand. "But this business of calling installations of this nature merely 'outpost number' such-and-such grates on me somehow. It seems that proper names would be more suitable."

Conway and Kincaid glanced at each other, and there was a twinkle in the captain's eye when he looked back at the colonel. "Yes, it is a mite barren, to say the least. Perhaps once you've assumed your rightful position as a regimental commander, you can use the power of your position to have something done about that. I can asssre you, the selection of names for these outposts is one of our primary concerns, and the obscurity of our title is most deleterious to the moral of the men assigned here."

Higgins nodded his head as if deep in thought. "I would assume that to be correct, Captain. Please be assured, it will be a priority matter with me when I am in command."

"That's truly heartening," Conway replied in a serious but approving tone that showed deep respect. "The fact that we are armed with single-shot Springfields instead of repeating Spencers is inconsequential to us, as are the lack of replacements, being paid on time, promotion when promotions are due, and the difficulty in securing sufficient equipment and supplies to keep us adequately stocked. Our principal concern is the fact that we are nothing more than a numerical dot on the vast map of military installations."

Had it not been for the colonel's position, from which he could see Flora leaning over the table as she arranged the serving dishes, Colonel Higgins may well have perceived the facetious tone of Conway's words, but as it was, his mind was occupied with other matters.

"Yes, I'm sure it is," he said absently. Then, catching himself, he glanced toward Conway. "If I may be so bold as to say so, Captain, you have a beautiful and absolutely charming wife."

"Boldness is the principle attribute of a distinguished soldier, Colonel, and truth is his moral guardian. Thank you for the kind remarks concerning my wife."

Major Delaney had easily detected the mental and verbal game that Conway was playing with his superior, and it was with a sense of contentment that he watched the flustered colonel struggle for an equally profound remark to match the one previously levied by Conway.

"Yes, of course..." Higgins stammered. "Moral...ah... integrity is...ah..."

Having removed her apron, Flora stepped to the entranceway of the sitting room at that precise moment and held her hands, fingertips pressed together, before her waist. "Dinner is served, gentlemen. Now if you will all be so kind as to join me at the table, we'll see if hunger can properly disguise the flaws in my cooking abilities."

Immensely relieved, Higgins surged to his feet while the others rose about him. "I'm sure you underestimate your own talents, Mrs. Conway," the colonel said, lapsing easily into the mode of flattery that had served him so well during his years on the banquet circuit in Washington. "I doubt that I have ever anticipated a meal with the relish I'm now experiencing, nor have I ever had the opportunity of enjoying it in more charming company."

"That remains to be seen, Colonel," Flora replied with a smile that was both engaging and slightly chilly at the same time. "Shall we dine, gentlemen?"

six

Throughout the course of the meal, it became increasingly evident to Kincaid why the Conways' marriage was so stable and secure. Having chosen a seat next to Flora after holding the chair for her, Higgins directed nearly every syllable he spoke in her direction, with fatuous admiration. And it was a marvel to see how well Flora handled the colonel, who obviously fancied himself a ladies' man, and who doubtlessly had a substantial reputation as a womanizer back in Washington. Flora deftly fielded the colonel's remarks by turning them to her advantage while avoiding offensive rejection. She feigned interest in the one-sided conversation, smiling, scowling, laughing, and scolding lightly as the situation dictated, while ever making it obvious that she was completely beyond the colonel's reach and definitely out of his league.

Conway seemed not to be aware of Higgins's total infatuation with his wife, and if he was, that concern was not revealed. After attempting to engage the colonel in conversation at the beginning of the meal and failing, he directed his attention to the other men at the table, and they talked amiably about a range of subjects. Delancy proved to be a perfect guest, providing intelligent insights and even displaying a sense of humor that seemed inconsistent with his otherwise stern countenance.

As Kincaid watched the colonel make a complete fool of himself, he remembered his own earlier conversation with Conway regarding jealousy in marriage. He remembered the captain's having said, "The basic element of love is trust, and since I love her completely, I also trust her completely. To tell you the truth, I would be more surprised if she weren't the object of admiration than angered by the fact that she is." Without doubt, Conway's statements were being put to the supreme test and were being borne out beautifully.

When the meal was finally over, the four officers retired to the sitting room for brandy and cigars while Flora made an overly long task of clearing the table and washing the dishes. Since it was obvious she had no intention of joining them, Higgins reluctantly directed his attention to Conway.

"That was an excellent meal, Captain Conway, made even better by delightful conversation."

"Thank you, Colonel. I wonder if the ability to cook and the ability to converse go hand in hand. Are you a good cook, Colonel?" Conway asked with a disarming smile.

"Heavens, no!"

"Then perhaps my observation is more fact than conjecture."

A puzzled look crossed Higgins's face as he tried to decipher the captain's meaning, and he failed to notice the satisfied smiles worn by Kincaid and Delaney. Abandoning the mental chore, Higgins puffed once on his cigar and looked at Kincaid, who was sitting directly across from him.

"Lieutenant? Did I hear you tell your first sergeant to have two platoons ready to move out on combat patrol tomorrow morning? As I recall, you issued that order shortly after we arrived, and stipulated the first and second."

"That's correct, sir. We have a suspicion that our presence is needed up north."

"Ah, my good Lieutenant," Higgins said grandly as he leaned forward to dust an ash from his cigar, "this man's army can neither travel nor commit itself on mere suspicion. We need concrete evidence before we take action."

"And what, sir, do we do if that concrete evidence is not yet in our possession? We may have to search out the evidence in order to take the appropriate action."

"Incorrect. And unnecessary, I might add." Higgins glanced at the two officers from Easy Company in turn, and there was a cunning look in his eyes. "Because I have the evidence we need, and fortunately your suspicions were correct this time."

"What do you mean by that, Colonel?" Conway asked cautiously.

"What I mean, Captain," Higgins replied while sliding a hand inside his tunic, "is this."

He produced a folded piece of paper that was obviously a telegram. "This arrived at Regimental Headquarters the day after I did, and I elected to deliver it personally. Rather than read the whole thing verbatim, I'll simply paraphrase. It seems some buffalo hunters were heading up north and were preparing to cross a Cheyenne reservation called the Clearwater. They saw a column of smoke rising from where the agency buildings were supposed to be. They saw the backs of two Indians leaving, and it looked like they were carrying something, probably stolen property. At any rate, they made them out to be either Sioux or Cheyenne, and part of a large war party, because the agency was destroyed and the agent and his entire family were killed. Their bones were found inside the burned-out trading post. Those things happen all the time, I suppose, but—"

Kincaid caught his breath and leaned forward sharply. "Colonel, what you've just told us is of extreme importance to the captain and myself. Check that telegram again. Are you sure it said the Clearwater Reservation?"

"Of course I'm sure," Higgins said rather sharply, while flipping the telegram open and trailing a finger down the yellow paper. "Right here. It says right here, in plain English, 'the Clearwater Agency.'"

"Does it give the name of the agent?"

"Yes it does, but I didn't think that was important, since he's dead anyway."

"It's more important than you could possibly know," Kincaid said evenly, dispensing with military formalities. "Look at it again and read the name to me."

"Lieutenant, I think you have the prerogatives of rank a little confused, which I'll excuse as the result of too much brandy," Higgins snapped. "Lieutenants do not *tell* colonels to do anything."

"Do it!"

The rigid look on Kincaid's face, the tenseness of his body, the commanding tone of his voice, and the fact that his hands had formed into white-knuckled fists seemed to convince the colonel that at that precise moment there were no junior officers in the room. His eyes went quickly to the telegram again.

"Yes, here it is. The man's name is Ira Griffin."

"Oh God," Kincaid whispered in the hushed room. "Oh God."

Conway was searching his mind as he watched the pained expression on Matt's face, trying to remember what was so important about the agent's name.

"Did you know him, Matt?" Conway asked softly.

"Yes and no, sir," Kincaid replied, turning toward the captain. "May I speak with you in the kitchen, sir?"

"Certainly. Excuse us for a moment, gentlemen," Conway said, rising quickly and leaving the room. Higgins stared at Delaney in confusion, and the adjutant shrugged his shoulders.

When they were safely out of earshot, Conway turned to Kincaid. "All right, Matt. What have you got?"

"Do you remember when we were talking with Windy over in the stables the other day, when he got back from Canada?"

"Yes, I remember. We were discussing a hunch he had."

"That's part of it, but more importantly, do you remember his saying he had some friends up there and that he was concerned for their safety?"

Conway pursed his lips in thought. "Yes, come to think of it, I do. I don't remember his mentioning any names, but he might have."

"He did." Kincaid paused and studied the captain's face. "His friend's name was Griffin, and he was the agent at the Clearwater Reservation."

"Oh Christ," Conway said softly. "I do remember now. Damn it! If we'd gone up there as he suggested, we might have prevented this from happening."

"Exactly. And the man who kept us from going is sitting in that room."

"That ignorant, insufferable son of a bitch," Conway muttered through gritted teeth, with a menacing glance in the direction of the sitting room. "I've a mind to go back in there and knock him flat on his fat, overstuffed colonel's ass."

"That was my first impulse too, sir. But with a man like him, it wouldn't accomplish anything more than the ruination of your military career. He'll get his in time, I'm sure, if Windy doesn't do it before then."

The mention of his chief scout and personal friend changed the expression on Conway's face to one of concern. "Damn, it's going to be rough having to tell Windy the bad news."

"I'm aware of that, sir. I'll tell him myself, the only question is when. If I told him right now, he'd be on his horse and heading up that way tonight."

"Yes, I'm sure he would. Tell him in the morning before you leave. While it won't take his mind off it, maybe the ride will help calm him down."

Kincaid nodded. "That's what I was thinking. But either

way, it's not going to be easy. A friend to Windy is like a god to anyone else."

"Yeah, I know. Come on, let's go back in there and be done with Higgins for one night."

The colonel glanced up hotly from where he was refilling his brandy glass, as Conway and Kincaid entered the room. "Well, I certainly hope this need for secrecy between you two is not a permanent condition. That's the first time I've ever had two junior officers walk out on me, and I certainly don't intend to tolerate it again."

"Our apologies, Colonel," Conway said, again in control of his emotions. "We were discussing a personal matter. At first light tomorrow morning, I'll be sending two platoons to the Clearwater agency to capture or kill whoever is responsible for the deaths of the Griffin family and the destruction of government property."

"Excellent, Captain. Excellent," Higgins chortled as the glass went toward his lips. "And I shall lead the expedition."

"You, Colonel?" Conway asked in surprise. "It sounds as if we're going to be up against some pretty desperate people, and if you don't mind my saying so, I think an experienced officer in the field, like Lieutenant Kincaid, should be in command."

Higgins wiped a dribble of brandy from his chin while watching Conway with glittering eyes. "The fact that we need a big victory, my dear Captain, is precisely why I must command. And that also is the reason I requisitioned a Gatling gun for this patrol. I am not the least bit ashamed to admit that I have a lot at stake here, personally. Inasmuch as we have a major uprising on our hands, the fact of my being the commanding officer who engineered the defeat of the rebellious element won't look at all bad on my service record. With the Gatling and your troops, we cannot possibly be defeated."

There was a disgusted, almost sick look on Conway's face. "And you would risk my troops for your own personal gain?"

"Risk? What risk?" Higgins asked in feigned surprise, while allowing himself a sly grin. "We have a few Indians who need to be taught a lesson, that's all. You have been more than generous with reminders of how skilled your troops are in combat, and it has been suggested that I see their performance in the field myself, which I intend to do." The colonel's eyes narrowed to puffy slits as he added with unnecessary emphasis, "And I will see that performance as their commanding officer."

"Colonel, either you are very foolish or totally insane, and I intend to wire Washington in the morning to verify which is the case," Conway said, turning his back on Higgins.

"Very well, Captain. But we will be gone at first light, as you said, and besides, your telegram will do no good. My contacts in the War Department have given me full rein for my actions on this Western tour, and I can assure you that those same contacts will not think too highly of your questioning my decisions. Particularly after I send a telegram of my own, detailing your truculent and insubordinate attitude." Higgins offered a placating smile. "Think about it, Captain. Think long and hard, because the decision you make may well cost you both your commission and your command."

Sensing that Conway was prepared to sacrifice both, Kincaid stepped forward. "Pardon me, Captain, but I'm afraid you have no choice. I am willing to serve under Colonel Higgins in the field"—he glanced at Higgins—"provided I have complete command of one platoon while, on paper at least, he is in command of the entire operation. Now, Colonel, I believe it's your turn to do some thinking. I am absolutely positive that Captain Conway is prepared to buck you all the way on this, and according to regulations, he is authorized to deny you command if he deems you unfit to perform that function. I propose a compromise: you are commanding officer of record, and I am commanding officer of the first platoon. Do we have a deal, Colonel?"

A flush crept into Higgins's cheeks as he reached for the brandy decanter again. "Well . . . I . . . I'm not used to having to lower myself to making compromises with a junior—"

"Do we have a deal or not, Colonel?" Kincaid asked bluntly. "If not, then I will risk my commission along with the captain's, and testify against you in the highest military courts."

"I think you'd better accept the compromise, Colonel," Delaney said in a flat tone, as if he were not emotionally involved in the outcome either way. "We both know the service record of these two officers, and doubtlessly, over the course of things, they have made some contacts within the War Department themselves."

Higgins hesitated, then swilled his brandy down and slammed the glass on a nearby table. "All right, compromise accepted. I am the commanding officer of record, and if you cross me on this, Lieutenant, you'll be digging latrines the minute I find out you have."

"Very good, sir. I won't cross you, but if I did, it would be because I prefer digging latrines over digging graves."

"Hah!" the colonel scoffed, shuffling toward the door. "You combat types have always been known to overexaggerate conditions in the field."

"Perhaps some do, Colonel, but I think you'll find that assumption to be incorrect in this case. I would like to make one final suggestion, if I may?"

Higgins paused in the entranceway and turned with a weary air, as if bored with it all. "Yes, Lieutenant? I'm listening."

"Leave the Gatling gun behind, sir. It will only slow us down."

"The Gatling goes where I go, damn it!" Higgins raged, his jowls quivering. "And that's final! Come, Major. It is time to retire."

Delaney stood and shrugged his shoulders helplessly, while the colonel stepped out into the night. "Please thank Mrs. Conway for the delicious meal, Captain, and thank you for the invitation. I apologize for the way things went, but as you can see, being the colonel's aide isn't all peaches and cream. Good night."

After Conway had showed the major to the door, he turned back toward Kincaid with a relieved smile. "Thanks, Matt. That's twice today that you've pulled my fat out of the fire. I would have gone all the way if you hadn't stepped in."

"I know you would have, Captain, as would I, given the same situation. But the way we've got it worked out is best all the way around. With Windy and me along, he can't foul things up too badly."

"Be prepared to take full command anytime you see fit," Conway cautioned, "and I'll back you all the way."

"If it means jeopardizing the safety and well-being of our troops, sir, please be assured that I will. Good night, Captain, thanks for the dinner."

"You're more than welcome, Matt," Conway said, watching Kincaid cross to the door, take his hat off the hat tree, and prepare to step outside. "Oh, Matt? One thing more: Did you notice that Higgins left and didn't even offer to take Flora to bed?"

Kincaid grinned broadly. "I noticed that. I'm sure she'll be crushed."

"Absolutely," Conway returned with a chuckle.

"Please give her my condolences. 'Night, Captain."

"'Night, Matt. After you've talked to Windy, tell him I'll see him before he goes."

"Sure thing, sir."

The first tinges of pink had just touched the eastern horizon when Kincaid parted the main gates of Outpost Number Nine and turned toward the tipi ring in the distance. He walked with little enthusiasm, even though the predawn stillness gave promise of an invigorating day. The prairie was coming to life, with the sounds of birds chirping and singing. The buzzing clatter of tiny insects hidden in the tall grass, wet with dew, seemed to transform a turbulent world into one of peace and harmony. Prairie flowers were in abundance, their petals hooded against the night chill, and the blackish-green of the grassland, as yet devoid of sunlight, seemed to indicate that the blossoms were defenseless in the hours of darkness. And yet there was a oneness of nature, as though all things lived and perished according to a preordained plan according to which there was no questioning the reasons why things lived or why they wilted and died.

It was in that environment of calm that Kincaid walked, hands in his pockets, head down, and mind aflame with the single question: Why? Why did it always have to be this way; men killing other men for reasons that had no justification? Had Griffin known the outcome, he would surely have given his assailants whatever they desired, just as the smaller plant adapts to shade in deference to its broad-leafed cousin. *Are we not all cousins?* he wondered, kicking a clump of sod with his boot, *cousins in the eyes of God and in the name of humanity? Or are we simply barbarians who rob, rape and murder as the mood strikes us? Is Colonel Higgins the living metaphor that serves to exemplify all that is wrong with mankind? A man who lives only to gain glory for himself, with total disregard for the needs and wants of others?*

He abandoned his speculations as he neared Tipi Town, the ring of Indian dwellings that stood a few hundred yards to the northeast of the outpost, and housed groups of transient, "pacified" Indians. Kincaid saw several small cooking fires blazing, with squaws moving around them like hunched-over ghosts, dreading the rising of the sun and the drudgery of another day. As he angled toward the tipi where he knew he would find Windy, a sense of overwhelming dread came over him, and for the first time that morning, he wondered what he would actually say.

"Good morning, Me-You," he said to the attractive Arapaho squaw tending a fire before the tipi, using the name Windy had given her in response to her eternal question whenever he told her he was going somewhere: "Me-You?"

Me-You smiled and nodded toward the antelope hide covering the entrance to the tipi. "Him not good happy today. Me like it here. Cook food."

"Thanks, Me-You," Kincaid responded with a cordial smile. "I'll drag that old bear out of his den and make him work for a living."

Obviously, Windy heard Kincaid's voice, because he said, "Is that you, Matt? Just a minute. Let me pull these worn-out boots over these tired old feet and I'll be right out."

Moments later, Windy pushed the flap aside and stood with a luxurious stretch. "Should be a beautiful day, Matt," he observed, stifling a yawn with the back of a fist, while examining the sky. "We movin' out this mornin'?"

"Yes we are, Windy. In half an hour. Colonel Higgins will be in command."

"That should be about as much fun as kickin' a mad grizzly in the balls. Why's that lard-assed son of a bitch in charge of combat patrol?"

"Because he's a colonel."

"Figures."

Then, in response to Kincaid's diminished tone, Windy squinted one eye and looked at him in the rapidly flooding dawn. "You all right, Matt? Sounds to me like somethin's wrong."

"There is. Come on, let's take a walk."

With the instincts of a frontiersman used to hearing bad news, Windy fell silent and moved in stride with Kincaid, who was now walking away from the tipi ring. After more than a minute of silence, he glanced across at Kincaid and said, "Spill it, Matt. I'm gonna have to know sooner or later."

"Goddammit, Windy, I wish I didn't have to be the one to tell you this," Kincaid replied, continuing to look down at his boots as they swept through the dew-slick grass.

"Somebody has to. Might just as well be a friend."

"If that's the case, I'd just as soon be your enemy."

"Naw, you wouldn't wish that on yourself or anybody else, Matt," Windy said, stooping to snatch a long blade of grass and place it in the corner of his mouth.

"No, I suppose not. But I'm afraid you've got some enemies now that we're going to have to deal with."

"Kinda used to that, Matt. And most of 'em are ten toes up and six feet down. Got anybody specific in mind?"

"No, not really. Remember the hunch you mentioned the other day about some problems up north?"

"Yup. I remember."

"Well, they've become a reality." Kincaid paused to glance at the scout. "Your friend, Ira Griffin, and his family have been killed."

There was no visible change in Windy's expression. He continued to chew the blade of grass as he stared straight ahead at the rising sun. But when he finally spoke, there was a deadly hardness in his voice.

"Who done it?"

"We don't know for sure, Windy. The colonel's telegram, the one he's kept in his goddamned pocket for two days, implicates either the Sioux or the Cheyenne. The agency is totally destroyed, and some buff hunters are supposed to have seen some people bearing the description of those two tribes riding away."

"Don't think so, Matt. Sioux, maybe, but not Cheyenne. That's their reservation, and they're too smart to shit in their own nest. Did they find the bodies?"

"Yes, but they had been burned in the trading post when it was put to the torch."

"Any fingers missin'?"

"Not that I know of."

"Well, if there ain't, then we can be pretty sure it wasn't the Cheyenne. They usually cut the fingers off their victims."

Kincaid couldn't help but marvel at the scout's lack of distress at the loss of his dear friends, and he was surprised by Windy's carefully calculated questions, in the face of such a revelation.

"I'm very sorry about the loss of your friends, Windy."

"Sorry don't buy whiskey, Matt. If Ira and his folks are

dead, that's something we can't change. Puttin' a little death on the people who done it is what I'm concerned about now. Goddammit, I had a feelin' somethin' was gonna turn shitty."

"Yeah, I know," Kincaid said absently. "And if it hadn't been for Higgins, we'd have had a patrol up there and maybe could have prevented it."

"'If' ain't no better'n 'sorry,' Matt. He'll get his, and if it has to come from me, so be it. I know he didn't actually pull the trigger, but he might just as well have, to my way of thinkin'. And he'll have to answer for that, after I'm done with the ones who actually did the killin'." The scout paused to stare at the northern horizon, and the muscles were tight along his firmly set jaw. "Ira Griffin was my friend, Matt. Nothin' more needs to be said than that. He had a purty wife and six of the finest kids you ever saw. There won't be no peace in my mind till I level a pair of sights on the ones who did 'em harm."

"I'm aware of that, and even though I didn't know any of them personally, I feel the same damned way. As far as the colonel goes, we'll just have to handle him in our own way by letting him think he's in charge. As far as you and I are concerned, things aren't going to be any different on this patrol than on any of the others. I wouldn't be surprised if Colonel Higgins falls victim to his own vanity."

"Just keep him as far away from me as you can, Matt, and don't let him get in my way whenever we catch up with the sons of bitches that killed Ira. If he does, he's dead."

"I can't predict what he's going to do, Windy, but I'll keep an eye on him the best I can."

"That's all I can ask. I'll be goin' to get my rifle now, and I'll join you in a few minutes."

Kincaid nodded. "Good. Your horse is already saddled and ready to go."

Windy nodded and started to turn back toward Tipi Town, but then he stopped and said, "Matt? Would we have time to get a telegram off to the War Department and receive a reply before we leave?"

"Should be able to. What have you got in mind?"

"Remember that war goin' on up in Canada that I told you about?"

"Yes."

"I'd like to know if some métis and Cree got their butts kicked. If they did, the Sioux just might be off the hook. Never know for sure till we get there, I 'spect, but I'd like to find out if we've got some blood-eyed Cree on our hands. From a distance they look a hell of a lot like Cheyenne."

"Sure, I'll send it right now. We don't always get a lot of cooperation from the MacDonald government up in Canada, and there's a little bad blood between our government and theirs because he's letting Sitting Bull hide out up there, but it's worth a try."

"Let's try. If we're up against the Cree, then we've got a real battle on our hands, to my way of thinkin'. They don't know nothin' about rules, and if they've come down on our side of the border, they just might be hell bent on killin' any whites they come across."

"Let's hope they haven't, then. I'll get that wire off right now."

The scout didn't reply. Instead he walked swiftly away to retrieve the big Sharps that generally did most of his talking for him.

seven

Attached to a lance that had been driven into the prairie sod, the bloody flag was outlined against the flame-red skyline as the sun sank from view. The silence of the plains was accented by the murmurings of crickets and other insects stirring from their day's slumber. Beside a small fire, an exceptionally large Indian sat trailing his fingers admiringly through the long blond hair of the young woman beside him, while sipping occasionally from the whiskey bottle in his other hand. The girl's blue eyes were fixed on the flames, and there was a hard detachment about them that belied the soft warmth of shadows dancing across her face. Rides Big Horses pulled Lisa toward him to smell her hair, and she made no move to resist him while yielding without enthusiasm. Her body was stiff, and she bent sideways at the waist, only to recoil the instant the pressure of the Indian's hand was released from behind her head.

Rides Big Horses grinned and glanced across at Johnny Singletree, who sat opposite him with Lorie by his side.

"Are these not magnificent war prizes, métis?" Rides Big Horses asked gloatingly. "They will keep our lodges warm for many winters."

Singletree, also with bottle in hand, massaged Lorie's thigh before turning her face to him with a less-than-gentle grip on her chin. Her eyes were swollen and red-rimmed from incessant crying, and her shoulders trembled as she sobbed even now. She cringed, trying to pull away, but the métis' grip held her firmly.

"They are as beautiful as the mountains and their eyes are the color of the lakes, but this one seems to have been overfilled by the winter storms."

Rides Big Horses laughed coarsely. "She has much *mischee*, métis. Your blankets will not be dry for many moons."

Perhaps it was in response to the Cree's humor, or merely the result of whiskey-induced anger, but Singletree suddenly released his hold on Lorie's chin and slapped her sharply across the cheek. The girl recoiled, but not in time to avoid an even sharper slap on the other side of her head. The métis held up one finger admonishingly and lowered his head to look directly into Lorie's eyes.

"No more," he said firmly. "No more. Go to my blanket and wait for me. I have words to say to the Cree chief."

Lorie hesitated, lips quivering and tears trickling down the sides of her face, and she appeared to be frozen in place. Singletree turned and waved impatiently at Lisa. "Take your sister to my blankets, and then go to the Cree's. We talk alone."

Lisa rose quickly, ignoring Rides Big Horses' testing squeeze of a firm, rounded buttock, and moved past the fire to kneel beside Lorie. She placed an arm gently around her sister's shoulders and helped her to her feet, and the two girls moved away in the darkness.

Rides Big Horses stared after them as he lifted the bottle once more. "They are sent from the gods, métis. They are a vision."

"They are twins and they will cause us much trouble, Cree. You should not have brought them here."

"They are my prize," Rides Big Horses snapped defensively. "I won them in battle. If you have no hunger for them, I will have two."

"Your prize in battle?" Singletree said. "Does a mighty Cree warrior consider killing one man and his children a victory in battle?"

Rides Big Horses watched the métis warily before responding. He was uncertain as to the other's meaning, and he had no intention of being made to look like a fool. "Remember, métis, it was you who told me to take what I wanted if the white man refused to give it to me."

"Yes, it was I. But I didn't tell you to kill the agent, his wife, and two of his children, burn the agency to the ground, and take four young ones captive. It was the whiskey that told you to do those things. Now the Americans will be looking for us with much more interest. They expect Indians to steal, and if that were all you'd done, they would only have made you go back to Canada. But now this will not be so. They will hunt for us as the eagle hunts the rabbit."

A crafty look came into the Cree's eyes. "But the eagle does not always have great medicine. The smart rabbit knows when to go to its lodge."

"We are far from our lodge, Cree. We are on the eagle's hunting ground."

Puzzled but not dismayed, Rides Big Horses said, "Then we will return to Canada. They cannot hunt for us there."

"We cannot return to Canada. We can only return to our homeland after we have found Louis Riel and he has told us what to do."

"*Kah!* This Louis Riel! He is nothing! The white man at the trading post knew nothing of him. If he were a great chief, his name would be on the lips of many."

"In Canada it is. In America it is not. That is why Riel is here and not there." Being more than sufficiently aware of the Cree's inability to think logically, Singletree switched to a simple statement of fact. "Riel is hiding here, causing no trouble and waiting for the right time to return. After what you have done today, we cannot do the same."

Rides Big Horses waved his bottle in disgust. "A Cree chief does not hide from his enemies. I have done nothing wrong. The Americans will think the Cheyenne did this thing, as you said."

"And who did you leave alive to tell them it was the Cheyenne?" Singletree asked with a weary smile.

Unable to think of an answer, the Cree remained silent and stared moodily into the fire. "We have talked enough. I drink now and then I take my woman. You take yours."

"And I will. After what you've done, I have nothing to lose."

A short distance away, beyond the ring of firelight, Lorie sat on a blanket with her knees curled up beneath her and her head pressed against her sister's chest. She was crying softly but quietly, and Lisa rocked her gently in the warmth of comforting arms.

"We have to be strong, Lorie," Lisa was saying as she stroked the long hair trailing down the other twin's back. "If we want to live, we have to be strong."

"I. . . I don't want to live. I want to die."

"No you don't," Lisa soothed her. "You just think you do right now."

"It was so . . . so horrible. What they did to Daddy and Mommy, Joe and Shelly. They're all dead. And . . . and what they did to us, they'll . . . do again tonight."

"Yes, they probably will. And if we fight them, it will only be worse. I don't think the one who has chosen you will be as cruel as the other. If he does it to you, try to think of something else, put it completely out of your mind. Think of Christmas, or your last birthday party—anything but what is happening to you. We owe it to our parents, our brother and sister, to live so that those who killed them will be punished for what they did."

Lorie lifted her head, brushed back the tears, and looked at her sister. "But . . . but how long will it go on? I . . . I can't stand it."

"Yes you can," Lisa replied, gently touching Lorie's cheek. "You can stand it and you *will* stand it. Daddy would expect us to be strong. I'm sure Mr. Mandalian will come looking for us, and he will take us away from them and protect us."

"Do you think so?"

"I know so. But we haven't got just ourselves to think about. Little Tommy and Sharon mean nothing to them. If we are killed because we are weak, they'll be killed as well. It's up to us and Mr. Mandalian."

Lorie's face brightened in an attempted smile. "I'll think about Mr. Mandalian. If . . . if he does it to me, I'll think about Mr. Mandalian."

Sensing hope, Lisa grasped Lorie's hands in hers while saying brightly, "That's it! Let's both think about Mr. Mandalian and never forget that he is coming to save us. We are all he has left of the family, and he needs us as much as we need him. After he finds us, he'll never let anything harm us again. Don't think about what happened to the others. We love them, and nothing can take that away. Think only about Mr. Mandalian on that big old horse of his, and how it's going to feel when he takes us into his arms and we know we're safe." Lisa had been speaking rapidly, trying to drive a sense of promise into her sister's mind. Now she slowed her rate of speech, emphasizing each word. "We must get through tonight, tomorrow, the next day, and every day it takes until we are found. Out there, somewhere, Mr. Mandalian is looking for us. And when you least expect it, he'll be here."

"How can you be so strong, Lisa? We're twins, the same age and all. But you sound like Daddy talking. Why can't I be strong like you?"

"You are strong like me," Lisa replied, glancing toward the fire and seeing the two men rise. She kissed Lorie quickly on the cheek and hugged her. "You are strong like me, only in different ways. I'll tell you about them after Mr. Mandalian saves us. They're coming now, and I have to go. Don't cry and don't scream if he touches you. Bite your lip and let your mind take you away to another place. If you do that, we'll live to see that other place. I love you."

With those words she was gone, running silently toward the Cree chief's blankets. She stumbled once, righted herself, and then vanished into the darkness.

It was visible from possibly three miles away—a black scar scorched on the otherwise featureless plains. A lone chimney stood like a solitary sentinel, abandoned by those over whom it had stood guard. A portion of a wall, half consumed by flames, stood charred and ugly above the jumbled ruins about its foundation, and wooden roofbeams, twisted and broken, jabbed skyward in a manner that suggested a living thing had been sucked into a black abyss and only long, pointed fingers remained above the surface. What remained of the agency was absolutely silent and devoid of life, with the exception of a pair of vultures strutting across the ashes of the trading post in search of something they could smell but not see.

Impatient with the pace being set in deference to Colonel Higgins's complaints of saddle sores and stiff legs, Windy Mandalian had ranged far ahead of the main body, and now, as his horse neared the agency yard, the two vultures lifted into slow, indignant flight, as if that which was rightfully theirs was being taken away. Windy slowed the roan and approached the burned-out buildings at a walk. His eyes swept over the ruins, but his face revealed no expression, gave no hint of the thoughts smoldering in his mind. Then the horse stopped, and he sat there with the Sharps cradled in one arm and a chaw of tobacco bulged against his motionless cheek. And as he looked at the remains of what had been, he remembered the way it had been when he last saw it: a place where a family, a good, happy family, had eked out a living and died a meaningless, brutal death—a family that had known love and shared the love generously, perhaps even to those who had come to kill them.

It took ten minutes for the twin columns of Easy Company to catch up, and during that time Windy had not moved. Even when Kincaid halted the platoons and rode up beside him with the colonel and the major flanking on either side, the scout remained silent and sat stock-still atop his horse.

"Looks like they did a pretty thorough job, Windy," Kincaid said in a lowered voice.

"Yup. Coyotes usually do." Windy replied simply.

Kincaid glanced toward the sun. "Looks like we've got three, maybe four hours of light left. What do you suggest?"

"Suggest?" Higgins echoed, urging his horse forward. "There's nothing to be suggested. We're going after the damned heathens, that's what! Hell, there's nothing we can do here."

Windy's eyes narrowed almost imperceptibly, while remaining fixed on the charred wreckage. "What I suggest, Matt," he said softly, "is that you tell that fat, frog-faced son of a bitch to shut up and stay the hell away from me."

"What?!" Higgins snapped. "If you've got something to say to me, mister, you damned well better look at me when you do."

Still no change of expression, no increase in volume. "If I did, you'd be a dead man."

"Damn it, mister! You don't threaten me. You're in the employ of the United States Army and under my command. I'll have you—"

"Matt. Get him away from me. He's got ten seconds."

There was no doubt that Windy meant each word, even though his tone was seemingly calm, and Kincaid reined his horse around to face the colonel. "Colonel Higgins, I suggest that you find whatever shade you can, sir, perhaps over by that wall. Windy will be wanting to bury the dead before we move out."

"This is preposterous! There aren't any dead around here, and even if there were, they'd be just that and nothing more. Stone dead!"

The hammer came back on the Sharps with a dull click. "Matt?"

Kincaid grasped the senior officer's reins and turned the mount while pressing his own forward. "Like it or not, Colonel, you're going over by that wall. If you don't, there *will* be some visible dead around here, but you won't be seeing them. Major Delaney? I suggest you come along."

"Why, I never! This will be in my first report!" Higgins sputtered, trying to regain control of the horse upon which he was being led away. "This is insubordination and—"

"And an attempt to save your life, Colonel. You write all the reports you want to when we get back. My only goal right now is to see that you live long enough to write them."

After Higgins had been seated by the remains of the wall, and was sitting there mopping sweat from his brow with dejected swipes of a damp handkerchief, Kincaid returned to Windy's side. "Are you going to want a burial detail, Windy?"

"Yeah. One grave will be enough, I'm afraid. There couldn't be much left."

"How about a detail to sift through whatever's left over there and see what we can find?"

"That's what I was thinkin', and let's start with the trading post. There were eight of 'em: Ira, his wife, and six children. Oldest was nineteen and the youngest was six."

"We'll get on it right away."

"'Preciate it, Matt. And one more thing—thanks for what you just did. I would've killed him, you know."

"I know that, and I wouldn't have blamed you if you had. I don't think anybody else would have, either. Let's get on with it and do what has to be done."

It was nearing dark when the last of the ash and rubble had been gone through. There were no remains to be found in any other buildings, but the partially incinerated bodies of four people were discovered in the trading post. The search detail laid the corpses out side by side and covered them with a single blanket. Windy stood over them, staring down.

"That's what's left of Ira, his wife, his son Joe, and his daughter Shelly. The two women were scalped and probably raped. Only thing that kept that much of 'em from the flames was that the roof caved in and the sod put the fire out. Same thing happen in the other buildings, Matt?"

"Same thing. We went over every inch of them and found only one body, an Indian who must have been shot trying to get into the family dwelling."

"What's he look like?"

"Hard to tell. He's burned pretty bad."

"No little kids? Two fourteen-year-old twin girls and two litter shavers, a boy and a girl about six and eight?"

"No. Do you think they were taken captive?"

"Might've been. You were tellin' me on the way up here about that telegram the lard bucket over there had in his pocket. Didn't it say somethin' about some Indians leavin' here carryin' somethin' in front of 'em?"

"Yes it did. Said it looked like they were stealing supplies."

"And they were seen leavin' toward the north?"

"That's right. The ones who saw them were coming from the south."

Windy glanced thoughtfully toward the north. "I left here five days ago. The colonel has had that telegram in his pocket for two days and it took us almost two days to get here. That means this place was raided about three days ago. Ain't much hope of any decent sign bein' left by now."

"No, I guess not."

"The High Plains are strange about keepin' secrets, Matt. One time they won't tell you a damned thing, and another time they'll talk your goddamned arm off. Once we get Ira and his folks buried proper, I'm gonna take a little sashay out yonder and see if the old girl's got a mind to talk. I probably won't be back till mornin', so maybe you and the others better make camp around here tonight."

"Just as well, I suppose," Kincaid said with a glance toward the burned-out wall. "Our commanding officer seems to have had about all he can handle for now."

Windy spat sideways and wiped his mouth with the back of a hand. "He had more'n he could handle before he took his daily constitutional yesterday mornin' Matt. Let's take care of Ira's people, then I'll be on my way. Oh, one more thing—ain't no fingers missin', so that likely lets the Cheyenne out. When they scalp, the Sioux take more and leave less, which wasn't the case here, so I think we can cross them off the list. That leaves only two tribes that might've been in this area."

Kincaid watched the scout and once again admired the calculating mind that had kept the plainsman alive through so many years alone on the prairie. "Who have you got in mind?"

"Blackfoot could've done it."

"And?"

"The Plains Cree out of Canada. Accordin' to that telegram you got just before we left, they took a purty good whippin', them and their métis friends. Could be they cut a trail for home, if they done this. Then again, maybe not."

"Well, I don't think we have enough evidence to count anybody out at this point," Kincaid said. "You take a look around and—"

"Lieutenant? I found a couple of things you might want to have a look at," said a corporal crossing the yard with two objects held in his left hand. One appeared to be a long black cloth, and the other a tiny object dangling from a leather thong attached to a small pouch.

"Yes, Corporal Miller. Bring them over here, please."

After the objects were handed to Kincaid, he examined the shawl and the tiny object, which was a carving of a bird of some kind. "What do you make of it, Windy?" he asked, handing the items across.

"The shawl was Mrs. Griffin's. I gave it to her myself before I left here last time. This other," he said, while his gaze again drifted to the north and his face turned blank, "is a Cree medicine pouch. That bird is a raven. Their three big gods are the turtle, the otter, and the raven." Windy turned to Corporal Miller. "Where did you find these?"

"The shawl was tucked away in a drawer, folded up real neat, but the dresser had been crushed by the falling ceiling. That little bag was around the dead Indian's neck."

"Thank you, Corporal," Kincaid said. "Have the burial detail carry the bodies of the Griffin family over to the grave that's been dug. When you're ready to close it, I want the entire command assembled for burial ceremonies."

"Yessir."

Kincaid turned to Windy, who was absently hefting the medicine bag in his hand. "Does that mean the Cree did this, Windy?"

"It means they were here, Matt. And that's reason enough to start lookin' for 'em," Windy replied, turning to place the shawl carefully in his saddlebags. "We're not all that far from the Canadian border, and—"

"Lieutenant Kincaid?"

Recognizing the voice, Matt glanced over his shoulder and answered, "Yes, Corporal Peterson?"

"I don't know what you want me to do with these, sir, but I sure can't just leave 'em here." Peterson swallowed hard and looked down at the objects in his hands. "They belonged to kids, sir, and they were hidden away in a secret trapdoor under the floor, where the family valuables were kept."

"Let's have a look at them, Corporal," Windy said, crossing the yard quickly with Kincaid following close behind. "I think I know who they belonged to."

Peterson handed over a hand-carved rendering of a horse and a rag doll with string hair, a button nose, and a painted-on smile. "That's all there was in there, Windy. Like they were treasure or somethin' extra special."

"Yes, they were. Special to a lot of people," Windy said, taking the toys while that distant, hating look came into his eyes again. "I gave them to two special little tykes five days ago. I thought they'd play with 'em, 'steada lockin' 'em up like they was goddamned gold or somethin'."

There was a hesitant crack in Peterson's voice when he spoke again. "According to the scuttlebutt I heard comin' up here, a whole family was killed by Indians. How old were the kids?"

"The ones I gave these to were six and eight. Nicest damned kids you ever saw, and kids that deserved a little bit more out of life than they got. Their pa was killed trappin' with me about six years back, and their uncle was raisin' 'em like they was his own."

Peterson looked at Kincaid. "I've fought a lot of Indians during my hitch out here, Lieutenant. Some of 'em bad, others maybe not so bad. You seldom see the things that make a family, but when you do, and you know those kids were killed, it makes you hate all over inside. It makes you want to kill, sir," Peterson said, glancing down at his boots. "It makes you want to kill real bad. Kids eight and six ain't old enough to have done nothin' wrong."

Thinking that Peterson, a veteran of many campaigns, might actually break down and cry, Kincaid touched his shoulder lightly and said in a gentle tone, "I know, Corporal, we all feel the same way. And I suppose the Indians whose children were massacred at Sand Creek by the Colorado Militia felt the same way. If such things could be explained, we might not be here trying to prevent them. People who do things like this"—Kincaid's other hand swept in an arc to indicate the burned-out agency—"are either too primitive and barbaric to understand the meaning of what they do, or too callous and sadistic to care. In either case, they must be caught and prevented from doing something as horrible as this again. And before we leave here, we will have caught them."

Peterson struggled to regain control of his emotions. "You bet we will, sir. And I hope I'm right in the middle of the fight when we do."

"Knowing you, Corporal, you probably will be," Kincaid replied, clapping Peterson on the shoulder. "Now get your squad and have them take their picket ropes from their saddles so we can use them to lower the bodies into the grave."

"Yessir."

Windy had moved away, and Kincaid caught up with him while he was placing the carved horse and the doll in his saddlebags with the shawl. He thought he heard Windy say, "A little yellow purse and a beaver pelt. That's all that's missin'."

"What's that, Windy? Were you talking to me?"

"No. No I wasn't, Matt. Talkin' to myself and some friends, mostly. Let's get this thing done, and then I'm gonna light out. Be back by dawn."

Windy had ridden nearly an hour and a half before the sun sank beneath the featureless horizon. He had kept the roan at a steady lope, knowing what he was looking for and realizing as well that he would never find it so close to the agency. His eyes constantly swept the plains around him while he kept the horse on a course due north, and the prevailing evening breeze coming out of the west told him of fair weather and his direction of travel. He knew there would be a full moon this night, and the cloudless sky promised visibility to the trained eye that would yield the information he sought, should he find the proper terrain to begin his search.

After the sun had disappeared, to be replaced by a rising moon, he rode alone at a constant, ground-eating pace through the gathering twilight. As a silvery brilliance spread across the vacant land, his eyes adjusted to the dimness and he reined the horse toward a rolling swell. Now he slowed the roan and rode cautiously, testing the air for the scent of smoke from a cooking fire, knowing he would not see the blaze until he was upon it, and then it would be too late to turn back, should the enemy be lying in wait.

The horse moved down the sloping banks until its hooves sank into the soft earth of the sandy bottom, and Windy knew he had found what he was looking for. Turning to the west, he followed the dry wash for two or three miles, always searching for any sign that would indicate the movement of a large number of horses staying below the skyline to avoid detection. When the scout finally gave up and started backtracking to his original starting place, he was slightly puzzled. The moonlight was brilliant now, and provided ample illumination for him to spot the remains of a fire. And if the Indians he was searching for had gone north as reported, then they would surely have taken the first draw, the one he was now working, and moved laterally to throw anyone in pursuit off their trail. And in that desire, they would surely head in a westerly direction toward the sparsely settled open lands, and away from the more heavily populated ground to the east.

When Windy reined in at the place where he had entered the draw, he paused to stare northward and search his mind for that inexplicable instinct that had served him so well. Could they have passed up this draw and gone on farther north? Not likely, but maybe. Could it be that they were confident no one would be on their trail? That would be an assumption no logical Indian could rely on totally. But then, not all Indians were logical.

Could they have gone toward the east? No, not likely. A Cheyenne, Sioux, or Blackfoot would never attempt to escape toward the east. Only if they were lost . . .

The word *lost* jarred Windy's mind. None of those three great tribes of the High Plains would ever become lost on their ancestral grounds. But what about the Plains Cree? Surely they would know east from west merely by glancing at the stars, but that didn't mean they would know what lay in either direction. Being new to the region, they might not know which direction was the best logical choice.

Even though he knew he was running out of time, Windy's mind was made up and he urged his horse forward once more to follow the ravine in an easterly direction. A mile, then two, of slow, steady, intense scrutiny of the sandy bottom passed by, and Windy judged the time to be somewhere near three o'clock in the morning. *A hundred yards more*, he decided, *and if I don't find anything I'll head back toward the agency*.

Fifty yards farther on, he found what he was looking for: the place where a large number of horses had come down the bank and turned up the ravine. The bottom was churned up by countless hooves, and Windy was equally as surprised by the size of the war party as he was by their direction of travel.

He allowed the horse to canter now, anxious to make up time but always wary of stumbling upon the enemy in the dark. He was fairly confident that with a three-day lead, they would have quit the ravine long ago, but when it came to tracking Indians, nothing could be taken for granted. Nearly a mile farther along the draw, he reined in beside a small mound of sand and stepped down. He cleared the sand away carefully with his hands, layer by layer, until he found the bed of ashes buried beneath. Then, on foot, he moved farther along, finding more mounds where fires had been extinguished, and he counted them until he found no more.

There were eleven fires in all. Now Windy counted back five mounds and dug again, this time in the central mound, the one he knew the renegade chief would have used. His fingers probed a five-foot ring around where the fire had been until they closed around a hard, round object, which he withdrew from the sand. Holding the bottle up to the weak light and running his fingers across the embossed label near the neck of the container, he read the label as if he were reading braille. It was the same label as the one on the bottle he and Ira Griffin had shared a drink from.

Having but one thing left to do, Windy quit the draw and walked up its sloping bank, moving slowly, hunched over close to the ground. Some fifty yards away he stopped and picked up a horse turd. First he tested it for hardness with his fingers and then broke it apart and held one half up to his nose. Satisfied, he dropped one half and knelt to pat the grass where a tethered horse had ranged on its rope and grazed in a tight circle. The feeding area was cropped low in comparison with the surrounding grass, and Windy made a mental calculation as to how much feed a horse would consume in one night and how much time it would take the grass to grow back. Searching the entire circle and finding it to have been grazed nearly down to the prairie sod, he knew the pony had been tethered in that one spot for a good deal of time. He trailed his fingers along the hoofprints in search of the crisp, hard outline that would tell him if the horse had been ironshod. The prints were ragged and uneven. Though there had been little doubt in his mind before, now Windy was absolutely certain he had found the campsite of the Indians who had destroyed the Clearwater agency.

Moving toward the draw once more with the remaining piece of dung in one hand and the bottle in the other, he walked quickly now, anxious to get back to his horse and return to the agency and begin the search at dawn from his present location. Then something caught his attention and he stopped. The grass was flattened in one spot, and it was obvious to his trained eye that one of the warriors had slept there recently enough for the grass not to have risen again.

Even though he felt the pressure of passing time, he knelt and searched the oblong swatch of depressed grass with his hands. Finding nothing, he started to rise again, but then he noticed something bright, like a flower that had been crushed beneath the blanket and hidden in the tall grass. Carefully, almost breathlessly, Windy's fingers went to the pink object, which he recognized as one of the ribbons he had given to the Griffin twins. His pulse quickened as he tugged at the ribbon, but it would not yield. Hope filled his mind and he leaned down inches from the ribbon to examine it closely.

And when he looked up again, there was a relieved smile on his face. The ribbon had not been accidentally lost; it had been purposely tied to a small clump of grass. His eyes swept slowly across the plains and resolve filled his mind. *One of them is alive, and she's out there somewhere, in the dark, just like I am. Is it Lorie? Or Lisa? Or both? Just hang on a little longer if you can, honey. Just hang on. I'll be coming for you at dawn. Please, just hang on.*

eight

Flora Conway was deep in thought and obviously troubled as she left her quarters and started across the parade, now shadowless and bathed in the midafternoon sun. She angled in the direction of the married enlisted men's quarters, her specific destination being the home of Connie Peterson. She had not seen the young woman since Connie had admitted to having been beaten up by her husband, and earlier in the day she had not attended a tea that Flora had given for the wives of enlisted men. It was not hurt feelings, however, that prompted Flora's visit to the Peterson home; it was a matter of personal concern for the woman's welfare and emotional well-being. Flora stepped into the shade of the porch roof and gently rapped on the door. After a reasonable wait, and in the belief that her knock had not been heard, she raised her hand a second time just as the door opened slightly.

"Connie? Are you all right?" Flora asked, bending sideways to look in at the young woman peering out.

"Yes . . . yes, I'm fine, Mrs. Conway."

"Now, Connie, we agreed on this a long time ago. The name is Flora."

"I'm sorry . . . Flora, I forgot. And, please accept my apologies for not attending the tea today. Something . . . came up and I couldn't make it. Thank you for the invitation, though."

Even though she felt slightly ridiculous, trying to talk to the woman through nothing more than a crack in the doorway, Flora smiled warmly and decided not to be turned away.

"I'm not here because you weren't in attendance. We all missed you and I just got a little concerned, that's all. Everyone needs to talk with someone once in a while, and I came by thinking you might like to chat for a few minutes."

"I'm really not much of a talker, Flora, as you know."

"Good," Flora said with a grin, "because I am, and I'm

always trying to search out a new listener. However, I generally prefer seeing the person to whom I'm speaking. It helps one tremendously to know that the person listening is still awake."

Suddenly aware of her rudeness, Connie pulled the door aside and stepped back. "Please come in. I . . . I guess I'm not thinking properly today."

"A malady occasionally suffered by all," Flora replied, stepping into the relative coolness provided by the heavy sod roof atop the ceiling. "Thank you."

As an automatic response and with no intention to judge, Flora's eyes swept over the small living quarters, and she was mildly pleased. The packed-earth floor had been swept and freshly dampened, cheery curtains graced the front window, and the furniture was neatly arranged and as spotless as old furniture can be made to be.

"My, but this certainly is a cozy arrangement you have here. I love those curtains."

"Thank you, I made them myself."

"You did? Are you fond of sewing?"

"Yes. It's my only pastime. May I offer you some tea?"

"I'd love some, if it's no trouble."

"No trouble at all," Connie replied, moving toward the stove, where a teapot had just begun to whistle. "I was making some for myself when you arrived."

While the tea was being prepared, Flora's eyes swept around the room again and she noticed a knitting basket placed beside a chair, into which a partially completed project had obviously been quickly stuffed.

"Please, Flora, have a seat there," Connie said, handing across a cup of tea. "It's Arnie's chair, and the most comfortable one we have."

"The male prerogative we women must always endure, I guess," Flora replied, while sinking into the chair with her tea cup carefully balanced on its saucer before her.

Connie resumed her seat beside the knitting basket. "I think it's rather nice myself. He's the one who provides for us, and when he comes home from patrol, hot, dusty and tired, it makes me feel good to think he's enjoying the one nice thing we have."

Flora smiled warmly, noticing that the woman across from her was speaking freely now. "And I concur completely. They spend too many miserable nights lying on the cold ground or walking guard duty, not to mention the fact that someone is generally trying to kill them. When they get home, they should have the best a woman can offer."

A wistful look came into Connie's eye, and she stammered once again. "I . . . I . . . try. Maybe not hard enough, but I try."

"You do excellently, I'm sure," Flora said quickly, wanting to divert the conversation from self-recrimination. "I see you knit as well as sew."

Connie glanced down at her work. "Yes I do. I suppose the two go hand in hand, when one spends a considerable amount of time making clothes."

"Clothes?" Flora asked. "Do you make your own clothes? I make my own sometimes, as well, and it's fun to talk with someone who shares the same avocation"

With undisguised admiration, Connie looked at the beautiful, well-dressed woman across from her. "I didn't think that on a captain's pay you would have to make anything." Then she blushed and looked down. "I'm sorry if that sounded as rude to you as it did to me."

"Please, it's our husbands who have to be concerned with rank, not you and I. But, to respond, captains are not exactly the most overpaid people in the army, either. I feel that every little bit helps, and besides, I genuinely enjoy it." Flora glanced at the basket. "What are you making now? May I see it? The yarn you're using looks absolutely beautiful."

Connie blushed as she looked toward the basket, and then quickly back at Flora. "Well . . . I . . . it's not anything, really. Just something I wanted to make."

"I'd love to see it."

After a moment's hesitation, Connie placed her cup and saucer to one side and reached into the basket and withdrew the material. There was a strange look in her eyes, both defensive and challenging in the same instant. "You'll think me a fool," she said, as she spread her work for Flora to see.

The craftsmanship was excellent, as was Flora's skill at hiding her surprise by allowing nothing more than an expression of delight to cross her face. Across from her, Connie was holding a little girl's nightgown knitted of pink yarn.

"That's beautiful, Connie. Absolutely beautiful. I wish I

were skilled enough to make things that small."

"You're not surprised?" Connie asked, watching Flora's face closely. "Especially after what I told you yesterday?"

"I'd be lying if I said I wasn't, but I'm even more delighted than surprised. It's darling, and if we couldn't at least dream our dreams, life would not be worth living. Have you made any others?"

"Yes I have. A whole trunkful, as a matter of fact. For boys as well as girls." Connie smiled weakly and added, "I began before I realized that I couldn't have children. Now that I know I never will have, I've settled on a family of four, in my dreams, as you say—two boys and two girls. That's what Arnie wanted."

"May I see some of the other things you've made?"

"Yes, of course. I've never shown them to anyone but my husband, and now I can't even show them to him, because he gets frustrated, then drunk, then angry if he sees me making something like this. That's why I wasn't at your tea; with Arnie in the field, it gives me time to work without fear of being caught and causing a fight between us. Just a moment, I'll get some things and show you."

When Connie returned a few moments later, Flora was absolutely stunned at the magnificent display of children's clothing draped over her arm. There were pants, dresses, blouses, shirts, and jackets, along with a variety of other items, such as bonnets, hats, and rag dolls.

"These are just a few of the things I made, but it's a sampling. Do you like them?"

"Like them? I think they're adorable! You are truly an amazing person, Connie. You are so gifted, so talented, I'll bet you could make a living doing that. Maybe even open up a little shop somewhere."

"Yes," Connie said in a barely audible voice. "That's what I intend to do. Just a moment, let me put these things away."

After Connie was seated again, she folded her hands nervously and looked up at Flora. There was a tightness around her mouth, as if she were about to cry, and mist glistened in her eyes.

"When you came here a while ago, you said everyone needs to talk to somebody, Flora, and you were right. I need desperately to talk to someone right now."

"Of course, my dear. Please, say whatever is on your mind, and I'll try to help in any way that I can."

"I'm . . . I'm going to leave Arnie. I'm going to tell him when he gets back from this patrol. I can't make him go through life like this, wanting children so badly and never being able to have them. Without me in the way, he could marry someone else, someone who can have children, or already has, and who's maybe widowed or something. That probably wouldn't be as good as having his own, but at least it would be something."

Flora's first impulse was to take the young woman in her arms and comfort her, but there was something about the look of determination on Connie's face that made her sense that such a display of affection would be mistaken for pity.

"I am deeply sorry to hear that, Connie. What would you do? Where would you go?"

"Home, to St. Louis. My parents live there, and as you suggested, I could open a little shop and support myself."

"Have you thought this over carefully?"

"Yes," Connie replied with a tired smile. "That is, if a thousand nights lying awake and thinking about nothing else is considered careful thinking."

"And your husband knows nothing about your decision?"

"No. But he's aware as I am that our marriage can't continue the way it's going now. It's destroying both of us."

"Do you still love him?"

Connie's lips were trembling uncontrollably now, and the tears in her eyes were no longer a secret. "Yes. More than anything in the world. I love him enough to leave him, if that will make him happy someday."

Unable to resist the impulse further, Flora rose and placed her arms around the young woman's shoulders, and drew her close. Connie made no attempt to resist; instead she rested her head against Flora's waist and cried openly.

"You poor, poor dear," Flora said, rocking Connie back and forth and making no attempt to wipe away the tears slowly trickling down her own cheeks. "I wish with all my heart that there were something, anything I could do to help, but I can think of nothing. You are a kind, good woman and don't deserve to have something like this ruin your life. If it would help, I'll talk to Warner and see if he—"

Connie pulled away quickly and looked up. "No, Flora. Please don't tell anyone, not even your husband. I've made my decision and I have to go through with it."

Flora smiled and stroked the young woman's hair reassuringly. "All right, Connie. I won't say a word to a soul. It's our secret, if that's the way you want it to be. And I'll pray to God that things work out right for you."

The sun was well above the horizon as Kincaid and Major Delaney walked away from the fresh graves that had been dug the previous day. It was the first time the two men had had a chance to talk alone, and Kincaid was finding the major quite an agreeable companion, and a surprising one as well. Matt would never have guessed that the bone-thin officer had served as a regimental commander during the Civil War, with the temporary rank of colonel, and had been decorated for valor in the field.

"After all that," Kincaid asked, when Delaney finished telling of his combat experience, "how did you ever happen to wind up as a colonel's aide?"

Delaney smiled. "You know the army as well as I do, Lieutenant. You go where you are sent. As I understand it, my transfer to the colonel's staff was the result of his personal request. I had never met the man before, but the word in Washington is that he likes to surround himself with people who have distinguished themselves in battle. It would seem, since he has never heard a gun fired, much less shot one, that he gets some sort of vicarious sense of valor out of it, as if the accomplishments of others were his own successes."

"I can see that already," Matt replied with an agreeing nod. "But what I can't understand is how you can tolerate such an insufferable person. I'm afraid I'd go stark raving mad if I had to be around him more than a couple of days. I just might, as a matter of fact, if this patrol turns out to be a long one."

Delaney chuckled with an easy smile. "It's all a game, Lieutenant. Except for ceremonies like inspecting your troops, I just shut him out of my mind. As I'm sure you've observed, he doesn't listen to anyone anyway, so he doesn't notice whether I'm paying attention to him or not."

"You're a well-disciplined man, Major, if you can shut him out of your mind. My congratulations."

"Thank you, and you are correct; I am a well-disciplined man. I was an accountant in civilian life, and I suppose that's the source of my mental self-control."

As they neared the burned-out buildings, Corporal Peterson hurried toward them and offered a crisp salute, which both officers returned.

"Lieutenant Kincaid, the colonel sent me to find you. He's hopping mad, sir, and he's raving about our not having moved out yet."

"Thank you, Corporal. I'll talk to him."

The two platoons were waiting by their mounts a short distance away, and Kincaid could see the colonel marching back and forth like an angry bear on a short leash. When they neared, Higgins stopped his pacing and glared at Kincaid.

"What the hell's going on here, Lieutenant? I was told we would move out at dawn, and it's more than an hour past that now!"

"We're waiting for my scout, sir. He should be back anytime now."

"You're holding up two complete platoons of mounted infantry just for one civilian?"

"No," Kincaid replied laconically, "for Windy Mandalian."

Ignoring Matt's inference, the colonel snapped a gloved hand toward the platoons. "I want those troops mounted up now and moving out within two minutes. We've got a war to fight here, and war waits for no man."

"Fortunately, in some cases. But since we do have a war going on, sir, where would you suggest we start looking for the enemy?" Kincaid turned and swept his hand toward the surrounding prairie. "Shall we start there, or there, or possibly over there?"

"I don't give a damn where we start, as long as we get started!"

"Which is exactly what we will do, sir—the minute Mr. Mandalian returns."

Higgins started to protest, but Delaney broke in, "The Lieutenant is correct, sir. He has assured me that Mr. Mandalian knows more about Indian fighting, and tracking those same Indians, than any three other men put together. I suggest we wait for his return."

"And I damned well didn't ask for any suggestions from

you, Major!" Higgins shouted. "The lieutenant's career is already in jeopardy, and very likely finished once I submit my report. Yours does not suffer the same peril, but by God it will, if you take sides against me!"

"The only sides I'm taking are those of good sense and prudence, Colonel," Delaney said without the slightest hint of perturbation. "You would do well to look into some of the same yourself."

"Lieutenant! Windy's comin'!"

All eyes went to the north, where a lone rider was approaching at a steady gallop. "Maybe we'll make your two-minute deadline after all, Colonel," Kincaid said with a hint of a smile.

Windy reined in and alighted in the same motion. "Sorry I'm late, Matt. Took a little longer than I thought."

"You're damned right it did," Higgins snapped. "You've tied us up for more than an hour now."

"You should have been tied up long before that," Windy said without looking at the colonel and maintaining his attention on Kincaid. "I'm purty blamed sure I found their first camp, Matt."

"Good. How far away?"

"'Bout a three-hour ride."

"Any idea how many?"

"I make it to be between sixty and seventy."

Kincaid whistled softly. "That many? Bigger war party than we thought."

"How could he possibly know that?" Higgins asked hotly, while edging forward to place himself in the center of the conversation.

Windy's head turned slowly and he looked at the colonel for the first time. "Against my better judgment and the needs of a hungry stomach, I'm gonna talk to you. The way I know that is 'cause I counted their campfires."

"So?"

"Near as I could make out, there were ten of 'em."

"And what does that prove?"

"Indians always build small cooking fires at night, instead of during the day, so the smoke can't be seen. With their fires bein' small, they usually build quite a few so they can cook their meat and get the hell out of there fast if they have to. Usually six warriors to a fire."

"Pretty damned poor intelligence for a military operation," Higgins scoffed.

"About right for the military mind involved," Windy said, breaking off a chaw of tobacco.

"How long has it been since they left, Windy?" Kincaid asked.

"Three days."

"Three days!" Higgins said with a derisive laugh. "How the hell could you know that? It might have been yesterday, for all we know."

Without saying a word, Windy turned to his saddlebags and drew out the horse turd, which he tossed toward the colonel. "That's how I know."

Higgins jumped back and brushed his uniform where the manure had struck his chest. "That's . . . that's . . . horseshit!"

"Right, Colonel," Windy said, working his mouth and spitting while stooping to retrieve the dung. "But this here's *special* horseshit. Special Indian horseshit," he continued, breaking the turd into quarters. "Look here, you might learn somethin'. See any sign of grain—wheat or corn or oats—that a white man always feeds his horse?" he asked, holding the feces overly close to the colonel's nose.

Higgins turned his head away in disgust. "Get that away from me! It's horseshit and nothing more."

"I figgered as much. Now look here real close and take a good whiff. Your nose and eyes'll tell ya—"

"Get that damned thing away from me!"

"I ain't askin' ya to *eat* it, Colonel." Windy said with a satisfied chuckle. "I just want you to look and smell. Anyway, it ain't got much odor left, so it can't be too fresh. And since shit passes through a horse like money through a soldier's hands, the grass ain't digested real well. Now you can see, if you look, the grass in this here turd is still kinda moist, not quite dry yet. It'd take about three days, in heat like this, to have that particular look and smell."

"Disgusting and totally unreliable."

Windy shrugged and tossed the turd aside. "Fine. You look for your Indians where you want to, and I'll look for mine where I know they are."

"Did they picket their mounts, Windy?" Kincaid asked, disregarding the colonel.

"Yup, they did."

"Couldn't have been in too big a hurry, then."

"Nope. Musta stayed there quite a while, "'cause the grass was cropped down to near bare dirt."

Higgins was not to be denied. "Assuming this theory of yours is correct, which I doubt, how do we even know those are the Indians we're after?"

Again, Windy's hand went to the saddlebag. "'Cause of this," he replied, pulling the whiskey bottle out and displaying it.

"So? It's a whiskey bottle. There must be thousands of them lying around here."

"Not like this one. Old Ira had a special brand of whiskey he liked to drink, and he saved it for himself and special friends, one of which I happened to be. Had it shipped out from back East. If there was a bottle like this around, you can bet it had to be stolen from Ira's place, 'cause he never threw none of 'em away."

"This is preposterous!" Higgins exclaimed, shaking his head in disgust. "An entire military operation based on one horse turd and an old whiskey bottle. What will we be seeing next, a handwritten message in Latin saying, "We did it. Come and get us'?"

"Don't read Latin, but I do read sign." Now Windy looked at Kincaid, and it was obvious he had no more to say to the colonel. "Found somethin' as good as a handwritten message, Matt."

"What's that?"

Windy's hand went to his shirt pocket and he pulled out the tiny strip of ribbon. "I found this."

"Oh God!" the colonel moaned with sarcastic dismay. "Now we've got a horse turd, a whiskey bottle, and a piece of ribbon!"

"Shut up, Colonel," Kincaid said sharply, without concern for the consequences. "You mentioned giving some gifts to the Griffin kids, Windy. Is that something from what you gave them?"

"Yup. It belonged to one of the twins, either Lorie or Lisa."

"Do you think some warrior took it from the house and lost it accidentally?"

"Nope. This wasn't lost by accident. It was tied to a clump of grass on purpose."

"Then you think one of them is still alive?"

"I'm sure of it. At least she was when they first made camp. I think they knew I'd come lookin' for 'em, and they were tryin' to tell me where they were."

"I hope they still are, and that no harm comes to them."

"Ain't no doubt about the fact that they've been bedded," Windy replied, the hard look returning to his eyes. "But at least they prob'ly ain't dead yet. We're gonna get 'em back."

"You're damned right we are. Sergeant Olsen, have the troops mount up. We're leaving immediately. Pass the word along that we know they are holding hostages, at least one young girl and maybe more! Should we cross their path, no one is to fire until we have made sure of the safety of whatever hostages might be still alive!"

Windy led his horse away to the water trough, while the soldiers swung onto their mounts. Unknown to Colonel Higgins, it was the very fact that Windy's roan was in need of water that surely saved his life. Higgins cleared his throat and looked up at Kincaid.

"I hope it is not necessary to remind you, Lieutenant, that our primary objective here is to bring an insurrection under control swiftly and decisively, and that is why I insisted upon bringing the Gatling gun along. Often in the course of a military operation, it is necessary to sacrifice civilians for the greater good of all. When we engage the enemy, it is my intention to bring all firepower at our disposal to bear at that time and, however reluctantly, be prepared for the loss of a few civilians in the name of the powers and responsibilities entrusted to us."

Kincaid stared at Higgins in disbelief. "You are incredible, Colonel. Do you know how old those girls are?"

"Age is not a factor."

"Like hell it's not! And I don't give a damn whether they were two old maids of ninety, or two young girls of fourteen, which they are. There will not be one shot fired until I am absolutely certain of their safety, or until the fate of this command is placed in total jeopardy. Is that understood?"

"Lieutenant," Higgins began in a menacing tone, "you seem to have a great deal of trouble remembering the chain of command."

"If those girls are alive, I am only interested in their safety. Now if you'll excuse me," Kincaid said, swinging gracefully into his saddle, "I have a patrol to lead."

"Hey . . . you . . . Lieutenant, damn you!"

Kincaid didn't look back, but if he had, he would have seen the colonel waddle to his mount, stab a boot angrily at a stirrup, miss, then finally hoist himself into the saddle and take up pursuit, his legs flopping on either side of his horse.

nine

The derivation of his surname might well have come from the expression on his face, as Major William R. Steele stared out from beneath the visor of his cap at a world he had never seen before. A full company of mounted Canadian militiamen was strung out in a formation behind him. But the look on Steele's face was not prompted by events of the moment; it was a perennial condition and the by-product of a humorless life.

Having lived his formative years at a boarding school in Berkshire, England, and later attended a military academy in the same town, he had known little of the joy that comes with feminine companionship, and had been a virgin until the age of twenty-six. A visit to a brothel at the climax of a drunken evening had been his first encounter with the opposite sex, and his only real memory of the occasion was the case of venereal disease he later had to cope with. From that point on, women had become objects of scorn rather than desire for the major, and he made the army his wife and became her dedicated servant.

Although it would not have been obvious to the casual observer, he was experiencing awe and wonderment as his eyes swept over the waving grass of the High Plains, which stretched before him in endless, undulating swells. It bore no resemblance to the neat and tidy farms of his homeland, which seemed so orderly with their rows of hedges and country lanes. Nor was there any similarity to the rugged, forested hills of Canada, now far behind them. Having never seen the American prairie before, he was spellbound by its vastness; he had never dreamed of a land so huge and yet so empty. A restless man, a man of action for whom time passed all too slowly, he felt somehow that he was being consumed by the plains, and that mile after mile passed by without any progress having been made. And always beyond lay the same featureless ground, rolling beneath an endless sea of grass.

"Major?" the captain riding by Steele's side asked tentatively. "Do you know where we are, sir?"

"Precisely," was the crisp reply.

"We are on American soil, sir. And have been for nearly three days now. I didn't mention anything earlier because I thought we would be turning back anytime. How much farther do you intend to go, sir?"

"As far as necessary, and we won't be turning back until our mission is bloody well accomplished."

The captain knew he was on shaky ground, but concern made him press onward. "Does Colonel Scripps know we're here, sir? What I mean is, do we have the proper authority to be here? This could be considered an armed incursion into a foreign country, sir."

"I don't give a damn what it's considered, Captain. I am following Colonel Scripps's orders to the letter. After we defeated the métis at Fort Howton, I was instructed to take one full company and find and destroy the forces of the Cree chief, Rides Big Horses, and his métis comrade, Johnny Singletree. That, my dear Captain Bullard, is exactly what we are attempting to do."

"But did the colonel know you intended to come here to find them, Major?"

Steele smiled coldly. "The question was never posed, therefore the need to provide an answer was unnecessary."

"What about the Yanks, Major? If we are discovered, surely they will be rather concerned about such questions. They may not look too kindly upon our presence."

"We are merely lost, that's all. We strayed across the border unintentionally, and after we've exterminated the vermin that are the object of our search, we will have done them a favor at no cost. Bloody decent of us, don't you think, Captain?"

Bullard shook his head at the major's simple dismissal of an incident that could have international ramifications, and studied the noonday sun riding high in a cloudless blue sky. "There may be more fact than fiction to what you just said, Major. About our being lost, I mean. Now that I can't see the mountains behind us, I don't know whether we're riding east or west. And with the sun at its zenith, there is absolutely nothing to give direction in this barren, godforsaken land."

"Trust me, Captain. I have matters fully in hand. At the present moment we're heading due south."

"How can you tell that, sir?"

"Instinct, my boy. Instinct."

The major's total confidence did not provide the ultimate panacea for the concerns troubling Bullard's mind. "I appreciate very much your navigating skills, sir, and in no way do I intend to question them. But if I were to hazard a guess, I'd say we are traveling more in a southeasterly direction than due south as you suggest, sir."

"Then it is you who are lost, my dear Captain, not I. Fortunately for yourself and the men of this expedition, I am in command here." Steele sighed contentedly and gazed about him. "Beyond that, the points on a compass are not of concern to me right now. What I find incredible is that it seems to take forever to get anywhere. One would assume that eventually one would see a mountain, a hill, even a big bloody rock. But this land seems determined to offer nothing but monotony. I'd say it's time for dinner and a cup or two of tea, what, Captain?"

"Whatever you say, sir. But we're running very low on firewood, and shortly we could be riding the pack animals ourselves. It might be foolish to waste our reserves on a noonday fire."

"Nonsense, Captain. We British are accustomed to having tea with our meals, and that is a tradition which you, our Canadian cousins, have wisely adopted as well. Surely this wasteland will suffer us a tree somewhere along the line. Halt the company and have dinner prepared."

"Yessir."

Rides Big Horses had become an increasingly impatient and angry man. Since the incident at the Clearwater Reservation, Singletree had not allowed him to approach any homesteads or tiny settlements to ask the questions that had been repeated so many times now: Do you know of a man named Louis Riel? Do you know where I might find him? The métis had taken that job upon himself, and always returned with negative results.

Their whiskey was long since gone, and the pleasure the Cree had once enjoyed with the free use of Lisa's body was now more an act of spite. And the fact that she would show no emotion had become a constant irritation. Somehow his manly pride seemed compromised. And yet he would not let her go or give her to the other warriors, who made no effort to disguise their interest. She was too beautiful to be merely the squaw of a Cree warrior.

Singletree had taken twenty of Rides Big Horses' braves with him to inquire once again as to the whereabouts of Riel, while the Cree chief was left behind with the others in a deep draw. There he brooded about the humiliation he was receiving at the hands of both the American girl and the métis. At that moment, though, it was his deep resentment of Lisa that was mainly on his mind. He realized he could not break her with physical abuse, and killing her outright would provide small reward.

He had noticed how she took care of the two smaller children each time the opportunity availed itself, as she was doing even now, while he stared at her. The little ones had become an increasing annoyance to him as well, especially Sharon, with her dirty face, runny nose, hair a tangled mess, and tears rolling incessantly from her big blue eyes. Rides Big Horses would have killed her several days before, had it not been for the objections of Singletree and the protection of Running Deer. As the Cree watched Lisa trail her fingers through the little girl's hair in an attempt to free the tangles, he realized he had the perfect means at his disposal of hurting Lisa while the métis was gone.

Rides Big Horses rose from his squat and walked to where the girls were, while Running Deer stood nearby with little Tommy by his side.

"Running Deer! Come! We will talk!"

The warrior hesitated, then moved toward his chief. "I am here. What do you want with me?"

"I am tired of the little ones. You and Sitting Crow will take them onto the great land, far from here, and let them go."

"Let them go? They would die in less than two days."

Rides Big Horses smiled coldly. "And they will die in less than that if my eyes fall on them again. They provide nothing, but only eat and cry. Take them away. I have spoken."

"They are but children, and—"

The chief's knife flashed in his hand, and he instantly grasped Running Deer by the braid on the left side of his head while pressing the knife point against his throat.

"Do you wish to die in their place?"

Having no difficulty in perceiving the chief's intentions, Lisa pulled the two children to her and held them tightly. She tousled Tommy's red hair and attempted to smile comfortingly, but she could muster little conviction. Sharon began to cry again.

The knife point punctured the skin of Running Deer's throat, and a trickle of blood ran down to his chest before he indicated with the slightest nod of his head that he would comply with the chief's wishes.

Rides Big Horses released the braid and took the knife away at the same time. "It is good. Take them now, before the métis returns. If you are asked by him, say only that they ran away. Nothing morc."

Running Deer's face was filled with contempt as he turned away, signaled to Sitting Crow, pulled Tommy from Lisa's grasp, and walked toward his pony. The other warrior did likewise, having considerably more difficulty dragging the screaming, hysterical Sharon away from her sister.

The Cree chief walked up to Lisa and stood beside her while he watched the two ponies gallop away. Then he looked at Lisa, expecting tears and pleas for mercy for the two children. For some time she continued to watch the swell over which the two horses had disappeared, then she rose and turned toward Rides Big Horses. The leer on his face showed he had the power to reverse his decision if his demands upon Lisa were met. Her eyes blazed in anger, but she revealed no sign of weakness.

"You are an animal," she said, clutching her skirts in either hand. "A filthy, worthless animal." Then she spat in the chief's face and walked away.

Rides Big Horses was too stunned to stop her. He stood there, staring after Lisa, mindless of the spittle sliding down his cheek. The other warriors who were gathered about him grinned covertly at their leader's immobility in the face of such humiliation.

When they had traveled nearly two miles, Running Deer and Sitting Crow pulled their horses up and stepped down. Running Deer leaned over Tommy and grasped the boy's tiny shoulders with big hands.

"You are free, little one," he said softly. "You are a brave warrior, and you will survive here better than you would with

Rides Big Horses. Here, this is for you." Running Deer pulled his knife from its sheath and pressed it tightly into Tommy's hand. "Use it wisely."

With those words, the warrior patted Tommy's head, then swung onto his pony's back and raced away with Sitting Crow following close behind.

The two children stood there alone on the vast expanse of prairie, and watched until the Indians were gone.

"Are we going to die, Tommy?" Sharon asked in a quivering voice. "I'm scared."

"Naw, we ain't gonna die, sis," Tommy replied with all the bravado he could muster. "Lisa told me that if we stayed together, Mr. Mandalian would find us. If she thinks he will, I do too. Come on, let's start walkin' and try to find a place to hide tonight."

With the knife in one hand and his other arm around his sister's shoulders, Tommy led her away to he knew not what.

Running Deer and Sitting Crow had seen it in the distance as they returned to the draw: a spiraling wisp of white smoke rising lazily upward and outlined by the deep blue sky above the horizon. They were not surprised by the air of excitement among their fellow Cree. Rides Big Horses was talking to five warriors who had obviously just returned from a scouting mission, and the chief paused to glance up sharply as the two Indians stepped down.

"They are gone," Running Deer said simply.

"It is good. Now we fight."

"Where is the métis? Has he returned?"

"Yes. I told him you had gone to search for the little ones. You have seen the smoke from their fires?"

Running Deer nodded. "Yes. Is it the Americans?"

"No. They would not be that stupid. It is the Grandmother's soldiers. They have come looking for us," Rides Big Horses smiled cunningly. "But it is we who have found them."

Just then, Singletree stepped from the rear of the throng of warriors and walked directly toward Running Deer.

"Did you find them?"

Running Deer could feel the chief's hot eyes on his face, and said, "No, we did not. They are little and there are many places to hide. We saw the smoke and came back."

"Then I can only wish them well," Singletree said, turning

toward Rides Big Horses. "We will split into two groups. By using the draws and staying away from the skyline, we can be on them before they know it. They are many, but they are unwary. We will strike quickly, kill as many as we can, and then be gone." His jaw tightened and he stared to the north. "They must have defeated my métis brothers, and we will make them pay for it with their lives. They have now ridden into our trap. We will strike hard and swiftly, driving off as many horses as we can. Let's go now, while they are still taking food."

Before moving to his pony, the Cree chief turned back to Running Deer. "You and Sitting Crow will take my war prizes and follow us until we go onto the plains. There you will wait until we have defeated the Grandmother's soldiers."

Running Deer shrugged and turned away with Sitting Crow by his side, and the chief watched them momentarily. Then he trotted to his horse and leaped onto its back in a manner that showed his thirst for battle and the renewed bloodlust coursing through him.

Divided into groups, the warriors separated; Rides Big Horses led one band along the draw to the west, and Singletree led the other to the east. In minutes they were gone from view, and only the eyes of a bird in flight could have detected them as they worked their way toward the Canadian militiamen.

Major Steele carefully placed the steaming cup on the ground beside him and bit off the tip of a cigar before leaning forward to light it with a brand from the fire. His troops lounged in scattered groups along the lee side of the prairie swell, and three sentries stood guard above. Steele puffed the cigar to life while glancing toward Captain Bullard.

"Nothing like a spot of tea to brighten one's day, what, Captain?"

"It does hit the spot, Major," Bullard concluded, blowing on the contents of his tin cup before sipping gingerly at the steaming brew. "This is a strange country, is it not?"

"Strange indeed. A man can see for miles upon miles. Reminds me somewhat of the Punjab region of India, except for the grass. I would challenge any artist to paint this scene," Steele said as his eyes swept the plains, "and bring some life to it."

"It seems to me that one would have to learn a different

type of warfare to do battle successfully here, sir," Bullard replied cautiously. "I rather suspect there might be a deceptive quality to all this visibility."

"Nonsense, Captain. War is war, no matter where it's fought. In Canada we have forests, mountains, hills, and meadows. We adapt to that. Here one can see his enemies the moment they crest the horizon, an excellent situation from a defensive point of view. I remember one time in Burma when I—"

Three sharp blasts rang out simultaneously, and two of the sentries collapsed, dead before they hit the ground. The third soldier dropped to one knee and raised his rifle to fire in the same instant that a fourth shot crashed into his chest and threw him backward to sprawl in the grass. The sound of pounding hooves and savage screams filled the air, and the militiamen scrambled to where their rifles had been stacked.

Steele lurched upward and pulled out his Enfield service revolver while yelling, "To your mounts, boys! To your mounts!"

Two waves of Cree, one to the left and the other to the right, swarmed over the crest of the swell and charged downward while firing from low on their ponies' backs and directing their shots into the pockets of soldiers running toward their horses. Others, stunned by the swiftness of the attack and too startled to fire, stared incredulously at the Indians bearing down on them. Soldiers were falling on all sides, and Steele snapped off two quick shots while Bullard leaped to his feet, waving his arms and screaming at the top of his lungs.

"Forget the goddamned horses! Assume the prone position and fire at will!"

Return fire, scattered at first and then becoming more steady, came from the ragged ranks of the militiamen, and a Cree here and there spilled from the back of his pony. The Indians had converged in a pincer movement, closing on either flank, firing as quickly as they could jack fresh rounds into the chambers. It seemed impossible to miss as they fired into their stationary targets, bunched together and still reeling from the overwhelming force and swiftness of the surprise attack. More soldiers slumped forward in the grass to lie motionless as the Cree mounts leaped over them and raced through the scene of what had been a peaceful tea break just minutes before.

While the main body of warriors whirled their ponies and

raced back for a second pass, a smaller group angled in the direction of horses tied to picket lines, and they leaned down from their mounts to slash the ropes with knives. Frightened horses, their eyes rolling in terror, raced away the moment they were free, while others, as yet still tethered, reared and plunged as scattered shots crashed into them.

Captain Bullard had been moving among his troops and fearlessly exposing himself to Cree fire, while settling his men in proper, defensive firing lines. The air was thick with burned powder, and the crashing roar of hundreds of rifles firing simultaneously was deafening, but he managed to direct the fire of two squads upon the Indians who were attempting to set the mounts free, and then he coordinated an organized defense on both flanks. The tide began to turn when the militiamen, firing from steady, prone positions, brought accuracy and superior firepower to bear and the Indians broke off the attack to race away in a westerly direction. As quickly as they had come, they were gone, with exultant shouts of victory fading behind them in the now still air. A deathly calm settled over the rolling swell, and only the moaning of the wounded and the muttered curses of soldiers recovering from their shock could be heard. Nearly one-third of the militia's horses had been set free, and they too finally slowed their headlong flight across the prairie and stopped several hundred yards away.

Miraculously, Major Steele had not been hit during the brief fight, even though he had remained standing, firing his revolver with cool, deadly accuracy. Now the weapon hung by his side and he stared in the direction where the Indians had vanished, his jaw set firmly and his eyes blazing with hatred.

Captain Bullard, who had suffered a minor scalp wound, walked slowly up the hill and stood silently behind his commanding officer for nearly a minute.

"We took rather heavy casualties, Major," he said softly. "Possibly twenty dead and that many more wounded. I'll have a complete report for you in a few minutes. Shall I send a detail after the mounts, sir?"

It seemed as though the major could not bring himself to lose sight of the place where he had last seen the enemy, and he continued to stare in that direction. "Where in the bloody hell did they come from, Captain?" he asked through gritted teeth. "Where? We had sentries out, didn't we?"

"Yes, sir. They were the first ones killed."

"Then how did the enemy get through, man? The sentries could see for miles in every direction from their vantage points. God damn it to hell!" Steele jabbed a finger in the direction of the horses, which had gathered in a protective group and settled down to graze. "I can see our mounts from here, and they must be a quarter of a mile away."

Bullard glanced toward where the horses stood, just as three more appeared, as if rising out of the very ground. "I think you've just had your question answered, sir. Do you see those three horses moving toward the others just now?"

"Yes, of course I do."

"Did you see them a few moments ago, sir?"

"No . . . no, I didn't." Steele replied, staring into the distance with a confused look. "Where in the bloody hell did they come from?"

"I think the problem with fighting in this open country is not what you can see at a great distance, but rather what you can't see at close range. By remaining deep within the swales and away from the crests, the enemy is able to get close without risking being seen. People who have never been exposed to such vast, open, and rolling ground as this, such as our three sentries, are lulled into a false sense of security, sir. If you stare straight to the horizon, everything seems to be flat, but if you look down at your feet, you notice you're standing on a rolling swell. While I've never fought there, sir, the Cree are known to inhabit the prairies of central Canada, which, while smaller, much resemble this country. I believe they have the advantage of experience on us here, Major."

Steele took up the riding crop hanging from a thong attached to his left wrist, and out of habit began a gentle tapping of his left thigh. The look of determination was there again, that dauntless expression of will to succeed at any cost.

"Well, my dear Captain, they have just lost that bloody advantage. We learn from our mistakes, and we have learned here today. We will not be taken by surprise again."

Bullard arched an eyebrow in surprise. "Pardon my asking, sir, but are you intending to continue this pursuit?"

"Of course I am, old chap!" Steele replied in an almost jolly voice. "We have engaged the enemy now, and the cat-and-mouse game is over. They fell into our trap once, and we returned the favor by duplicating their tactical error. Both sides are even now. One battle does not a war make, Captain, and the next time we shall emerge victorious. Chin up. That was a bloody good little scrap today."

A heavy weariness came over Bullard, and he sighed while looking down at his dead and wounded, now being collected by those who had escaped uninjured. "'Bloody good' might well be a more literal assessment of what happened than you intended, Major."

"Death and blood are inevitable in war, Captain. Be a good chap now," Steele said, walking briskly away, "and send a platoon to collect our mounts. We'll be riding to the hounds before the hour is out, and the fox shall be run to its den."

Bullard, born in the province of Quebec, watched the British officer stride away. There was something about English officers that galled him to the marrow of his bones. It was a trait he had seen demonstrated on many occasions. They had such a sense of propriety about them, of dignity and absolute correctness. To them, loss invariably constituted a victory if one survived it, and was considered merely a learning experience. A victory was nothing to be unduly heralded, because that was the expected result in the first place. They seemed to believe that the traditions of chivalry held as much weight on the frontiers of Canada and the United States as they had in King Arthur's Court, around his vaunted Round Table.

Bullard looked about him, surveying the string-straight horizon, and he could not help but think he was standing in the middle of a huge round table himself at that very moment. Unfortunately, he remembercd sadly, the table upon which he stood was spread with dead, wounded, and dying. He shook his head disgustedly and walked down the hill to carry out his orders.

ten

Judging from the condition of the rotted cottonwood, it must have been uprooted years earlier and carried in the swift, angry flow of a flash flood to lodge against the bank of a draw. Subsequent years of spring and fall floods had carved a deep indention in the bank behind the cottonwood. It might have passed for a cave, and it was within that cool recess that Sharon now lay staring at the grasshopper in Tommy's hand.

"I don't want to eat bugs, Tommy," she said weakly. "I hate bugs."

"This isn't a bug, it's a grasshopper."

"That's still a bug."

"They're simple to eat, Sharon, honest they are," Tommy replied, imploring his sister. "It's been two days since the Indians left us, and we've got to eat. Here, I'll show you. You don't chew 'em or nothin'. You just close your eyes and swallow." With those words, Tommy shut his eyes, opened his mouth, and tossed the green insect as far back in his throat as he could, while swallowing as deeply as possible. After several repeated swallows, he grinned, opened his eyes, and looked at his sister. "See there. Kinda tickles when they go down. Here," he continued with as much enthusiasm as he could muster while reaching into his pocket, "try one."

"I don't want one. I want a drink of water."

"I'll find some water for us tomorrow, Sharon, I promise I will. But I ain't got none right now. Please, Sharon, you got to eat, and this is all we got. Except I found some wild onion and I dug up some bitterroot. Pa showed me how to clean the bark away so somebody could eat it if they was real hungry. I like grasshopper better."

"I don't want to eat. I just want to die. Mr. Mandalian ain't never gonna find us."

"Sure he will. It'll just take time, that's all. Tell you what—

if you'll eat this grasshopper I've got in my hand, I'll eat part of the grass snake I killed today with that knife Running Deer gave me."

Childish curiosity came to the little girl's eyes in spite of exhaustion and despair. "You're gonna eat a raw snake?"

"You bet I am. But only after you have some grasshoppers."

Sharon eyed him warily. "How many?"

"Six."

"And if I do, you'll eat a snake?"

"I said part of a snake."

Sharon sat up and accepted the dead insect to examine it closely. "I bet it crunches in your mouth."

"I done told ya, you don't chew it. Just swallow hard. Come on, try it."

Sharon raised the grasshopper to her lips, closed her eyes, opened her mouth, and then stopped.

"Tilt your head back. It'll be easier," Tommy said, inching forward.

"I can't do it, Tommy. I don't care how many old snakes you eat."

"Go on, tilt your head back like I said." He was close to her now, waiting with one hand poised as Sharon tilted her head back. "That's it. Now open your mouth wider."

The little girl expanded her mouth to its widest, holding the grasshopper just beneath her lower lip. Tommy tapped her hand with his palm and the insect popped into her mouth while he instantly shoved her jaw upward. Sharon swallowed instinctively with a muffled scream, and Tommy leaned away to place his hands on his thighs with a satisfied smile. "See there? You done it."

"You cheated!" Sharon blurted, swallowing again to make certain the grasshopper had gone down. "Now you have to eat two snakes!"

"All right, I'll eat two. After you eat all your grasshoppers. That wasn't so bad, was it?"

"It felt funny. Will . . . will you help me eat the other ones?"

"Sure I will. Then I got me a snake to skin. And tomorrow we'll leave here and try to find some water. But right now we gotta eat what we got."

Later, when the setting sun had sealed off the cave in total darkness, Tommy lay there with his arms around his sleeping sister and stared at what would have been the opposite wall in daylight. He was experiencing a fear he had never known before, a fear not only of the dark, but of what lay ahead with the next day's rising sun. He wondered how much longer they could go on, and he was certain they would find no water the following day.

He closed his eyes and the tears seeped from the corners of his eyelids as he squeezed his sister more tightly while holding the knife in one hand behind her neck.

"Please, Mr. Mandalian. Please find us tomorrow," he whispered softly, his voice muted against Sharon's hair. "I can't do it much longer."

Then the exhausted little boy fell asleep and the heavy knife slowly slipped from his grasp.

"Kincaid? May I speak with you a moment?" Higgins asked as he placed his plate of beans to one side and took up his coffee cup.

Kincaid stood and walked toward the small fire beside which the colonel sat, and squatted to sit crosslegged in the grass. "Yes, Colonel? What can I do for you?"

"What can you do for me?" Higgins asked with a haughty but discouraged snort. "Shall we begin with a hot bath, a decent meal, laundered uniforms, and a good, stiff drink?"

Kincaid smiled and forked in another mouthful of beans from the tin plate in his hands. "Well, sir, the beans are fairly warm and the coffee's hot. While I can't honor your other requests, that is something positive to consider."

"Positive! I've never heard of anything more negative in my entire life! How much longer is this charade going to continue?"

"Charade, sir? I thought this was what you wanted. Service with a combat unit in the field, a sort of reorientation, as it were, and a chance to distinguish yourself on the field of battle."

"Yes, I suppose you're correct, but I had expected a little more action and a little less drudgery. The only things we've battled so far are heat, flies, filth, and indigestion." Higgins shifted his bulk uncomfortably. "Not to mention a sore ass."

"All of the above go with the occupation, sir. I think it would be accurate to say that for every five minutes of action, there are five days of searching and enduring. Perhaps you will come to appreciate that fact once we've caught up with the foe and have engaged them in battle, if that's what it comes to."

"If that's what it comes to!" Higgins scoffed. "You're damned right, that's what it's going to come to! I didn't ride all this way and subject myself to the extremes of discomfort just to shake hands with the enemy and walk away."

"I have vivid recollections of times when I would have preferred to do that very thing, but each situation is different, and I suppose we'll find out soon enough about this one. According to Windy's calculations, we've gained some ground on the Indians who raided the agency. We couldn't be more than a day and a half behind them, two days at the most."

Higgins took a sip of his coffee then tossed it aside in disgust. "Swill. Not even fit for stockade fare. As I suppose you have observed, Lieutenant, I am not particularly fond of that Mandalian fellow. He dresses like a savage, has the manners of a mongrel, and has no respect whatever for authority. I have no idea how he ever managed to weasel his way into the military community, but I'll have to tell you straight out, he would never be a member of a regiment under my command."

"Then it would be your loss, Colonel," Kincaid replied evenly, "not his."

Higgins adjusted himself to a more comfortable position and glared at Kincaid. "I see. There has been little question throughout this ordeal as to where your allegiances lie, and so be it. I called you over here to attempt to talk with you like one civilized military officer with another, but I see that is not to be. Now I'm forced to deal with you in the manner to which I am accustomed, as senior officer to junior officer. I have come to have serious reservations about your judgment and particularly your total faith in the opinions of Mr. Mandalian, which are spurious at best, and I am quite prepared to take full command of this entire operation."

Kincaid smiled easily. "You might be prepared to take command from the standpoint of rank, Colonel, but there is no one west of the Mississippi less qualified to take command than you."

"Simply a matter of judgment, and in this case a prejudiced opinion," Higgins retorted, his face reddening. "I can see nothing that we've accomplished so far that an absolute moron could not have engineered."

"Incorrect, sir. And only an absolute moron would be so shortsighted as not to appreciate what Windy has done. He has led us to what was very likely the Indians' most recent camp, where we are now, and he's done that more by instinct than by having fresh sign to follow. He has done it by thinking like an Indian and directing our actions accordingly. The lay of the land and the need for cover generally dictate an Indian's course of travel. No one knows the means to accomplish that, and thereby predict the other fellow's moves, better than my scout."

Kincaid might just as well have said nothing beyond his first two sentences, as the colonel had not been listening anyway. "Are you calling me a moron, Lieutenant?" Higgins asked with a hot-eyed stare.

"I have only laid down those conditions that would establish one to be a moron, sir. Anyone wishing to label himself thusly, in view of those criteria, is entirely free to do so."

Higgins lurched forward at the waist, then struggled clumsily to his feet. His jowls quivered with rage as he jabbed a pudgy finger down at Kincaid. "You, Lieutenant, are under arrest for insubordination! Corporal of the Guard!"

Kincaid waited in silence while the colonel glanced frantically about him. "Corporal of the Guard!"

"You're wasting your breath and jeopardizing our position, Colonel," Kincaid said softly. "Maximum silence should be maintained at all times, and especially after dark. Beyond that, my troops have been instructed to take orders from no one but myself or Windy Mandalian."

"You . . . you superseded my authority!" Higgins spluttered.

"You have no authority here, Colonel. We made an agreement to that effect in Captain Conway's sitting room. And spare me any more threats about ruining my military career. Per our agreement, you are to be the commanding officer in charge only on paper, should we be successful in this operation. I'm sure that condition would be changed, should the opposite happen to occur. In return for that consideration, I am the commanding officer in reality. Should that fact ever slip your mind again between now and when this patrol is over, I will be forced to write a report of my own when we return. I don't think your conduct to this point is conducive to favorable opinion, sir, and please be reminded that Captain Conway will back me up one hundred percent. As would Major Delaney, I suspect, if asked to do so."

"Major Delaney? So you've attempted to undermine me even with my own adjutant?" The colonel's eyes narrowed.

"You are a devious man, Lieutenant, but so am I. My day will come, and I warrant you, I have far more influence with the powers that be than you do, or anyone else in this godforsaken place. I am on a first-name basis with generals and senators back in Washington, Lieutenant, and that is where the ultimate decisions are made."

Kincaid smiled again. "Fine, and I congratulate you. But look around, Colonel; do you see any senators or generals here? Have you seen any fancy carriages, well-bred ladies, or cut-glass chandeliers in the past few days? No, I'm afraid you haven't. What you *have* seen is two platoons from Easy Company, trying to do a miserable job under even more miserable circumstances. At this moment you have no more influence than the lowest private in the entire army, sir, and I'm certain you have even less common sense."

"This is not only insulting, Lieutenant, it is an absolute outrage! I demand an apology!"

"I apologize, sir, for telling you exactly how I feel about you and for the fact that you alone have to live with the truth."

Higgins twisted away sharply, stumbled and nearly fell, then stalked away into the night. Kincaid continued to watch the pear-shaped figure until it was lost in the darkness, then he heard Windy call him.

"Got a minute, old son?"

"Sure, Windy. Let's go over to the cookfire and grab a cup of coffee. You could probably use one by now." Kincaid looked at the scout with concern as they walked down the sandy draw. "How long's it been since you've had some sleep?"

"Since the last time I needed any," Windy drawled, forking a chaw of cut-plug from his cheek and tossing it aside. "Cup o' coffee does sound mighty good 'bout now."

"What'd you find," Matt asked, filling two cups and handing one to Windy.

"A whole damned bunch of stuff. Now all I gotta do is figger out what it means. You remember when you caught up with me here, I said it looked like them featherheads we been chasin' split into two groups, one followin' the draw to the west and the other to the east?"

"Yes, I remember. What about it?"

"Well, after I left you here, I had me a couple hours to scout around afore dark. They split up, like I said, but they joined up again about a mile north of here."

"What would be the point in that?"

"To lay down an ambush, I reckon."

"Upon whom?"

"That's where the figgerin' part comes in," Windy replied, tilting his hat forward to scratch the back of his head. "Looks like there was a purty good battle on the lee side of a big, rolling swell over yonder. Empty casings scattered all over the damned place. Plus some dried-up blood on the grass, twenty-one fresh graves, thirteen dead Indians, and six horses that ain't gonna shit no more."

"Do you think it was one of our units that got jumped?"

"Don't reckon so," Windy replied, taking a casing from his pocket. "Ever seen one like this before?"

Kincaid took the brass casing and turned it in the firelight. "No, I don't think I have. It certainly wouldn't fit a Springfield or a Spencer."

"Nope, sure wouldn't. But an Enfield, now, it should cozy up purty nice to that."

"An Enfield?" Kincaid said, surprised. "That's a British-made weapon, isn't it?"

"Yup. And used by the Canadian militia. Thirty caliber."

"What the hell would they be doing here?"

"Chasin' the same people we are, I 'spect. It's Plains Cree we're after, Matt, for sure, and not Cheyenne or Sioux. Those lads stretched out over on that hillside proved that. They must be on the run purty good now, or they would've come back for their dead. Don't figger it's us they're runnin' from, though, 'cause if they knew we were on their trail, they wouldn't have took on them Canucks."

Kincaid studied his cup in thought. "Well, if the Canadians lost twenty-one in one skirmish, I'd say they're a mite outclassed against an outfit that only lost thirteen."

"Yup. The fightin' we've got here is a mite different from what they're used to up north. The Cree, on the other hand, ain't called Plains Cree for want of a better name. They're used to prairie fightin'. 'Sides that, they're being led by a white man, or at least a breed."

"You never cease to amaze me, Windy. How in hell could you possibly know that?"

"Not much to it, really," the scout replied with a dismissing shrug. "The tracks here in the sand was still mighty good when

I showed up, and it was plain as the nose on your face that he was wearin' moccasins."

"So? What do the Plains Cree wear? Button-up shoes?"

Windy allowed a chuckle as he sipped his coffee. "Nope. Be a lot easier to track if they did, though. But our white feller—or breed, or whatever—might just as well have been. Indians always mount from the right side of a horse, without fail." The scout grinned. "He mounted from the left, like we do."

"Yeah, sure, Windy, you old bastard," Kincaid said. "Anyone would have spotted that in a minute. Even Colonel Higgins, I'm sure."

"Heard ya talkin' to the old shithead. Sounded like you've just about had it with him yourself."

"Long ago, Windy, long ago. But up until tonight, I had hoped a little diplomacy might work. Now he can go fuck himself, as far as I'm concerned. Any decisions made for these two platoons will be made only by you or me. Speaking of which, what's our next move?"

"Well, the Cree are definitely headin' west now, and either they're plumb lost or they're lookin' for somethin', like I said afore. And don't forget, we've got them Canucks on our hands too. Looks like they headed west as well, and I wouldn't be one damned bit surprised if they met somewhere along the trail, most likely with the Cree suckerin' 'em into another trap. I reckon we should split into two patrols, with one platoon trailing the Cree and the other trailin' the Canucks. Could be the Canucks might bait our trap for us."

"Sounds good to me. I'll take the first and you take the second. I'll go after the Cree, and you take up the trail of those Canadians. We'll leave at first light in the morning."

"Just a minute, Matt, old son," Windy said with a sly glance. "Who gets the colonel? Him and his goddamned Gatling gun?"

"You do, of course," Kincaid responded with a wide grin. "I think if you two spent a little time together, you could strike up a real nice friendship."

"Yup. Just like two dogs and one bone. 'Night, Matt, you're a real sweetheart."

The afternoon sun beat down with blistering intensity, and it seemed even hotter than the day before as the first platoon worked its way westward. The two point men, a hundred yards to the front and spaced widely apart, were but a shimmer in the distance, and their blue uniforms were wet with sweat that rapidly dried and turned to faint white streaks of crusted salt. The heads of the normally spirited mounts drooped noticeably in the heat, and sweat-foam had formed around the rear edges of their saddles.

Abruptly, one of the point men halted and raised his rifle above his head. Kincaid halted the platoon and waited for the soldier to check out whatever had aroused his suspicions. As he sat there, he glanced around and saw the sharp banks of a ravine of sorts, which obviously was prone to flash flooding, and he turned to Peterson.

"Corporal? Take two men and go over and check out that draw for sign while we're waiting. Looks like a good place for an Indian night camp."

"Yessir. Hayes! Canfield! Fall out and come with me!"

Peterson cantered away with the two privates behind him, then slowed his horse as he neared the draw. He turned his horse and rode along the edge for several yards before finding a suitable place to descend the bank, and when he did, he turned his mount and all three men disappeared from Kincaid's view. Watching the ground closely for sign, Peterson walked his horse along the sandy bottom, glancing up every now and then and deciding to quit the draw just beyond the big cottonwood lodged against the bank fifty yards away. As he neared the snag, he was certain there had been no Indians along that stretch of the ravine in the recent past, and he glanced up to find an egress route. Then his eyes caught something and he reined the mount in sharply.

There were tracks in the sand, fresh tracks that no Indian could possibly have made, unless he was wearing shoes and had incredibly tiny feet. Puzzled, Peterson swung down and knelt to examine the footprints more closely. Just up the bank, the tracks were more clearly visible, and he could determine that two children had recently been there. His heart skipped a beat as he glanced a little farther up and saw a black hole that appeared to be a small cave of some sort. Peterson scrambled toward the opening. After peering inside, he worked his way into the small opening, and when his eyes adjusted to the dim light, he could make out the scuffmarks of tiny shoes on the water-packed earth. Off to one side he could see the skin of a snake, which he took up and tested for moisture. It was still damp and clammy, and the corporal knew it couldn't have been left there more than a day before.

Peterson squirmed quickly from the hole and cautiously crept along the bottom, looking for tracks leading away from the cave.

"What the hell you up to, Corporal?" Canfield asked. "Looks to me like the sun's got to ya."

Peterson made no reply, but continued his search until he found two sets of tracks again, and the place where feet had scrambled, slipped, and then scrambled upward again. The corporal mounted the bank in a frantic crawl and stood on the lip to shield his eyes and search the prairie to the south. He saw nothing but shimmering heat waves. Turning, he descended the bank with leaping strides and raced toward his mount to swing up into the saddle.

"Two kids were here yesterday, or maybe even early this mornin'!" he said excitedly as he reined his horse around to face the pair of privates. "White kids. We've gotta go after 'em. They won't last long in heat like this!"

"Shouldn't we tell the lieutenant, Corporal?" Hayes asked. "He don't much like to have us go traipsin' off on our own, without permission."

"I ain't traipsin' nowhere, private," Peterson replied with urgency filling his voice as he urged his horse up the steep bank. "You go and tell the lieutenant what we've found. Canfield, you come with me. We might not have much time. Hayes, you ask Lieutenant Kincaid to send a squad to this point and have 'em fan out, just in case me and Canfield miss those kids."

Spread fifty yards apart, the two soldiers worked their way south, riding slowly and searching intently on either side. If the children had left any trail in the grass, it was not to be found, and after nearly a mile, Peterson's heart sank and he turned in the saddle to glance backward. A full squad of soldiers was spread out behind them, slowly working its way in the same direction.

Unknown to Peterson, only three hundred yards ahead of him and off to his right, two delirious children were stumbling forward, mindless of their direction of travel. Every time the little girl, who was mostly being dragged, fell to her knees, her brother would stop and help her to her feet and then urge her onward. Their lips were parched and cracked, and swollen tongues filled their bone-dry mouths.

Even in his delirium, Tommy thought he heard the sound of hoofbeats approaching behind them, and he turned with the knife in his hand.

"Indians comin' . . . sis. Gotta . . . gotta . . . hide."

Sharon had again dropped to her knees, and Tommy pushed her down in the grass, then flopped beside her with the knife pressed forward. He tried to focus on the twin objects approaching, but his eyes would not respond, and all he could make out were two men riding toward them and slightly off to the left.

Peterson was nearly abreast of them now, and in seconds he would have passed by where they lay, but from the corner of his eye he saw something glint in the deep grass, like sun reflecting off metal. His head jerked in that direction, but whatever had made the flash of light had disappeared. He wondered if the heat was causing his mind to play tricks on him, or if he had just imagined having seen the flash.

Deciding that neither was the case, he rode cautiously in the direction from which the flash of light had come. Thinking it might have come from a rifle barrel, he eased his Scoff out of its holster and drew the hammer back as he stared between the horse's ears for any movement in the grass. Suddenly, and no more than twenty feet in front of him, Peterson saw something leap from the dense cover. Instantly he leveled the revolver as his finger closed on the trigger. The sights lined up on a little red-haired boy, staggering forward in desperate lunges, carving harmless swaths in the air with a large knife, and the corporal's heart sank as he realized he had been but a heartbeat away from sending a bullet crashing into the young boy's chest.

"You killed my ma and pa!" the boy screamed hoarsely. "You killed 'em! You killed 'em!"

Stepping quickly from the saddle and turning his horse away, Peterson approached the boy warily, sidestepping a feeble thrust of the knife, then grabbing a shrunken arm as the blade passed by.

"I didn't hurt your folks, son. Honest I didn't. I'm a soldier and I'm here to help you," Peterson said gently as he removed the knife from Tommy's hand. "Let's put that away, you won't need it anymore. Hayes!" the corporal shouted over his shoulder. "I found 'em! Get over here and give me a hand!"

Then Peterson knelt and lifted one of the boy's eyelids with the tip of his thumb, while testing his forehead for moisture with his other fingers. The skin was bone-dry and strangely chilled, while the retina was constricted to a tiny dot. The corporal knew the child was but a few hours from dying of sunstroke.

"Grab your canteen and bring it over here!" he snapped in Hayes's direction, as the private stepped down from his plunging mount. "Then look over there in the grass. There should be another one."

Before Hayes had reached him with the canteen, Peterson had gently lowered the boy down and was removing his kerchief, which he dampened and sponged around the parched lips before squeezing several droplets onto a searching tongue. Moments later, Hayes carried a little girl forward and lowered her to the ground beside the boy.

"Get your bedroll and spread it out, then hold it over these kids," Peterson said, without looking up from where he worked over the girl with the damp cloth. "We've got to get 'em some shade or they'll be dead within the hour."

"God, but they look awful, don't they?" Hayes asked, pausing for a moment and staring down at the children.

"Hell no, they don't!" Peterson snapped. "They look beautiful 'cause they're still alive. Now get that goddamned bedroll!"

An hour later, Peterson again stood before the relatively cool cave in the draw, with Kincaid standing by his side, and both men looked in at the two children stretched out on a cushion of blankets.

"Don't give them too much water too quick, Corporal," Kincaid cautioned. "They'll ask for it, but don't give it to them. Just keep on like you've been doing, a little bit at a time."

"Yessir. I ain't aimin' to see them little shavers get away from me now. They were damned close when I found 'em, but they're gonna make it just fine now."

Kincaid noted the loving tone in the corporal's voice, and a single glance told him he was looking at no wife-beater or common drunk. "You are to be congratulated, Corporal. You saved their lives. I'll admit I wasn't exactly pleased when I saw you heading south, but you used your best judgment, and that's what I expect of my men."

"Thank you, sir, and I apologize for not waitin' for you. But seeing those kid's tracks, out here alone like this, was more than I could take. I couldn't have waited a minute longer if it had meant the firing squad."

"I understand that. As I said, you did the right thing. Keep working over them like you have been, and they should come around in an hour or so. When they do, call me."

"Yessir. Sir? Do you think these are kids from that trading post at the Clearwater?"

"Yes, I believe they are."

"And they were just left out here on the prairie like this to die?"

"Renegade Indians have been known to do that, Corporal. And worse. Take good care of them," Kincaid said, offering a congratulatory tap on the corporal's shoulder.

It was nearing nightfall when Kincaid was summoned by a private dispatched at Peterson's request. The two children were sitting on the lip of the cave when he arrived, and he was relieved to see that the ashen look had gone from their faces.

"Well now, how are you doing?" he asked with a pleasant smile as he leaned down to rest one arm on his knee. "You had us scared there for a while. My name is Lieutenant Kincaid, and this is Corporal Peterson. He's the one who saved your lives." Matt offered his hand. "What are your names?"

Sharon looked at Tommy with her wide blue eyes and remained silent while the boy accepted Kincaid's grip. "Pleased to meet you, sir. My name is Tommy Griffin and this here is my little sister, Sharon."

"Pleased to meet you, Tommy and Sharon. How old are you two?"

"I'm eight," Tommy replied pridefully. "She's only six."

The taunting tone of her brother's words prompted Sharon to work up enough courage to speak. "Tommy's a liar, Mr. Kincaid."

"Come now," Matt said with a chuckle as he ruffled the little boy's hair. "Your brother here is a brave man, and brave men don't need to lie."

Tommy glanced sharply at his sister. "Am not!"

"Yes you are!"

"Now, now, let's not argue. What makes you say that Tommy's a liar, Sharon?"

"He lied to me twice!" Sharon said.

"In what way?" Kincaid asked, secretly marveling at the resilience of children and at their easy dismissal of near-death in favor of resolute determination to settle an old score.

"He said he'd eat two snakes if I ate six grasshoppers. He only ate one!"

Kincaid couldn't help but laugh. "Well, that's not so bad. I think one snake is worth six grasshoppers any day. How else did he lie to you?"

"He said a friend of ours would find us," Sharon replied with a slight pout. "And he didn't."

"And who would that friend be?"

"Mr. Mandalian."

"Well now, I guess Tommy's clean on both counts. Mr. Mandalian did find you, in a manner of speaking. If it weren't for him, we wouldn't be here right now."

"Really, sir?" Tommy asked in wide-eyed excitement.

"For a fact. He wouldn't give up until he knew for sure we'd catch up with the Indians who took you captive."

"See there, Sharon! Lot you know!"

"That's enough now, you two," Kincaid said, leaning forward once more. "I've got to ask you some questions, and then I think you should try to sleep. You've got a long ride ahead of you in the morning."

"Where are we going, sir?"

"Back to Outpost Number Nine. That's where Mr. Mandalian stays."

"Will he be there?"

"No, not for a while at least. Now listen closely. Mr. Mandalian is trying to find your sister, or sisters. Are they still alive?"

Tommy looked down, and his lips quivered as he scuffed the toes of his boots together. "Yes, they're alive, sir. But they're not being treated very good."

"I imagine not, son, but the main thing is that they're still alive. If that's the case, Mr. Mandalian will get them back to you. Now did the Indians who took you captive happen to say where they intended to go? Did you overhear anything that might help us find them quicker?"

Tommy searched his mind. "No. they talked Indian-talk a lot, and we spent most of the time with our friend, Running Deer. He's the one who took us away from Chief Horse, and he gave me his knife."

Kincaid caught his breath and looked closely at the little boy. "Did you say Chief Horse, Tommy? Try to remember now—did he have any other names?"

"I think so, but I forget 'em."

"Try to remember. It's very important. Could it have been Chief Rides Big Horses?"

Tommy crinkled his face in thought, then his eyes lit up. "Yes, that's it. Chief Rides Big Horses. I heard him say that's who he was after he killed Ma and Pa out in the yard in front of our house. Then he said it other times too, when he was braggin'. He brags a lot," Tommy said disgustedly.

"Yes, I imagine he does," Kincaid replied, then rose to his feet. "You two try to get some sleep now. I've got to talk with Corporal Peterson."

While the little ones scrambled back into the cave, Kincaid turned and walked down the draw with Peterson by his side. In the back of his mind he remembered the conversation he'd had with Captain Conway and Flora several days before, regarding the Peterson marriage, and the follow-up conversation with Conway just before Colonel Higgins's inspection of Easy Company.

"Fine kids, aren't they, Corporal?" Matt asked as they walked side by side.

"Sure are, sir," Peterson replied in a distant tone.

"It's going to be tough on them, losing their mom and dad like they did."

The corporal swallowed hard. "Sure is, sir. And it's a damned shame."

"We're going to have to find a place for them to stay back at the outpost until we can get them properly settled," Kincaid said with a sideways glance at Peterson. "A good home and somebody to give them the love they'll need to get through the adjustment period. I know Maggie would do it, and so would Mrs. Conway, but I'd like to see them with a younger couple. Just can't quite place my finger on who. . . ." Matt concluded, his voice trailing off.

Peterson watched the lieutenant cautiously. "How about my wife and me, sir? We've always wanted children, and we could give them a good home until you decide . . . decide on somebody else."

"That's an idea. I never thought of you two."

"Don't imagine you did, sir," Peterson said with a hint of dejection. "I know I've been mean to her a time or two, and it ain't no secret around Number Nine. We've got our problems, sir, but we ain't bad. Them kids back there'd be as snug as a bug in a rug with us. I promise you that."

"By God, that's a thought," Kincaid said, nodding his head agreeably, as if the notion had not occurred to him. "Sure your wife wouldn't mind? Might be a bit of a chore, taking care of two youngsters."

"She'd love it, sir. Absolutely love it."

Kincaid clapped a hand on the corporal's shoulder. "Good. Then it's settled, and you can take them back. Tomorrow morning, you and your squad will provide an escort for those kids, and when you get there, tell Captain Conway about our conversation here this evening."

Strangely, a troubled look crossed Peterson's face and he walked in silence for several moments before looking across at Kincaid. "Don't get me wrong, sir. It'll be an honor to take those kids back to the outpost, and I'll damned well get them there without a hair on their heads being touched. But as soon as Connie has 'em tucked in bed, I want to come back, sir."

"I appreciate that, Corporal, but I think we can manage without you."

"I'm sure you could, sir. But I've got some business to settle with that Rides Big Horses, myself, and when the battle starts, I want to be there. If possible, I want to be the one to take him with guns, knives, fists, or rocks, whichever he prefers."

"I admire that, and as soon as you get fresh mounts and a little rest, I'll expect you back here. Angle west and figure we've traveled at least two days. But as far as taking Rides Big Horses yourself, I'm afraid you'll have to stand in line for that, Corporal."

Peterson glanced up in surprise. "Why's that, sir?"

"Because you'll have to get around Windy first. The Griffins were like his own family to him, and the only thing on his mind right now is sinking a knife in that Cree's belly. I don't think there'll be much left for you after Windy's through with him."

Peterson smiled knowingly. "No there won't, Lieutenant. I don't care who gets that son of a bitch, as long as it's someone who cares about those kids back there."

"Rest assured that Windy does, Corporal. Rest assured that he does probably more than anybody alive right now. I imagine there's some other Cree needing a little killing for what they've done to the Griffin family. We'll save you one. Have a good ride, and I'll see you when you get back."

eleven

Windy Mandalian was pushing the men and mounts of the second platoon harder than he would have liked to, but he was certain that since the Canadians had already fallen into one trap, they would very likely fall into another. His concern in that regard was twofold: first, he didn't like to see men die needlessly, be they Canadian, American, or Indian; second, and perhaps more important, if the Cree did attack again, he would have found his prey, and he wanted to be close enough to counter-attack. He judged his force to be approximately half the number of those opposing him, and a diversion, should it develop, could well offset the numerical disadvantage.

The trail left behind by the Canadians was easy to follow, and with the exception of having to remain constantly alert to surprise attack, Windy was little concerned about the direction in which the Cree had gone. The fact that the Canadians went due west after they broke camp, and then veered to the northwest each day, indicated that they were hopelessly lost, and Windy had no doubt that the Cree were aware of that fact as well, and that they would strike when the opportunity best suited their needs.

According to Windy's calculations, by maintaining a steady pace, he would have the Canadians in sight by no later than noon the following day—or their remains, at least, should the Cree get to them first.

The Gatling gun was taking a severe jolting as it rattled across the prairie on its carriage, but Windy could not have been less concerned, and he would have been delighted to see the entire contraption fall apart. Such was not the case with Colonel Higgins, who doubtlessly viewed that weapon as the instrument with which he could achieve the major slaughter he envisioned and the one that would spell a major victory in the Eastern newspapers.

The colonel urged his horse up beside Windy's and looked across at the stone-faced scout. "You, sir, are a maniac! Slow this column down immediately! I didn't order that Gatling gun brought along just to see it strewn from Wyoming to California!"

Windy offered no reply and continued forward at a steady canter that was intended to cover the greatest distance possible in the shortest period of time while causing the least wear on their mounts.

Under the guidance of the colonel's inexperienced hands, his horse was constantly alternating between a smooth gait and a spine-jolting trot, into which it had fallen now, and Higgins's jowls flapped while he held his hat on with one hand.

"I said slow down, goddammit!" he demanded in a tooth-jolting chatter. "And I mean now!"

Windy worked the tobacco in his cheek, spat unconcernedly, and glanced at the colonel. "You could do that horse a mite of harm, trottin' it that way."

"Me? Do *it* harm? I'm afraid you've got that a little bit backwards, Mandalian," Higgins managed, while attempting to right himself after having been bounced off to one side of the saddle.

"Give it a little head, then pull it in real slow-like and keep it there," Windy said, watching the horse work its foam-flecked mouth against the pressure of the steel bit. "You're keepin' the reins too damned tight, and all it wants to do is keep up with my horse."

More out of desperation than appreciation, Higgins followed Windy's advice and the horse immediately settled into a smooth canter. Windy smiled as the colonel adjusted himself in the stirrups once more, settled his hat, and stared out over the horse's ears with little confidence.

"He knows more about what he's doin' than you do, Colonel. Just quit tryin' to steer the son of a bitch, and leave him alone. Now you wanted to say somethin' to me?"

"You're damned right I do," Higgins snapped. "I want this column slowed down immediately."

"Maybe to somethin' like a trot?"

Higgins grimaced. "No, a fast walk."

"Can't do that, Colonel. Got places to go and asses to kick."

"Do you have any idea what this pace is doing to my Gatling gun?" Higgins asked, risking a backward glance to make sure the carriage was still in one piece. "It can't take this kind of beating much longer."

"Guess we'll find out for sure, next day or two. If it can't, it oughtn't to be here in the first place. You're ridin' with the mounted infantry, not the goddamned artillery."

"That piece was designed for use by rapidly moving forces in the field, like this one."

"Then it should get along fine," Windy replied, shifting the chaw to his other cheek. "Cause we're movin' as rapid as we can. If it don't, you give them people who built it hell in that report of yours."

An instantaneous flash of anger swept over him, and Higgins raised his gloved hand above his shoulder and commanded, *"Company, hoooooo!"* while reining in his own mount. The soldiers behind swerved their horses, narrowly avoiding a collision with the colonel while maintaining the same pace behind Windy. The only rider who slowed and then stopped beside the enraged, florid colonel was his adjutant, Major Delaney. He remained silent while the Gatling gun rattled by, and then looked across at Higgins, who was staring glumly at the rapidly receding column.

"Maybe if it had been a full company, they would have stopped, sir," he said, attempting to conceal a grin. "As it is, that's only one platoon."

"I don't give a shit if it's one man or a whole goddamned regiment, Major! When a colonel gives the order to halt, they're dammed well supposed to halt!"

Delaney watched the platoon moving steadily away. "In that case, I guess the best thing we can do is catch up and tell them that. Shall we, Colonel?"

"I don't particularly like your tone of voice, Major. I'm putting you on report as of now, and effective when we return to the outpost."

"I'm the only son of a bitch that stops, and I'm the one who gets put on report," Delaney said with a soft chuckle and a shake of his head at the irony of it all. "Aw, hell, out here, who gives a damn anyway. Come on, Colonel. I'd like to put a little less distance between myself and that platoon up there."

"Any idea where we are, Major Steele?" Captain Bullard asked, his eyes sweeping over the monotonous terrain ahead. "We lost their trail yesterday and we've been riding blind, if you'll pardon the expression, all day today."

The first traces of exasperation were visible on Steele's face, and he mopped perspiration from his brow with the back of his hand. "Of all the bloody goddamned miserable places to attempt to conduct a campaign. To be entirely candid with you, Captain, I haven't got the foggiest notion where we are, and if that business about lost people going around in circles has any validity to it, I would expect to see the graves of our dead any moment now."

"Thank you for your candor, Major," Bullard said with sincerity. "I had not the slightest bit of trouble maintaining a westerly course until approximately ten o'clock this morning. After that, the sun was nothing but a flaming nuisance, as it shall remain until it sets again this evening."

With his customary British optimism returning, Steele touched his horse's flank with the crop and moved forward once more while saying, "I would say our only ray of hope is that the bloody thing sets behind the western horizon in this godforsaken land the same as it does in the civilized parts of the world. Shall we press on, Captain?"

Bullard signaled for the company to move out once more, while resuming his customary place by the major's side. "Sir, we have about four hours of light left to us today, and tomorrow we'll start anew. But our rations are running extremely low and I suggest we consider turning back the day after tomorrow, if we haven't found the Cree by that time."

"Turn back, Captain?" Steele asked with an arched eyebrow. "I have no intention of turning back, if by that you mean returning to Canada. My entire career is on the line with this endeavor, as is yours, I suspect. We have no choice but to achieve victory, or there is no point in going back at all." The major hesitated and smiled. "That is, my dear chap, if we could find our way back in the first place."

"Then I'll have to put the troops on half rations, sir."

"By all means. Half rations it is. Perhaps we'll find some wild game that's as lost as we are, and we'll live on fresh meat if we have to. But one thing must always be at the forefront of your mind: I have never suffered a defeat in the field, and that record shall remain intact even if we have to wander around here for the remainder of our bloody lives. Is that clear, Captain?"

"Clear beyond any need for clarification, sir. Perhaps one

day we will be known as 'the lost legions of Canada,'" Bullard said without humor. "It will be most comforting to know that we aren't lost to the minds of schoolchildren."

"That's the spirit! Jolly good, old chum!" Steele chortled with a slap of the crop against his leg. "But not to worry; we shall snatch victory from the jaws of defeat yet, you'll see. Someone once said, 'Losing is for losers.' Bright fellow indeed. I don't intend to see myself, you, or the men of your command in that category, however. Now back to the business at hand. In two hours, send a patrol forward to find a suitable campsite for the evening. We should be well secured by nightfall."

"Yessir," Bullard replied without enthusiasm. The Englishman's "jolly good" attitude was grating on him more and more with each passing mile.

Shortly before the sun began its plunge toward the horizon, Bullard selected a five-man detail and sent them forward to find a high point that would lend itself to the needs of a secure defense. It was with little enthusiasm that the detail quit the main body of troops and rode alone to the front. Nearly blinded by the slanting rays of the setting sun, they shielded their eyes as they moved forward at a canter, and soon they disappeared into a swale, only to emerge minutes later and then fade from view once more. Then they were lost to Bullard's eyes completely, which he closed and uttered a silent prayer.

A half hour passed by, then a full hour, and still there was no sign of the detail, which normally would have returned to direct the company to their night's bivouac.

"I wonder what happened to them, sir?" Bullard asked, with an obvious hint of worry. "They should have been back by now."

"Yes, it seems that they should have been," Steele replied. "Perhaps they had difficulty finding a suitable location, which is entirely understandable, considering the conditions."

"To my way of thinking, one of these rolling hills would have been just as good as the next, sir."

"I suppose so. But it's standard procedure to send a bivouac detail ahead in the interest of the security of the main command. Therefore, I intend to continue the practice until events dictate otherwise."

"At the risk of seeming insubordinate, sir, I'm afraid 'standard procedure,' as we've known it in the past, has little bearing on the present set of circumstances." Bullard was watching the major's face intently as he spoke, and now he added, "It would seem to me that flexibility and adaptability are what we must concern ourselves with until—"

"Good God, man, look down there!"

Lying at the bottom of the draw into which they were now proceeding were the bodies of five men, stretched out neatly side by side. As the company drew near, they could see that each man had an arrow in his chest, and their blood-red skulls were made even more red by the dying rays of the golden sun. A broad swatch of scalp had been removed from each man, and the effect of the scene was made even more grotesque by the fact that their hands were folded neatly across their chests, as if they were enjoying a comfortable nap.

Both the major's and Bullard's eyes quickly swept over the surrounding terrain, but the prairie was peaceful and calm, revealing no secrets in the settling twilight.

"They're playing a game with us, Major," Bullard said, trying to control the emotion in his voice. "Those five men were arranged that way by the Cree to tell us they can do anything they want, when they want. We aren't following them, sir. They're following us."

The captain braced himself, thinking the major might say something like, "Jolly good show. At least we've made contact with the enemy again," but Steele offered no response for long moments, as though his normally indomitable spirit had taken a blow to the solar plexus.

"Yes, it appears they are, Captain," Steele finally said through gritted teeth. "We've got to find a way to meet them in open combat, but they're too cowardly for that kind of warfare. If we could just sight them once, we would annihilate them and be done with it. Have a detail retrieve the bodies of those men and bring them to the top of the rise just ahead of us. We'll bivouac there tonight. Have the company move forward and establish a picket guard."

"Yes, sir." Bullard started to turn away, then hesitated. "Has it ever occurred to you, Major, that what we began as a pursuit mission has now taken on entirely defensive characteristics?"

"We are on the march and moving forward, Captain," Steele replied sternly. "That is not a defensive characteristic. The tables will turn very soon, mark my words, and then we shall be on the attack. Until that time, we shall continue on as we have. The hour grows late, my Canadian friend, let's get cracking."

It was shortly past noon the following day when Windy caught his first glimpse of the rearmost portion of the Canadian militia as they appeared briefly on a distant swell and then were lost from view. He had seen the five freshly dug graves earlier that morning, and he had pushed the platoon even harder in an effort to catch up. There had been no spent cartridges, no evidence of a battle, and he suspected what had happened to be an old Indian ploy, namely to make the enemy hungry enough for revenge that they would leap at the slightest bait, to get them sufficiently thirsty for Indian blood that they would abandon good sense and logic in a desperate attempt to even the score. And he also knew the bait would be offered in the heat of the day, after mounts and men had become weary and were off guard.

Another fifteen minutes passed, and when Windy caught sight of the entire company once more, he veered the platoon off to the left to provide flanking support for the unsuspecting Canadians. They crested one swell, then another, and Windy's heart sank as he pulled his horse to a stop and watched approximately twenty warriors show themselves briefly at a distance of some two hundred yards from the militiamen, then turn and gallop away as if fleeing for their lives.

"Don't fall for it," the scout muttered, but he knew the admonition had been uttered in vain.

Major Steele had been brooding all morning long, and even though Bullard had tried to engage him in conversation, it was to no avail. The major was hungry for battle, itching for the chance to take the offensive, and so dead set was he upon victory that no other thoughts or words seemed capable of penetrating his brain. And when he saw the twenty warriors, he jerked his horse's head up and his eyes glowed with delight.

"Well, would you bloody by Jesus believe that? We've cut their trail, Captain!"

"That can't be the main force, sir," Bullard responded quickly. "There had to be at least three times that many when they jumped us the first time."

"When you're fishing, my friend, you take whatever happens to be on the hook. Have the bugler sound the charge! By damn, we'll run the bloody fox to ground!"

With those words, the major spurred his mount forward, and Bullard, against his own better judgement, gave the signal for the call to charge.

The faint strains of the bugle call drifted back to Windy, and he slapped the loose end of his reins against the big roan's flank and sunk his heels home. "Shit!" he said as the horse bolted into a run. "We're three hundred yards too damned late."

Up ahead, Steele was riding perhaps twenty yards in front of the main command and lashing his mount with his crop in quest of greater speed, while Bullard's mount was running ten yards to the rear.

"We're gaining on them," Steele exulted, seeing the Cree no more than a hundred yards away on what appeared to be tiring ponies as they raced across a flat stretch of prairie in the direction of another hump on the floor of the plains. "Their mounts are no match for ours!"

A sense of dread filled the captain's heart as he saw how quickly and easily they were catching up with the fleeing Indians. It was all too pat, too easy. Less than a day before, the Cree had been in charge, capable of striking at will, and now they were caught off guard? Committed to whatever lay ahead, he glanced once toward the company strung out behind him, pushing their mounts for all the speed they could get, then he pulled out his revolver as they pounded up the rise. If everything was as it seemed, the Indians would be within range the next time they came into view.

Just as Steele's horse crested the prairie swell, the first shot rang out and the major's mount buckled instantly, sending Steele catapulting over its head. Bullard had topped the rise as well, and he felt a terrible impact against his right shoulder and could sense a spinning, weightless sensation as he slammed from the saddle. The remainder of the company was committed as well when they surged above the horizon, and a withering fire coming from the Indians lying prone below decimated their ranks, spilling mounts and men on all sides.

Dazed, Bullard wobbled to his feet and screamed, "Dismount! Seek what protection you can find and commence firing!"

Fully one-third of the company had either been killed or

wounded in the first volley, and those remaining leaped from their horses to skid, belly down, in the grass. The twenty mounted warriors who had served as decoys whirled their ponies on churning hooves and swung back to attack from the flank, and Bullard again risked his life to stagger up the hill and coordinate the defense. But he knew there was little hope for saving his command. Below and off to the left, he could see Steele crawling toward the relative safety of his dead horse and slipping in between its twisted legs while firing the revolver in his hand. The Cree at the bottom of the swell continued to lay down a steady barrage, and the mounted warriors were taking a deadly toll as they raced their ponies back and forth to fire down on the easily discernible targets spread out on the crest.

Then a stunned Captain Bullard heard firing from somewhere off to the left, and his head snapped in that direction with the thought that they were being brought under attack on another front. What he saw was unrecognizable to him at that moment, but there were approximately thirty soldiers streaking downward on bay horses, and their blue uniforms were resplendent in the brilliant sunlight. A tall man wearing buckskins and riding a big roan horse was in the lead, and when they reached the bottom of the swale, he threw his hand up and the unit pulled their horses to a plunging stop to leap down and advance on foot.

Caught completely by surprise, the Indians broke off the ambush and retreated toward ponies being held in the distance, where they swung up on their mounts and raced away, while being joined by those mounted warriors plunging down from the crest. Several scattered shots were fired at fleeing targets, and then silence settled over the plains.

Bullard went immediately to the major's side. "Are you all right, sir? It looked like you took one hell of a spill."

"Yes, I did at that, Captain," Steele replied with a slight grimace as he massaged his leg. "Must have twisted my knee." Then he noticed Bullard's blood-drenched sleeve. "You're hurt far worse than I am, Captain. Here, let me take a look at it."

"Nothing more than a flesh wound, sir. I'll tend to it myself."

Steele heaved a dispirited sigh and twisted around to look at the fallen men and horses scattered about him. "I'd say I rather led with my chin, wouldn't you, Captain? Bloody stupid of me, but the humiliation of it all had stolen my better judgement."

"Yes, sir, I'd say it did. And to be quite frank with you, Major, you are no longer in command of my company. I'll risk whatever repercussions there might be for my actions in assuming command."

"And you are entirely correct in doing so, Captain. Perhaps I have outlived my time. As you indicated earlier, it appears that I'm not adaptable enough to deal with a situation that does not adhere to military maneuvers with which I am accustomed."

"Don't be too hard on yourself, sir. We all make mistakes."

"Yes, that's true," Steele replied, gazing into the distance. "But on this mission I have made more than a generous amount. If the rank of colonel were offered to me now, which I admit was my ultimate goal at the outset, I would refuse it without a second thought."

"I don't think you're in much danger of having to make that decision, Major," Bullard replied frankly.

Steele smiled weakly. "Are you sure you're not British? A remark like that could only come from an Englishman."

"Absolutely certain, Major."

"Pity. How many did we lose to my stupidity?"

"All I can say is that we suffered heavy casualties. I haven't had the chance to make a full reckoning."

"I see. Who were the lads who came to our rescue?"

"American army, I think, sir. One of them is approaching right now, as a matter of fact."

Steele looked up to see Windy Mandalian swing from his horse and step to the ground, then drop his reins and cross the remaining steps on foot. "Can't tell a hell of a lot by them uniforms," Windy said easily as he squatted and rested his elbows on his thighs, "but from the looks of things, I'd say one of you boys is in charge of this shindig. My name is Windy Mandalian."

"And I am Major William R. Steele, and this is Captain Charles Bullard. It is a pleasure to meet you, sir. While I happen to be responsible for this entire affair, Captain Bullard is now the officer in charge. We'd like to thank you for a judicious application of muscle at the appropriate time."

Windy worked his chaw, spat, and tilted his hat back. "I

reckon you're aimin' to say you're glad we showed up when we did?"

"That I am."

"That's what I thought. Glad to be here. You boys been takin' a purty steady thumpin', ain't ya?"

"Unfortunately, yes."

"Canadian, ain't ya?"

Steele hesitated. "Canadian militia."

"Fur piece from home, ain't ya?"

"Yes we are," Steele replied with obvious resignation in his voice. "We were in pursuit of two renegades, a métis named Johnny Singletree and a Cree chief who calls himself Rides Big Horses. I offer my sincere apologies for crossing the border without—"

Windy's body stiffened noticeably, and his eyes went cold. "Never mind that apology shit, you can tell that to somebody else. You just mentioned a name that's got a mite of personal interest to me."

Puzzled, Steele asked, "Johnny Singletree?"

"No, the other one."

"Chief Rides Big Horses?"

"That's the one. A Plains Cree who linked up with the métis?"

"One and the same."

"So he's the one," Windy said softly, while continuing to stare at Steele without seeing him.

"Pardon me, sir?" Steele asked, stunned by the deep look of hatred in the plainsman's eyes. "Are you familiar with Rides Big Horses?"

"Nowhere near as familiar as I'm gonna get," Windy replied, straightening and turning toward his horse. "Let's get this outfit of yours patched up and move on out of here. We've got some Indians that need to be taught a little lesson. I'll send some men over this way with our medicine kit."

Steele watched Windy ride away, and then twisted his neck to look up at Bullard. "I think we just might have found the man who knows his way around this wasteland, Captain," he said as he struggled upright to stand on one foot. "Tend to yourself and our wounded, and I'll be up there as fast as I can hobble on one leg."

"May I help you, sir?"

"Not on your bloody life, mate. Get to it now, I think I smell victory in the air."

The first person Windy encountered when he rejoined the platoon was, predictably, Colonel Higgins. "What is the meaning of this, Mr. Mandalian?"

"Meaning of what?"

"Why didn't you deploy the Gatling on that rise and use it to our full advantage?"

"I used it to our full advantage. It's keepin' the tarp dry."

"If it had been used for the purpose for which it was designed, we would have had that entire renegade Indian tribe pinned down instead of letting them escape as they did!"

"If I had used it at all, Colonel, it would have been a waste of shells. They were beyond the damned thing's effective range. Besides that, if we had taken the time to set the son of a bitch up, them Canadians over yonder would have been so much pork, skinned and ready for saltin', by the time we got one round out of the miserable bastard."

Higgins's head snapped toward the rise. "Canadians? Did you say Canadians?"

"Thought that's what I said."

"What in hell's name are they doing here?"

"I think they're wonderin' that same thing themselves," Windy said, dismissing the colonel and turning abruptly to the assembled soldiers. "I need a volunteer."

Private Fitzpatrick stepped forward. "I volunteer, Windy."

"Good boy, Fitz. I want you to hightail it over to Matt and his platoon. Ride southwest, and you should cut their trail by nightfall. Tell him to angle northwest toward the marsh—he'll know where it is—and to be there no later than midday tomorrow. Whilst you're talkin' to him, tell him we're gonna have us a bunch of Cree boxed in. One of em's name is Rides Big Horses. Tell him we just done saved them Canucks' bacon and that they're gonna give us a hand, and that we'll be apporaching from three fronts, his, mine and theirs. You got that, Fitz?"

"I . . . I think so, Windy."

"Then get on your horse and ride. Don't let me down now, hear?"

"I won't," the young soldier replied, leaping into his saddle. "We'll be there when the shootin' starts."

"Good boy. Don't miss it, should be quite a show."

Higgins edged forward again. "Just what in hell's name is a foreign army doing on United States soil, I'd like to ask?"

"Gettin' their butts whupped, mostly, would be my guess. I'm goin' up and talk to 'em right now. Let you know when I get back," Windy replied, reining his horse around.

"Just a damned minute," Higgins shouted, waddling toward his horse. "I'm going with you. This is a breach of an international treaty!"

"Forget your treaty, Colonel. We've got one more war goin' on now than we need. If I see you up there, I'll cut off your balls and shove 'em up your ass."

With those words, Windy was gone. Higgins's foot lowered from the stirrup and he stood watching the scout canter up the slope.

Captain Bullard's arm was supported by a sling, and Major Steele stood with one leg braced stiffly in front of him and a bandage strapped tightly to his knee. Windy had squatted and smoothed out a mound of dirt to provide a platform for the map he intended to draw with the knife in his hand, and he spoke as he worked.

"You fellers been a mite lost the last few days, ain't ya?"

"That would have to be the understatement of the decade," Steele said somewhat contritely.

"Can't tell direction on the High Plains?" Windy asked, squinting upward against the afternoon sun.

"Sir," Steele began patiently, "there is no direction that could mean anything here. Everything is the same, so what is there to find?"

"Could have a point there, but if you'd knowed where you was goin', you just might have had a few more filled saddles when you leave."

Steele winced visibly while Windy moved over to take up a clump of grass. "Gonna give you a two-minute lesson in how to find your way back to Canada. See this head of seed here?" he asked, turning the bulging stem upward.

"Yes, of course we see it," Bullard replied. "But grass is grass, isn't it? Miles and miles of the damned stuff."

"Sure it is, but it's more 'n that. It's a weathervane, the same kind you see on top of some old homesteader's barn. 'Round these here parts, the prevailing wind is generally from the west. Not always, but generally. If she shifts to the south, you're in for some thunder and hail. If she shifts to the northeast, you're most likely gonna have a downpour like a cow pissin' on a flat rock.

"Now look here. The seed head of this grass, just like the flowers, grows facing the southeast and away from the prevailing wind. Always the same, and you can't never miss."

Windy moved over to a large anthill.

"Now, the little critters that built this are called bulldog ants. They bite like hell and will sure get your attention, but the main thing is to look at their entranceway. It, too, always faces the southeast to catch the morning sun and keep the wind from pluggin' up the hole." Windy straightened and dusted off his hands. "Same goes for the cottonwoods you see growin' in some of the draws around here. Once the top branches get above the tops of the rises, they flag away from the wind, and the leaves are thicker on the southeast side 'cause they ain't dried out from the breeze. Ain't nothin' to it. No matter where the sun is, even if you've got cloud cover, you can always tell where you are. And once you know where the southeast is, the rest of it's dumplin's and gravy."

Steele and Bullard were truly astounded, and they stared in disbelief at the seed head and the entrance to the anthill, both of which faced in the same direction.

"That's incredible!" Steele finally managed. "Here we've been muddling along, trying to tell direction by the sun, when all the time we've had a map right at our bloody feet!"

"That you have," Windy replied, popping a fresh chaw of tobacco in his mouth and working it in place. "'Sides that," Windy continued with a grin, "the sun ain't always reliable; only seems to be on the job half the time. Now, I've got to tell you boys somethin' serious, since you know your way around and all. I've got me a United States Army colonel down there that's got a feather up his ass a yard wide. He ain't particular fond of you fellers bein' on American soil, and if he had his way, our two countries would be at war with each other before noon tomorrow.

"Now here's the way I see it. If you throw your troops in with mine—what there is left of yours, anyway—and help me put those Cree bastards out of business, that just might take some starch out of his britches. Whatcha think?" Windy asked, spitting sideways and squinting up at the two officers.

Steele cleared his throat and leaned forward slightly. "We

came here for two things, Mr. Mandalian, and each of them has a name: a Cree called Rides Big Horses and a métis renegade named Johnny Singletree. We will cooperate in any way to see them dead or in our custody."

"Thought that might be your answer," Windy replied, moving over to his makeshift map table. "Now here's what we're gonna do."

twelve

Captain Conway watched his wife move her mashed potatoes about disconsolately with her fork, and the absent-minded activity seemed a perfect match for her mood throughout the entire meal.

"You're unusually quiet this evening, Flora," Conway said, glancing up from his roast beef. "Is something troubling you?"

"Nothing I can tell you about, Warner," Flora replied with little enthusiasm.

"Well, now, I thought we had a no-secrets agreement working all these years. If that's been declared null and void, I'd certainly like to know about it." Conway winked as he lifted his fork. "Otherwise I might find some secrets of my own to keep."

"Please, Warner," Flora said, looking up with a plea for understanding in her eyes. "It has nothing to do with you and me. It has to do with something we talked about earlier."

"Earlier?" Conway asked, ceasing his chewing and pursing his lips. "The fact that I need new shirts for my uniforms? No, that couldn't be it. The color of the outpost walls? No, you've always liked dull brown. Let me see now—"

"Warner, please. I know you're trying to cheer me up, but it's no good. What we talked about earlier, and what has me depressed now, has nothing to do with the color of the outpost walls! It's the Petersons."

"That's the secret?" Conway asked in surprise, a look of concern crossing his face. "I don't mean to sound callous, but if that's the secret you're keeping from me, I think you should know that nearly everyone on post is aware of their marital problems."

"I know they are, dear, and that's making it especially rough on Connie. And I think it's driving her to a decision she doesn't really want to make."

"Yes? And what would that be?"

Flora picked up her fork before laying it down again with frustrated emphasis. "As I said previously, dear, it's a promise, a secret promise I made that keeps me from telling you, and I can't violate that."

Conway watched his wife closely. "I'm not asking you to. But I'd like you to keep one thing in mind. The morale of the married men on this post is invariably commensurate with the degree of happiness they are deriving from their marriages. When a marriage goes south, so does the man who happens to be directly involved. What I'm concerned with here is maintaining a fighting force, a group of men who are dedicated to principles we were sent here to uphold. I know that women's problems are better left to people other than myself, but when they directly involve this command, I become directly involved myself."

"Well, I . . . I . . . can't tell you anyway, no matter what the consequences. I made a promise, and I'll keep that promise."

Conway tried to shrug it off. "Have it your way, I certainly didn't mean to pry. But when a man's wife wears her problems like a tattoo on her forehead, and yet won't discuss them, it's a little difficult for her husband to simply ignore her plight."

"I'm sorry, darling," Flora said with an attempted smile. "I know you have important things to think about, and I don't wish to trouble you with—"

A sharp rapping came at the door, and Conway glanced up at his wife before craning his neck in the direction of the sound. "Now who do you suppose that could be?"

"I have no idea. Let them in and we'll see."

After taking the linen napkin from his lap and touching the corners of his mouth, Conway excused himself, stood, and crossed to the door, which he opened and stood away from in the same motion.

"Yes?"

"Pardon for botherin' you, Captain," said a soldier standing in the shadows, "but I'd like to talk to you for a moment, sir, if you can find the time. Lieutenant Kincaid's orders."

"Corporal Peterson! I didn't recognize you in the darkness. Please come in. Has something gone wrong with the patrol?" Conway asked as he ushered the noncom into the room.

"No, sir," Peterson replied, dragging the hat from his head

as he stepped into the captain's quarters. Seeing Flora rise the the table, he said "Evenin', Mrs. Conway. Sorry to disturb your dinner."

Flora offered a genuine, congenial smile. "We were quite finished, Corporal. No disturbance at all. Won't you please have a seat?"

"No thank you, ma'am, haven't got time for that," Peterson said, crumpling the hat in his hands. "'Sides that, I've got some special people waitin' outside. Lieutenant Kincaid told me to come straight here, so here I am."

"Special people?" Conway asked, moving around to look at Peterson. "And who would those special people be?"

Peterson grinned affectionately, then tried to check himself. "Well, sir, they might not be special to you, but they sure are to me. They're the dirtiest, smellin'est little rascals you ever saw, but they're beautiful right down to their toes, in my eyes."

Conway cleared his throat and glanced once at his wife, then back at Peterson again. The soldier was obviously bone-weary and badly in need of a shave, his uniform was salt-caked from days in the field, and he wasn't particularly sweet-smelling, but instead of revulsion, those factors aroused an instinct of protectiveness in Conway.

"Corporal, you've obviously been on a difficult assignment, if I may request an answer, who are these special people to whom you are referring?"

"May I show you, sir?" Peterson asked, a light shining in his eyes.

"Certainly. Please do."

"Be back in just a minute, sir. 'Scuse me, Mrs. Conway."

With those words, Peterson darted for the door while the captain and his wife exchanged questioning glances. A moment later he returned, ushering two shy and frightened children before him. They both clung to the corporal's legs, one on either side, and stared up at the tall officer and his beautiful wife.

"Captain, Mrs. Conway, I'd like for you to meet Tommy and Sharon Griffin." Feeling their grip on his trouser legs, he glanced down at the children and then looked up again with a self-conscious grin. "As you can probably guess for yourselves, we got to be purty good partners on the ride back here. All right, kids," he continued, pushing the children gently to the front, "stand up here and meet some special fine folks.

This is Captain Conway—he's the man in charge of this outfit—and his wife, Mrs. Conway. Tommy, shake the captain's hand. Sharon, a little curtsy would be nice."

The Griffin children complied, and it seemed rather strange to see two such ragged little people adhering to propriety and acceptable manners.

Conway shook Tommy's hand while Flora returned Sharon's curtsy. The little girl grinned and Tommy said, "Pleased to meet you, sir. A friend of ours, Mr. Mandalian, works for you. Mr. Kincaid told us that."

"He certainly does, Tommy, and he's a friend of ours as well. It's a pleasure to meet you."

The look on Flora's face was an admixture of delight and sadness as she looked at the children while standing with her hands folded in front of her. Her husband had told her of the massacre at the Clearwater Reservation, and she knew instinctively that the two unwashed little faces before her belonged to a pair of orphans.

"You children must be starved," she said, kneeling and taking their hands in hers. "Do you like roast beef, potatoes with gravy, and beans? Then, after your tummies have settled a bit, maybe some pie?"

The children tried to restrain a show of enthusiasm, but the look in their eyes told differently. "Yes, ma'am," Tommy said, "we sure do. We ain't—"

"Haven't," Peterson corrected.

"—haven't had food like that in a long time."

"Then you will right now," Flora said, rising again and looking at Peterson. "Corporal, while I'm reheating their dinner, I wonder if you would mind asking Connie to come over and help get Tommy and Sharon washed up? They can have a nice hot bath later."

"Be a pleasure, ma'am. I'm sure she would love it." He looked at Conway and said, "Captain, I haven't got a lot of time, 'cause I've got to get my squad back to the platoon. Could you walk with me across the parade so we can talk?"

"Certainly, Corporal," Conway replied, taking his hat from the hat tree. "Let's go."

As they walked, Peterson reported everything he knew about the patrol up to the point of his departure, and he passed along the opinion expressed by Kincaid that the renegade Indians would soon be captured or killed. Conway listened intently, asking occasional questions, then he thanked Peterson and started to turn away.

"Sir? One thing."

"Yes, Corporal?" Conway asked, turning back to face Peterson again.

"About those kids, sir. They're orphans now, you know, and they ain't—ah, excuse me." Peterson grinned. "I've got to get out of that habit. And they *haven't* got anybody to take them in. Lieutenant Kincaid suggested that Connie and me take care of 'em until you could find a . . . better place for 'em to live. He told me to tell you that. I hope you can see your way clear to agree with him, sir. For our sake, as well as the kids'."

Conway smiled and offered his hand. "That sounds like an ideal arrangement to me, Corporal. If your wife has no objections, I certainly haven't."

Peterson pumped the captain's hand vigorously. "She won't, I can guarantee you that. She's got more clothes stashed away right now than they could wear out in a year."

Puzzled, Conway asked, "Clothes?"

"You bet, clothes, sir. I'll tell you about it some other time, if that's all right with you. Right now I'd like to get inside and tell Connie the good news. Can I come back to your quarters with her and watch those little tads have their first decent meal in God knows how long, sir?"

"Of course you can, Corporal." Conway hesitated and then added, "We'll have a drink together."

"Thanks, but no thanks, sir. I won't be needin' that anymore. I quit drinkin' as of right now."

Conway smiled in the darkness. "Good for you, Corporal. See you in a few minutes."

Kincaid saw the lone rider streaking toward them, and he halted the platoon to await the soldier's arrival. A twinge of concern passed through his mind, and he wondered briefly if Windy's unit had been ambushed. As the rider drew near, Matt recognized Private Fitzpatrick, and when the young soldier pulled his mount to a plunging, skidding stop, he allowed a couple of seconds for Fitzpatrick to catch his breath.

"Riding your mount a little hard, aren't you, Private?"

"Had to, sir. Got a message from Windy."

"Go ahead."

"Them Canucks got jumped by the Cree, and they're shot up pretty bad. If it hadn't been for the second platoon, they'd be history by now. Anyway, Windy told me to tell you to angle toward the marsh. He said you'd know where it was, sir."

"I do. We can be there by midday tomorrow."

"That's when Windy said he wanted you to be there. Now here's the plan the way Windy told it to me. He doesn't figure the Cree know it's there, being' new to these parts and all, and they're headin' in that direction right now. Since you can't ride a horse across it, he plans to trap them there, with the first platoon to the south, the second to the north, and the Canucks comin' straight up the gut."

Kincaid thought for a moment and then nodded. "Should work, if we can keep them going in that direction. The marsh is horseshoe-shaped on the eastern side, and if we can drive the Cree into the middle of that, they'll have only one escape route. It'll have to be done fast, though, because once they realize what's happening, they'll try to break out."

"That's Windy's thinkin', exactly. I suppose we'd better stop talkin' and get on over there, huh, sir?"

"Yes, we'd better. Fall in somewhere among the ranks, Private. I wish we had a fresh mount for you, but I'm afraid we don't."

"He'll make it, sir," Fitzpatrick replied, patting the horse's lathered neck. "He's got a ton of heart and lots of miles left in him."

"I hope so. Let's go."

"What time do you make it to be, Captain?" Steele asked, squinting at the sun.

"I'd say about ten o'clock, sir."

"That's about what I figure. Mandalian said we should expect a little action around noon, didn't he?"

"Yes he did. By that time he thinks the Cree will know they're riding into a trap and will try to break out, probably straight at us."

"Good. Excellent, in fact. I hope they do," Steele replied, rising on his stirrups to check the line of soldiers riding parallel to him on either side and spaced ten yards apart. "A rather unusual formation, wouldn't you say, Captain?"

"Yes it is, sir, but no more unusual than the man who

suggested it. That Mandalian seems to have a nose for what Indians might do next."

"He's unorthodox, to say the least, but then, conventional tactics don't seem to have worked too well for us so far. I'm afraid we've been slightly out of our element, and my bloody pig-headed attitude about following accepted military procedures has cost us a lot of good men."

"Don't be too hard on yourself, sir. No one else with our limited experience in this type of warfare would have known what to do any more than you did."

Steele's jaw tightened and he stared straight ahead. "Thank you, Captain. I don't usually accept any form of compromise regarding my performance, especially from junior officers, but since you are now in command, I suppose I can indulge in that luxury."

"I'm afraid that's not the case, Major," Bullard replied while watching Steele's face closely. "I am not the one in command. You are."

"What?"

"That's a fact, sir. Now that we've linked up with the Americans and we know what the hell we're doing, I think the most experienced and best officer available to us should be the one commanding. In my opinion, sir, you're that man."

"Nonsense, Captain. You took command away from me, and rightfully so. After all the troops I've cost us, I have no right to expect those yet surviving to respect my decisions."

"They're soldiers, sir, not townspeople voting on a new mayor. They are trained to take orders from the top, as am I, and it's not up to them to question your decisions one way or the other." Bullard smiled and added, "Besides that, Major, I know we are going to be successful, and I want that victory to be yours. And that's the way it will show on the record when we get back to Canada. If the situation were otherwise, your military career would be finished, and on top of that, you genuinely deserve this victory. If it hadn't been for your taking the chance that you did by coming here, Rides Big Horses and Singletree wouldn't be riding into the trap they're riding into right now."

Steele's eyes narrowed as he considered the captain's words. "Is that your final decision, Captain?"

"Yes it is, sir."

"Fine. Then would you be a good chap and ride down our left flank and space it out a bit more? It seems to me that the troops on the end are closing in and not maintaining the separation suggested by Mr. Mandalian."

"Yes, sir. Right away, sir," Bullard replied with a grin.

The sun had reached its zenith when they crested a rounded knoll and Steele could see a strung-out line of blue in the distance off to his left and a matching one, similar in configuration, off to his right. He judged the distance to be approximately an eighth of a mile, and from their angle of progress he could see that the pincers maneuver was slowly closing. Then they were moving down again, and he lost sight of the American troops, but he continued to watch his own point riders. Two ducks glided overhead, wings set in preparation for landing, and Steele felt a familiar tingle run up his spine.

Then, up ahead, the point riders suddenly raised their rifles above their heads in a horizontal position, then jerked them down sharply.

"Prepare for battle!" Steele yelled, turning his head and shouting the command down both flanks. Rifles came up quickly and chambers were checked for fresh rounds, while the three point riders came pounding back toward the main force.

"They're comin', sir!" the rider nearest to Steele shouted as he jerked his mount around and fell into line. "And they're comin' hard!"

"Let the red bastards come," Steele said firmly as he cocked his revolver. "I've been waiting for this a long time."

The first wave of Cree burst into view and were instantly met with a barrage of rifle fire that sent warriors spilling from their ponies. Numerous horses went down also. Stunned, the Cree hesitated momentarily on the crest, and another volley tore into their ranks before they peeled off to the left.

Kincaid had closed quickly to the right when he heard the shots, and the first platoon sealed off the escape route while pouring deadly fire into the milling Indians. The Cree wheeled their ponies and raced back toward the marsh, and as the enemy fled before them, Kincaid turned his mount toward the Canadians and rode along the line until he identified the man he thought was in charge, then turned his horse in beside the major's.

"Good afternoon, sir, I'm Lieutenant Matt Kincaid, Easy Company, United States Mounted Infantry."

Steele returned the salute with a hint of surprise on his face. "Good afternoon to you, Lieutenant. I'm Major William Steele, Third Mounted Brigade, Royal Canadian Militia. May I express my apologies for being on American soil without the proper invitation?"

"Certainly, sir," Kincaid said with an affable grin, "once the business at hand is completed. Be sure and have your men watch those warriors you hit with those first two volleys. Check and make sure they're dead. They have a cute way of coming back to life after you've gone past, and it might cost you some dead or wounded if you aren't careful."

"Thanks for the reminder, Lieutenant. Consider it done."

"Fine. I'd better get back to my platoon now. Nice to meet you, sir," Kincaid said, saluting once more and riding back down the line.

Steele was pleased, and he smiled to himself as he wondered if he would have been as cordial to the lieutenant, had the circumstances been reversed.

Off to the right, there was one man who was not the slightest bit cordial and had no intention of being so. Colonel Higgins had succumbed to something nearing a raging fit when he heard the firing, and he was certain that the outcome of the battle had already been decided.

"You've stolen it from me, Mandalian! You and that god-damned Kincaid! I've endured the most miserable period of my life without significant complaint, in the belief that I would be at the forefront of the battle, and now the whole thing's over and I haven't fired a single shot! We had an agreement that this was supposed to be my victory!"

Windy glanced off to the right, mentally calculating the distance between themselves and the tip of the marsh. He figured it was approximately one hundred yards. Then he stared straight ahead and studied the terrain.

"This shebang ain't over yet, Colonel. Not by a long shot. We're the next to be tested. If you know how to shoot that Scoff of yours, you'd better get the damned thing out."

The absolute conviction in Windy's voice stunned Higgins, and he impulsively pulled the revolver from its holster and gripped it with a testing flex of his fingers. As best he could remember, it was the first time he'd had the weapon in his hands with the intention of firing it.

"Pull the hammer back, Colonel, 'cause here they come," Windy said in a flat and deadly tone.

Higgins looked up from his examination of the Scoff to see Indians racing across the crest before them and angling toward the opening between the second platoon and the marsh. The veterans of Easy Company quickly brought their Springfields to bear and fired seconds after Windy's Sharps belched flame and blasted the lead rider from his pony's back. Again the Cree's attempted escape was thwarted by withering fire, and their charge faltered, with warriors and mounts spilling onto the grass.

Higgins aimed, closed his eyes, and pulled the trigger, but instead of the jolting blast he had anticipated, the hammer clicked down on an empty chamber. He cocked the hammer a second time and pulled the trigger, but again nothing happened. By the time he tried a third time, the firing had died about him, the Cree were gone, and the empty click of metal on metal was the loudest sound to be heard.

"Works better with shells in it, Colonel," Windy said matter-of-factly as he reloaded the Sharps. "'Lessen you wanta throw it at 'em."

Higgins's face reddened, and he slammed the Scoff back into its holster. The crotch of his pants was a darker blue than the remainder of his uniform, and the colonel touched the wetness with a gingerly squeeze as he felt the urine slide down his thighs.

Windy shoved the last shell into the magazine and cradled the Sharps in the crook of his arm once more. "Don't worry about it, Colonel. Least ways, ya didn't shit 'em."

The three units joined forces on the lee side of the last prairie swell before the plains sloped down to the marsh below, which was fringed with rushes and tall grass. The wetland was formed by a natural basin fed by an artesian spring, and was the catch-basin for spring and fall runoff fed to the marsh from the draws and ravines leading downward from the north and west.

With its water shimmering like a mirage in the desert, the marsh was at least four hundred yards in width, and shaped like a wide horseshoe. Spread directly across the center of the grassland breasting the marsh were the combined forces of Easy

Company and the Canadian militia. Below them, at a distance of possibly one hundred and fifty yards, the Cree were backed up to the open end of the horseshoe and confined to a narrow neck of land. Cottonwood trees flourished in the wet draws leading to the marsh, and fringed its edges as well, providing the beckoning sight of shaded coolness.

Kincaid, Windy Mandalian, Steele, Bullard, Delaney, and Higgins were gathered toward the center of their troops, and Kincaid glanced across at his scout.

"Windy? Let's step aside for a moment. I'd like to talk with you."

"Sure, Matt," Windy replied. "Them boys down there ain't goin' nowhere for awhile."

When they were out of earshot, Kincaid turned and looked at his scout. "I wanted to take you aside and tell you this, Windy, because I think it's news that you should hear by yourself."

"I'm listenin', Matt."

"Tommy and Sharon are all right. We found them yesterday, or I should say Corporal Peterson found them, and he's taken them back to the outpost."

Windy offered no response, but Kincaid thought he could see a slight tremor at the corners of the crusted, battle-hardened scout's mouth as he gazed into the distance. The chaw of tobacco lay motionless in his jaw, and if he blinked his eyes, it went undetected by Kincaid. A full minute passed before Windy turned to look again at the officer.

"Them little shavers mean a lot to me, Matt. Their pa asked me one time if I'd be their legal guardian if anything ever happened to him. I told him I would, and I guess I am. They're the kids of an old trappin' pardner of mine, and his brother was raisin' 'em like they was his own. Don't think they ever knew he was their uncle, not their father."

"There's no reason for them ever to know differently, Windy. Let them remember their past as it was, a life of love and happiness. The future will take care of itself."

"I know that, Matt, and I'm thankin' ya for the reminder. But our problems ain't over yet. At least one and maybe two of old Ira's kids are down there right now with them Cree. I kinda figger I'm their guardian too, now that the family's gone."

"And rightfully so. We'll get them out somehow." Kincaid

paused to study the scout's face. "Do you know who's holding them hostage?"

"Yup, I do. The slime off a snake's belly who goes by the name of Rides Big Horses. He's the one what killed both Scotty and Ira." Windy's jaw tightened, and his eyes were hard once more. "He's mine, Matt. All mine."

"And you have a right to him. If those girls are still alive, do you think they held them back when they tried to break out? I cautioned my men to watch for them, but none of us saw any girls."

"I reckon they did. There ain't no horse with two people on its back that can do the same as with one. If the Cree had broken through, the girls would have been at the center of the pack."

"I thought as much. Well, one thing's for certain, we've got them trapped and there's no way out. Unfortunately they've got hostages, or we could take them right now."

"Offer them a chance to surrender, Matt," Windy said in a distant tone, as though he had something else on his mind.

"Surrender? They'd never do that."

"They will, under the conditions you're going to offer them."

Kincaid eyed Windy closely. "Conditions? What kind of conditions?"

"First they set the girls free. Then I fight Rides Big Horses to the death. If he wins, the rest of 'em get off scot free. If he loses, the rest of 'em surrender peacefully and take whatever punishment they've got coming."

"You sure you want to do that, Windy?"

"Never been more sure. You arrange it, I'll do it."

"All right. But, goddammit, be careful, you old son of a bitch. I can't afford to lose you."

Now Windy worked the tobacco and spat. "I can't afford a loss like that myself, Matt. Let's get to it."

They saw the Gatling gun being wheeled into position as they walked back up the hill, and heard the slide open and close in preparation to fire. The other officers were still standing in a group, but Higgins was off to one side, supervising the positioning of the Gatling.

"What the hell's going on here?" Kincaid asked as Higgins walked over to join them.

There was a strange glint in the colonel's eyes as he stared down at the Indians. "This is the perfect place to use the Gatling, Lieutenant. This is the exact situation it was designed for."

"There is one white girl being held hostage, and possibly two. Not one shell will go down that barrel until I am certain of their safety, and if events transpire as I think they will, there will be no need for your Gatling gun."

"What do you mean by that?" Higgins demanded.

"Because we're going to offer them a chance to surrender, Colonel. If they do, this situation is over."

"Over?" Higgins asked with glazed eyes. "Over? Just like that? Over?"

"Yes, over. I would like to see this thing settled as peaceably as possible."

It appeared that Kincaid's words hadn't registered in Higgins's brain, and he walked away as if in a daze. Matt watched the colonel momentarily, then turned to Steele to explain the conditions Windy had laid down for surrender. The other officers listened intently while Kincaid spoke, but Windy stood off to one side with his bowie knife in hand, testing the sharpness of its steel blade with a callused thumb. Delaney happened to glance up once while Matt was talking, and drew in a sharp breath.

"Matt! Watch out!"

All heads jerked toward the Gatling just as Higgins slammed the butt of his revolver down across the head of the private who was standing guard over the weapon. Frenzied now, the colonel leaped onto the platform, gripped the trigger handle with one hand, and began turning the crank with the other. The Gatling's clustered barrels revolved, spitting flame and smoke in a deafening, continuous roar. Bullets snapped in the air, and leaves torn loose by slugs slamming into cottonwoods could be seen drifting down below.

"There will be no surrender!" Higgins screamed. *"There will be no surrender!"*

The Cree instantly returned fire, and the troops, strung out belly-down along the rise, lifted their rifles and lined up sights. "Hold your fire!" Kincaid yelled, running toward the Gatling carriage. "Hold your fire!"

Matt was but five steps from the colonel when a Cree round ripped into Higgins's throat and he was lifted in a twisting, spinning arch to flop on his back and slide partway down the lee side of the hill. His arms trailed limply by his sides, and his head was twisted beneath one shoulder. Just one glance at the gaping hole in the colonel's neck told Kincaid that Higgins was dead, and he let out a weary sigh while bending forward at the waist and placing his hands on his knees.

"You came to fight and you lost, Colonel," he said softly. "Now the only victory you stand to achieve is one your soul is going to have to win for you."

thirteen

"Be watchin' 'em real close, Matt," Windy said while staring straight ahead. "After what Higgins done, I 'spect they just might be a little jumpy."

Kincaid nodded and raised the rifle higher to make sure the Cree saw the white flag of truce tied to its barrel, a banner that in more mundane times served as Private Boswell's undershirt. Windy was stationed off to his left as they rode downslope, and to his right were Major Delaney and Major Steele, while above them every rifle in combined command was trained on the Cree, who were now cautiously watching the approaching contingent.

"You Americans certainly have a strange way of doing business with Indians," Steele said through gritted teeth. "In Canada they wouldn't be given this choice."

"We're not in Canada," Delaney responded, also staring straight ahead. "But they *are* your Indians. What would you do with the guilty ones?"

"Hang the bastards."

"Then perhaps justice has no boundaries."

Two lead riders, followed by a ten-warrior escort, had swung up on their ponies and were coming forward to meet Kincaid and those flanking him. With five yards of separation left, both sides stopped, and there was silence for several moments. Then Kincaid spoke, emphasizing each name and title in the knowledge that Indians were generally impressed by authority.

"My name is Lieutenant Matt Kincaid, commanding officer of this military district. To my right is Major Bradford Delaney, special envoy from the War Department in Washington, and to his left is Major William Steele, sent here as the representative of the Canadian government." Kincaid paused for effect, then added, "To my right is Windy Mandalian, perhaps known to some of you as The Snake. His reputation speaks for itself."

The rider on the right smiled and nodded his head, while the large Indian to his left remained impassive. "I am Johnny Singletree. Major Steele and I have seen each other before, but it has always been done while looking down the sights of a rifle barrel. This is Rides Big Horses, chief of the Cree Nation. You have come to us under a flag of truce, so say what you have to say."

Kincaid lowered the rifle and laid it across his lap. "We are here to offer you terms of surrender. We have you boxed in and there is no possible means of escape. Either you accept our terms of surrender, or you will die here, far from the hunting grounds of your ancestors."

"We have two of your white women," Rides Big Horses said with a sneer curling his lip. "If we die, they die as well."

Kincaid could sense Windy's slight shift in his saddle at the mention of the two white women, and he spoke quickly to ease the building tension.

"We know that, Rides Big Horses. If necessary, they will be sacrificed, but if so, not one Cree will leave here alive. Is that understood?"

The firmness of Matt's tone seemed to jolt the Cree chief, and he lapsed into silence again while Singletree said, "What are your terms of surrender?"

"The two white women are to be turned over to us immediately. If they are unharmed, the Cree chief will be given the opportunity to fight to the death for the freedom of his people. If he wins, you will all be set free. If he loses, you will be subject to Canadian laws that govern the prosecution of murderers." Again, Kincaid hesitated. "That penalty, according to Major Steele here, is death by hanging."

The métis and the Cree both remained silent until Rides Big Horses finally spoke. "And who of your number would be foolish enough to fight me?"

"Me," Windy replied bluntly. "We each choose one weapon. You get first choice."

Rides Big Horses studied the weathered scout, obviously some years his elder, and his chest swelled perceptibly. "You?"

"Yes, me. If you accept the terms, name your weapon."

The Cree chief laughed in disgust. "An old man has come to do a young man's work. I accept. I choose lances on horseback."

Windy nodded, showing no emotion. "And I choose knives, if neither of us is killed by the lance."

"Let me say this one more time," Kincaid interjected. "Your people will surrender peaceably if Mr. Mandalian wins. My people will let them go if he loses."

"That is understood," Singletree replied.

"And the white women are to be set free, regardless of the outcome."

"They will be brought to you right now," the métis said, turning and waving an arm to summon the girls forward.

The girls were escorted forward between two mounted braves. While Lisa walked straight and tall, Lorie was hunched over and seemed to cower. Her sobs could be heard even from that distance, and her body shook uncontrollably. The fact that Lisa's arm was around her shoulders was of little apparent comfort to Lorie. The two braves, Running Deer and Sitting Crow, stopped off to the side of the group in the center of the meadow, and Singletree looked again at Kincaid.

"They will stay there until the fight is over. I have learned from the way my people are treated in Canada that no white man can be trusted. They are as much yours as they are mine. Let the warriors prepare for battle." With those words, the métis stripped the bloody flag from the lance he held in his right hand, and tossed the weapon to Windy. "Use this in your fight with the Cree. It has brought only misery and heartache to my people."

Windy caught the lance in midair and turned its tip forward. "I have no fight with your people, métis. My fight is with the coward who calls himself a Cree chief, when the only true chief his people have is a good man named Swift Otter."

Rides Big Horses grimaced. "I am the chief of the Cree. Swift Otter is an old woman who would give our land to the sons of the Grandmother in England."

Windy had not looked at the two girls until that time, but now he glanced in their direction while asking Singletree, "Can I talk to 'em? I want to make sure they're all right."

"Yes, you can talk to them."

Windy swung down from his saddle, stabbed the lance into the ground, and walked to where they stood watching him, as two drowning people might watch a log floating in their direction. When he was still ten steps away, the twins could contain themselves no longer, and they rushed forward to hug the grizzled scout. It was the first time during the entire ordeal that Lisa had allowed tears to come to her eyes.

"Thank God you're here, Mr. Mandalian," Lisa said, pulling away to look up at the tall scout. "Thank God. I've prayed for the sight of you for so long."

Lorie tried to speak, but no words would come forth and she continued to cry with her head pressed tightly to Windy's chest. Windy pulled Lisa to him again.

"Well, the old boy must've heard ya, honey, 'cause here I am. Sorry it took so long. Are you girls all right? What I mean is, when I finally get you out of here, are you gonna be able to make it?"

"We'll make it, Windy," Lisa replied with conviction. "Now that you're here, I know we'll make it. Just get us away from them as quickly as you can."

"I'm aimin' to do that right now. It ain't gonna be purty, so I want you girls to look away. You've seen enough bad things to last you a lifetime."

Windy hugged the girls tightly one final time and then turned away, but Lorie would not let go of his waist, and he had to pry her arms loose.

"Come on, Lorie," Lisa said, taking her sister's hand. "We're safe, now that Mr. Mandalian is here. Let him go and do whatever he has to do."

Lorie followed her sister with stiff-legged reluctance, while continuing to stare pleadingly over her shoulder at Windy. The scout crossed again to his horse, swung onto his saddle, and took up the lance once more.

"I'm ready when you are, Cree. Lance and knife. Nothing more."

Rides Big Horses sneered, turned his pony away, and rode toward the warriors waiting in the distance, with Singletree and his escort following behind. Windy, Kincaid, Steele, and Delaney went to the opposite end of the meadow, where Windy took off his gunbelt and handed it to Kincaid along with the Sharps.

"You ready for this, Windy?" Kincaid asked, watching the scout loosen the bowie knife in its scabbard.

"Been ready for six years, Matt. Killed lots of folks in my time, but damned few who deserved it as much as that Cree son of a bitch over yonder."

"I agree. Good luck, partner."

"Sorry, old son, but luck ain't gonna have nothin' to do with it."

Windy turned the roan, while hooking the butt of the lance just beneath his right elbow. The Cree was waiting across from him with his weapon held in a similar manner, and the two opponents were no more than fifty yards apart. Windy nodded, the Cree returned the nod, then both horses bolted forward at a gallop.

On the first pass, Windy deflected the chief's thrusting jab with the lance, knocking it upward while slamming the butt of his own weapon into the Indian's stomach. He heard a surprised grunt escape the Cree's lips as he reined his horse around in a tight circle.

On the second pass, the Cree's lance tore into the side of Windy's shirt and ripped the skin open along his ribcage. The buckskin quickly turned red, and the Cree smiled in cruel triumph as he wheeled his pony and confirmed that he had injured his opponent.

Windy seemed not to notice the wound as he leveled the lance again and urged his horse forward. When the two horses were but ten feet apart, he shifted the tip of the lance and aimed it directly at the lower portion of the Indian horse's throat, and the steel blade sank deep into the animal's chest just above the shoulders. The horse's front legs buckled immediately, and the surprised Cree raised his lance in an attempt to maintain balance on the tumbling animal. Windy snatched the weapon from Rides Big Horses' hand as he raced by, then turned to watch the Indian's mount flop over in the grass, the self-styled chief leaping away to roll twice before landing on his feet. Windy tossed the lance aside as he stepped down from the roan, pulled the huge bowie knife from its scabbard, and advanced toward the Cree, who stood facing him with weapon in hand. The horse lay off to one side, legs twitching, with the lance shaft protruding from its chest and the blade slammed neatly into its heart.

"Now we're down to a man's game," Windy said, closing warily on the Indian, his legs spread apart, bending slightly at the waist while shifting the knife from hand to hand.

The Cree sank into a crouch and began circling, but the haughty look in his eyes had changed to one of grudging respect. *"Aiiieeeee!"* he screamed, lunging forward with a thrust of his knife.

Windy brought the heavy bowie knife down swiftly in a chopping motion as he stepped to one side, and the razor-sharp blade completely severed the thumb from the Indian's right hand. Blood spurted forth in a great red gush, and Rides Big Horses stared at the stump of his thumb in stunned surprise, then switched the knife to his other hand and made a second, desperate lunge. Again the bowie came down, this time opening a deep gash on the Cree's forearm. A panicked look came over the Indian, and in that moment's hesitation, Windy whipped his knife forward and down to cut the Cree's left ear from the side of his head.

The Indian held his mutilated right hand to the spurting patch of red where his ear had been, and backed away, staring down in shock at the severed ear, lying in the grass like a large grub. His head jerked up when Windy spoke to him in Cree.

"Hear me, you slime from the bowels of a mad dog! You are a murderer, a liar, a coward, and a thief, and before I send you to the Distant Place, I will make of you such a sight that your ancestors will turn from you in disgust and horror. The Snake has spoken, and may his name ring in your ears as Wendigo comes to eat your soul."

The Indian made a feeble, backwards swipe with his knife, which Windy easily sidestepped before smashing the butt of his bowie against the Cree's nose, breaking the cartilage and laying the nose against the side of Rides Big Horses' cheek. Blood now ran freely down the chief's neck, from his nose into his mouth, and was dripping from both hands. Still, Windy made no effort to kill the grotesque figure trying to circle him once more.

The Cree lunged forward again, hacking and chopping with the knife, which nicked Windy's shoulder as he danced to one side, hit the Indian with his opposite shoulder, and then sliced half of the other ear away as the Cree spun and stumbled backward. Rides Big Horses was gasping for air through his blood-filled mouth, and he tried to raise his knife hand, but was unable to do so.

"Finish it, Windy," Kincaid said. "He's had enough. Kill him, for God's sake, and get it over with."

At the sound of Kincaid's voice, Windy hesitated as if awakening from a dream, then stepped forward and plunged the bowie into the Cree's throat. Jerking the blade free as the Indian dropped to the grass, the scout turned and walked away while the Cree warriors stared in silence at their fallen chief.

"Goddamn, but he's one tough bloke," Steele said just above a whisper. "Never seen anything like that in my life."

"Nor have I," Delaney added. "I knew he wasn't a man to be fooled with, but I never expected anything like that."

Kincaid watched Windy walk away, and knowing he would want to be alone for a few minutes, he looked at the two officers, who continued to gaze in wonderment at the dead and disfigured Cree.

"Windy's probably one of the kindest, most gentle men you could ever hope to meet, but he's also one of the most deadly, cold-blooded people you'll ever know when somebody mistreats one of his friends."

"You point out his friends to me before I leave here, Lieutenant," Steele said with a grim smile, "and I'll damned well make sure they sleep on a feather bed tonight."

Kincaid chuckled. "Not a bad idea, Major. Now let's get on with this and be done with it. They're your Indians on our soil, but I assume you would have legal jurisdiction over them. How would you punish those guilty of murder and most likely rape?"

"Line them up and have one of the girls point out which ones molested them, which ones took part in the killing you told me about at the agency, and which ones, if any, treated them decently. The guilty ones hang, the innocent go free." Steele's eyes went to the warriors waiting in the distance. "I came here for two men. One of them is dead, and the other is over there. Other than that, my business is concluded, and the others are free to go back to Canada, as I intend to do."

"Fine. Sergeant Olsen?" Kincaid called to the sergeant waiting up on the hill. "Come down here, please."

When Olsen arrived, Kincaid said, "Select a detail and line those Cree up over there. Take their weapons and stack them up in a pile. The innocent ones get their guns and horses back; the guilty ones are to be hung immediately."

"Yessir."

Fifteen minutes later, forty-eight Cree were lined up, and the four officers, along with Windy and Lisa, walked the row. Of the twenty Cree who had taken part in the raid, and of the thirteen who had taken part in the rape, only six remained alive. Lisa pointed them out, one by one, until they got to Running Deer and Sitting Crow.

"These two were especially kind to us, Lieutenant," Lisa said. "They took care of the children, and if it hadn't been for them, Tommy and Sharon would surely have been killed. They don't deserve any punishment."

"And they will receive none, Lisa," Kincaid replied, placing a hand lightly on the girl's shoulder. "They will be taken care of." Now Kincaid looked at Running Deer. "When we found the little boy, he said one of you had given him a knife to protect himself and his sister. Are you the man he was referring to?"

"Yes I am."

"Then I thank you for your kindness. As I understand it, your people are having a difficult time up in Canada. There's an Arapaho reservation about four days' ride due west of here. Your language is similar to theirs, and I think you would be welcome there. If you wish to remain in the United States, I'll make the necessary arrangements."

"Thank you, Lieutenant," Running Deer replied, "but we will return to our homeland with our people."

"Fine. It's your choice, and I wish you good luck."

They moved along the line again, and the last man to be confronted was Johnny Singletree. "What about him?"

"My sister was given to him. If he did to her what the Indian did to me, then he should hang along with the others. But to tell you the truth, Lieutenant, I never saw him do anything wrong, and he wasn't there when my parents were killed."

"Lorie?" Kincaid asked, turning to the girl who was watching silently from some distance away. "Come over here, please."

With obvious reluctance, Lorie moved forward to stand beside Kincaid. "Yes . . . Lieutenant?"

"This man's name is Johnny Singletree. Did he hurt you or harm you in any way while you were a captive?"

Lorie looked at the métis and there was something of a shy smile about her face. Singletree smiled at her in a pleasant, handsome way.

"No, Lieutenant, he never touched me. He tried to help me all he could, and he said I should make it look like I was his, so that awful Indian would leave me alone." She bit her lip and looked tenderly at her sister. "I'm not strong like Lisa, Lieutenant. She was abused the whole time, yet she is the one who kept me going. If I had been given to the Indian instead of to this man, I would have gone crazy. No, he didn't hurt me, and I thank him for that."

Singletree regarded Lorie with something approaching affection. "You talk much in your sleep, little one. I wish you more pleasant dreams in the nights to come."

Kincaid turned to Steele. "Major? This is one of the men you came here to get. Do with him as you will."

"Lieutenant," Steele replied in a distant voice, "I came here thinking I was cock of the walk. Sad to say, at the expense of many men I found out differently. The métis and I will be enemies again, I'm sure, but right now I'd just as soon let him go free with the innocent ones." The Englishman touched the corner of his cap with the riding crop. "Could be we're wrong in the way your people are being treated, but I have nothing to say about that. If we do have to fight again, let's bloody well do it in Canada, old sport, where I know my way around."

Singletree nodded. "The grievances between our two peoples are many, and one day we will probably meet again on the field of battle. But when we do, and if we do, I'll not forget what you've done here today."

"That's good of you," Steele replied with a slight smile, while unconsciously tapping his crop against his thigh. Then he glanced at Kincaid again. "It looks like we have six for the rope, Lieutenant. Shall we carry on?"

"I would like to thank all three of you for your patience in this whole tiresome affair," Major Delaney said as he swung onto his saddle and looked down at Kincaid, Conway, and Windy Mandalian. "While I regret the fate suffered by Colonel Higgins, there is no one to blame but the Colonel himself. 'Killed in action' will be the sum of my report, and I suppose some of his friends back East will see to it that he gets a posthumous medal or award of one kind or another. If so, that will provide the final twist of irony as regards the life of Colonel Higgins. Best of luck to you."

Conway and Kincaid saluted while Windy allowed a nod of his head as the major's horse cantered away, with two escort squads from the third platoon following close behind.

"Not a bad sort, Captain," Kincaid said as the major disappeared from view, "all things considered."

"No he isn't, Matt. He's a fine officer, as a matter of fact."

Then Conway turned to the scout. "Got your speech all set, Windy?"

A pained expression crossed Windy's face. "Ain't much on makin' speeches, Cap'n, but whatever I've got to say, I guess I'll have to say it, so let's get it the hell over with."

"Fine with me," Conway said, leading the way into his office. "I'm sure there are some mighty anxious folks waiting in here for your decision."

There was a strained silence about the captain's office as the three men filed into the room and Conway took a seat behind his desk. The four Griffin children, freshly scrubbed and wearing new clothing that was the product of Connie Peterson's needlework, stood along the wall, with the corporal and Connie stationed at one end of the line. Flora Conway was seated on one of the chairs, and Windy took up his usual position near the window while Kincaid stood near the door.

"First of all, Corporal," Conway began, taking up a pencil and turning it in his fingertips, "I'd like to commend you on returning to your unit as you did. Even though you arrived too late to have any effect on the outcome, it was a very conscientious act on your part."

"Thank you, sir," Peterson replied rather nervously. "I felt I was only doing my duty, sir."

Conway nodded. "Yes, I'm sure you did. As I understand it, you intend to quit the service after this hitch is up. What are your intentions if I might inquire?"

"That's correct, sir," Peterson replied with a glance at Windy. "A lot of what I intend to do depends on Windy. I worked in my father's print shop before I joined the army, and now he wants to retire. He's offered me the entire business, if I'll come back and take over. That's what I intend to do, sir . . . if I have a family to support."

"I see. Where is this print shop located?"

"New Haven, Connecticut, sir. The most beautiful place on earth, to my way of thinking. Fine place to raise children, what with the good schools, churches, and mannerly people around there."

"I'm sure it is." Conway watched the Griffin children closely. "Would you kids like to live in a New England town, see the snow in the winter, watch the leaves turn color in the spring and fall, and maybe go fishing when school's out?"

The two little ones nodded eagerly, while the twins, strikingly attractive in new dresses, smiled demurely.

"Fine. I guess the final decision is up to one man. Windy was given guardianship over you children by your parents, and any decision he chooses to make will be legal and binding. You know better than I how much he thinks of you, and I'm sure any decision he makes will be in your best interest." Now Conway looked at the scout. "Windy?"

Windy shifted uneasily against the wall, and then stood to his full height. "Only a few things I want for you kids, and they're the same things you had before—a good home, hot meals, clean clothes, and a mom and dad to love ya. I can't give you those things, but the Petersons there can." Windy looked down at little Tommy with mock sternness. "And if that little rascal there on the end needs a whuppin' from time to time, I'm sure the corporal can handle that as well."

A low round of chuckles filled the room, and Tommy's face reddened as he glanced down. Peterson reached out and placed a protecting hand on the boy's shoulder.

"Far as I'm concerned, the six of you are a family from this here minute on." Windy paused before adding, "With one condition."

"What's the condition, Windy?" Peterson asked, puzzled.

Windy watched them in silence for a few moments before grinning as he said, "The one condition is that I get invited back for some clam chowder on a cold winter evenin'."

"You're on, Windy," Peterson said, striding forward to pump the scout's hand. "You'll be welcome anytime, you and the lieutenant and Captain and Mrs. Conway, everybody."

"What's clam chowder?" Sharon whispered to Tommy.

The little redheaded boy leaned down and replied, "You're gonna like it, sis. It's soup made out of grasshoppers."

SPECIAL PREVIEW

Here are the opening scenes
from

EASY COMPANY ON THE OKLAHOMA TRAIL

the next novel in Jove's exciting
High Plains adventure series

EASY COMPANY

coming in February!

one

The door to the orderly room flapped open and Sergeant Ben Cohen turned to greet his commanding officer. Captain Warner Conway looked a little ruffled this morning—not that he didn't have the right. There was usually enough going on at Outpost Number Nine, this isolated, undermanned, undersupplied wart on the Wyoming plains, to ruffle better men. If better men there were—an unlikelihood in Sergeant Ben Cohen's estimation.

"Good morning, sir," Cohen said briskly.

"Good morning, Sergeant Cohen."

Captain Conway took the mail from Cohen's desk and walked crisply to his office. Cohen poured the CO's coffee without being asked. He knocked and then entered, placing the cup at the precisely correct spot near Conway's right hand.

The letter from Regiment was in Conway's hands, and he frowned, reread a key paragraph, and shrugged. Cohen, of course, had already read the letter when he opened the mail, but he stood nearby with an expression of polite diffidence.

"Well," Conway said, drumming on his desk. "I guess I'll have to cut Matt Kincaid loose for this project." The captain muttered, "Damn," and placed the letter temporarily aside.

That was all the discussion there would be between Cohen and Conway. The CO knew full well that Cohen had scanned the letter, and now that Conway had voiced his intentions, Cohen would notify Lieutenant Matt Kincaid that his presence was required in the captain's office. They knew each other well, these two strong military men, so alike and yet so different.

Cohen was built like a bear, his temper was hot, and although he was the perfect soldier around Warner Conway, he could be hell on wheels with errant enlisted men.

Conway almost never lost his temper. He was a composed,

thoughtful man with handsome, weathered features. Tough as nails he was, underneath, but that facet of his personality seldom showed through.

"There's something you'll want to look at, Ben. Regiment's got nothing better to do than inspect Number Nine again. You've got three days to get ready."

Sergeant Cohen took the second letter and held it. Neither of them remarked further on the inspection. Conway knew full well that Cohen's men were ill-equipped—that they had patched blankets, worn-out boots that wouldn't even hold a shine, that their uniforms were faded and torn—but he made no comment. It was Cohen's responsibilty to see that the inspection was passed, and if he knew Ben, somehow Number Nine would pass with flying colors.

"I'll be damned!" Conway said, slapping his desk with delight."

"Finally some good news, sir?" Cohen asked as Conway read the letter in his hands slowly, smiling.

"John Fairchild's written to me."

"Major Fairchild, sir?"

"The very same. There's a soldier for you, old John. He pulled my bacon out of the fire at Cross Keys. Came riding through a Confederate artillery barrage to pull us out. Old John . . ." The colonel's face was glowing with reverie. "His son's been assigned to Number Nine, Ben." Conway shuffled through the rest of the mail. "Yes, here are his orders. John Fairchild, Jr. There's good news for us, Ben. A sharp young second lieutenant just when we need someone."

"Yes, sir. We won't miss Lieutenant Kincaid so badly, then."

"We'll miss him, Sergeant. Always miss Matt when he's not around. I wouldn't tell him that," Conway said with a smile. He was fond of First Lieutenant Matt Kincaid. Matt was a professional and a hell of a man. "Better send someone on over to his quarters now."

"I was on my way, sir," Cohen answered.

Captain Conway had tilted back in his leather chair, holding his coffee cup absently. "John Fairchild's boy. I'll be damned. . . ."

Matt Kincaid was with Lieutenant Taylor at the paddock when Cohen found him. "The captain wants to see you, sir," Ben said.

"Oh? Good news or bad?"

"How much good news do we get?" Taylor asked wryly. He stroked the nose of his bay gelding. The bay was coming along nicely after taking a Cheyenne arrow, which had gone completely through its neck.

"I couldn't call it bad news, sir," Cohen answered after considering the question, "but you'll be moving."

Matt lifted an eyebrow and tugged down his hat. Nodding goodbye to Taylor, Kincaid strode with Cohen back across the parade to Captain Conway's office.

"He's waiting for you, sir," Cohen said, and Matt tapped on the doorframe and entered.

"Matt, good morning. Coffee?"

"I'd appreciate it, sir." Matt seated himself at the captain's gesture and waited as the captain found the communiqué from regiment. Matt scanned it briefly. "Oklahoma?" he asked with surprise.

"That's it, Matt." Conway rose and stood near the large wall map, which he glanced at briefly. "As you know, the Dakota Confederacy tribes are starting to straggle back from Canada. In their minds, it seems, all the fuss over Custer and the Little Big Horn is over."

"Only in their minds," Matt put in. It was far from over to the War Department in Washington. That battle had frightened people badly, and overnight had changed the entire Indian policy. They were no longer so sure just who had the upper hand on the Western Plains.

"Most of the captured Indians are being quartered at Pine Ridge and other similar large reservations," Conway went on, "and there's quite a number of Cheyennes. Too many. Washington has the word that some of these bands, finding themselves on reservations, are talking about picking up the hatchet again.

"There's a medicine man called . . ." Conway glanced at the letter. "Wovoka. He's actually a Paiute, they say. Wovoka is talking up the Ghost Dance again, and actually has held one ceremony. The longer these Cheyenne are penned up, Matt, the more influence a Dream Singer like Wovoka is bound to have." Conway perched on a corner of his desk.

"So we simply transport them?" Matt asked.

Conway's eyes flickered. "Militarily it's imperative, Matt. The potentially hostile force is growing in size. Many of these people counted coup against Custer at the Greasy Grass. Yes, we're separating them. There's a band of about forty warriors, plus women and kids, dogs and horses under Dancing Horse. You've heard of him?" Matt shook his head. "Well, you'll find out. He's a tough old fox, Matt. Don't underestimate his intelligence."

"I never underestimate any hostile, sir."

"I know you don't, Matt, but be careful. Regiment wants you to escort these Indians to the agency at Darlington, in the Indian Nation."

"That's between the Canadian and the Washita, isn't it, sir?"

"That's right. Just north of the Washita River. Now it's true that the South Cheyenne, like Dancing Horse's people, used to range that far south on their hunts. They tangled with the Seventh under Custer once, along the Washita. Still and all, they are going to make a hell of a fuss about having to leave their homeland and the green north."

"It's understandable."

"It is. But you be careful, Matt. Pick your own personnel. Regiment has indicated that they are sending three Indian scouts to meet you at Pine Ridge, so take that into account. A platoon-sized force, I think, don't you?"

"Yes, sir," Matt sighed, and got to his feet.

"This may amount to nothing more than a summer excursion, Matt," Conway said, rising to walk toward his lieutenant, "but it could turn out to be a hell of a mess. Just watch yourself. Please."

"I intend to, sir. Thank you."

Ben Cohen was in the enlisted barracks when Lieutenant Kincaid arrived. The first sergeant was going through trunks, examining saddles, blankets, and weapons, groaning and cursing as he went.

"Something the matter, Sergeant Cohen?" Matt asked mildly.

"You're goddamned right. . . ." Cohen was facing away from Kincaid as he began to speak, and as he came around, his voice broke into rigid courtesy. "Nothing, sir. There's an inspection around the corner, that's all."

"Be nice if they would issue something worth inspecting, wouldn't it?"

Cohen gave the lieutenant a look of gratitude. "You don't know the half of it, sir."

"Anybody want to beat this inspection?" Kincaid asked,

glancing around. "I'm herding some Cheyenne down to the Nation. Volunteers accepted."

Private Malone had been hanging back in the corner, as if to fade into the wall. "How's that work, Sarge?" he asked Cohen. "Locked trunks for men not able to stand inspection?"

"That's right," Cohen said.

"Let me be the first to volunteer," Malone said. He grinned, and Kincaid, despite himself, grinned back. Malone was branded as a troublemaker, and had spent more time sewing on corporal's stripes and ripping them off again than anyone could total. He couldn't hold his liquor worth a damn, and when he drank he fought, but there was no liquor along that Oklahoma Trail, and Malone was a topnotch, veteran soldier.

Platoon Sergeant Gus Olsen had just entered the barracks, and he glanced at Cohen, who was still throwing things aside in disgust. Then the sergeant looked to Kincaid.

"I'd like to ride, sir."

"I'd like to have you, Gus, but you're needed here. There's a green officer coming in. Son of a friend of the captain's. He'll need some breaking in."

Wolfgang Holzer was standing rigidly at attention beside his bunk as Cohen tore through the barracks, tossing much he found into a pile that he intended to have burned.

Reaching Holzer's area, Cohen stopped in amazement. The man's bunk was tightly made, his uniform meticulously pressed, his clothes and blankets cleaned and patched, his boots as glossy as obsidian.

"Why can't you all take care of your equipment like Holzer?" Cohen asked in exasperation. "If I had a platoon of Holzers—"

"You'd have the prettiest, most screwed-up platoon in the U.S. Army," Malone said in a slow drawl.

"Button it, Malone," Cohen growled, more because he didn't care for his men popping off in front of officers than for any other reason. After a moment's consideration, Cohen had to admit reluctantly that Malone was right. Wolfgang Holzer was a born soldier—born for the German army—but an overzealous recruiting sergeant had signed Holzer as he stepped to the docks in New York, not bothering to find out, nor caring, probably, whether Holzer could speak English. The man was efficient, respectful, and neat as a pin. But Holzer's uses were limited.

"I'd like to take Corporal Wojensky, if it wouldn't cripple

you or Olsen," Matt said to the first sergeant.

Cohen shrugged. "Fine by me. Sergeant Olsen?"

"We'll make do," Olsen said affably.

"I know I'm leaving you short, Sergeant," Matt apologized, "but I need some experienced men, and Wojensky can speak the lingo."

"Some." Gus Olsen grinned. "At least 'eat,' 'drink,' and 'want to go to bed with soldier?'"

Cohen stepped outside with Kincaid, after first ordering Malone and Stretch Dobbs to burn the torn blankets and bits of uniform he had stacked to one side.

"So now you'll have two shavetails to mother, won't you, Sergeant?" Matt asked. He stood on the porch, looking out across the parade. Maggie Cohen was just leaving the sutler's store with a parcel. "There's some money spent," Matt said, nodding.

"Knowing that woman," Cohen said with pride, "it's something for the pot or something for me. She's not the sort to throw money around, my Irish girl."

Returning to the former topic, Cohen said, "I don't mind the green ones, Lieutenant. I guess I've broken in half a hundred in my time—that's the way I look at it, that I broke them in. But most men are smart enough to realize that out here it's learn or die. Most of 'em have learned. Mr. Cambury, now, he's sharp as a tack, and eager to learn. Of course, his thoughts aren't always with us."

Matt smiled. Tad Cambury was expecting his bride-to-be in a matter of days, and the young second lieutenant was understandably distracted.

"And I expect this Mr. Fairchild will be the same. An army brat, Point man. His father's a great friend of the captain."

Four Eyes Bradshaw was waving excitedly to Ben from the orderly room, and Cohen excused himself with a few muttered phrases about clerk-soldiers.

Matt watched him go and then turned toward his own quarters. If Cohen had inspection on his mind, Matt was even more engrossed in his own problem.

Oklahoma.

He wondered if someone had already informed Dancing Horse that his people were being taken to the Indian Nation, or if they had left that chore for Matt as well. He knew how the Cheyenne chief was going to take it; he knew there would be resentment and more than a little anger.

He supposed it was a sort of compliment that Captain Conway had chosen him for this job, and not Taylor or Fitzgerald; but then it was a compliment he could have done without.

With a sigh, Matt went into his quarters and began packing.

The enlisted barracks was bustling with activity when Corporals Wojensky and McBride entered. Malone was busy packing, as was Stretch Dobbs. Holzer was dusting under his bunk, and Rafferty was digging through his trunk.

"They got him," Wojensky announced.

"Got who?" Malone asked, turning, hands on hips. The cigar between his lips was cold.

"Kip Schoendienst. Four Eyes just got the word from regiment."

"From regiment?"

"That's right. A couple of regimental MPs picked him up sitting on a riverbank fifty miles south, holding his head and moaning."

"Christ—regimental MPs. They'll have to court-martial him, won't they, Wojensky?"

"I do believe so," Wojensky said with a shake of his head.

"Damned fool," Reb said.

"What happened?" Private Trueblood was new to the post and had missed out on the episode.

McBride shrugged. "It wasn't much. It happened in town three nights ago. We had a few drinks and Kip had a few more. All of the sudden he hops up and says, 'Yippee! I'm bound for Texas to herd them longhorn steers.' And off he went."

"You let him go?" Trueblood asked, astonished.

"Hell, I was in no shape to stop him. Besides, how in the hell was anybody to know he was serious? I guess he went out, got on his horse, and headed off, singing cowboy songs."

"If he'd straggled in on his own," Malone explained, "or if we'd been able to find the silly son of a bitch, he might've got off with company punishment. Hell, Kip's a good kid. Green, but he's a soldier."

"Regiment has a record of it now," Wojensky said. "The captain'll have to court-martial him, likely."

"He could get ten years. Hard labor!" Trueblood said with a shudder.

"If he's lucky," Malone said soberly.

"What's this about an inspection, Gus?" McBride asked.

"Regimental," Olsen told him. "Best start cleaning up now. Everyone else is."

As he said that, Malone shoved his blankets into his footlocker and padlocked it shut.

"Everybody?" Wojensky asked.

"Not Malone. He's going riding to the Indian Nation."

"To be a cowboy?"

Olsen laughed. "No. You'll find out, I expect, Wo. You volunteered for it while you were gone. Lieutenant Kincaid's leading a party of Cheyenne down."

"Shit!" Wojensky sighed. "Well, maybe it beats standing inspection." He looked at Holzer, who was flicking the dust from his spare boots with studious concentration.

"Holzer's going too," Olsen told him.

"Then what in hell's he doing that for? Wolfie!" Wojensky called. When Holzer's head came up, the corporal flipped his hand over, indicating that Holzer should simply dump his gear into the locker.

"Inspection!" Holzer called back with a smile. Then he continued with what he was doing.

"Who else is going?" Wojensky wanted to know.

"You, Malone, Dobbs, Holzer, and Rafferty, as of now. Not you, Red—Kincaid's hoping nothing comes up that he'll need a bugler for. And what would we do without sweet reveille?"

"Suits me." McBride shrugged. "I get homesick far from Number Nine."

"I thought you were breaking somebody in on that damned horn," Malone said.

"I was." Reb glanced up. "Kip Schoendienst."

The stagecoach rolled on after changing teams at Carmody Wells. Dust streamed out behind the stage, a long, yellowish plume that drifted for half a mile and more across the dry grass plains. The road was dry, and Gus McCrae worked his six horses, making good time. He had only two passengers, both originating at Fort Laramie. They sat facing each other now, one a young man in the uniform of a second lieutenant, the other a frosty-eyed young woman named Pamela Drake.

"Will we make it today, then?" Pamela asked. She held tightly on to the leather strap on the wall of the coach, grimacing with each jolt.

"We should." John Fairchild smiled and once again measured Pamela Drake. He found her worth the measuring. Tall, elegantly dressed in green silk and white lace, with eyes of an extraordinary deep green, her hair was auburn, swept back, and hung with ringlets. Her lips were full and there was a subtle, mocking sensuality to them.

Pamela Drake returned Fairchild's glance for a moment, then turned her eyes to the empty, unbroken land outside. The long grass was flattened by the gusting wind. Far in the distance, Pamela saw a low knoll where a bedraggled, half-dead oak stood. Except for that, the land was as flat as the sea, and as interminable.

"It's a dreadful place, isn't it?"

She looked at Second Lieutenant Fairchild once again. He nodded. A young man of twenty-one, he had closely cropped blond hair that curled against his scalp, and a mustache that hovered over a slightly cynical mouth.

"It's a springboard," Fairchild commented.

"I beg your pardon?"

"Simply a place to be gotten through, Miss Drake. May I call you Pamela?" She smiled and nodded. He went on, "For myself I see Wyoming as an opportunity to begin carving out my career. I have a leg up out here," he said with a wink.

"A leg up?"

"Pull, that is." Fairchild shrugged and glanced away. "My old man soldiered with Captain Conway."

"Oh. Is that the way careers are carved out in the army, Lieutenant Fairchild?"

"It's the way they're carved out everywhere, Pamela," he said, leaning far forward, looking steadfastly into those deep green eyes.

"Yes, I suppose so, Lieutenant—"

"Look here, I can't properly go on calling you Pamela if you're going to insist on calling me Lieutenant Fairchild. John, please!"

"All right—John." She smiled and glanced demurely down at the floorboard of the Concord stage. The coach hit another pothole and Pamela was jolted from the seat. She collided with John Fairchild, and his arms went around her.

He picked her up carefully, his hands staying on her waist moments longer than necessary. "Thank you," she said breathlessly, straightening her hat.

"Can't you slow down a little?" Fairchild called out the window, but the coach kept on at the same frantic pace; it was doubtful that McCrae even heard the shout.

"That's all right." Pamela smiled faintly. "I suppose I must get used to all this. After Tad and I are married, we will spend a lot of years on the plains, I expect."

"I expect so." Fairchild was silent, looking out the window. "Not much of a get-around for a woman, is it?"

"I'm sure I don't expect more, as long as I'm with my husband-to-be."

"No, of course no."

She found herself suddenly fascinated by John Fairchild's hands. The sunlight streamed through the window and illuminated the golden hairs on his freckled knuckles. She caught his gaze on her, and started as if he had poked her.

"I'm sure I don't know what's the matter with me." Pamela patted her curls.

"It's the long ride, the unfamiliar surroundings," he said comfortingly. Yet the gleam in his eyes was hardly comforting. She knew it for what it was; Pamela Drake was used to having men look at her hungrily.

She turned her head away. What *was* getting into her? A bride's nervousness, she supposed. Alone in a strange land . . . what was she doing here! She closed here eyes tightly. The stagecoach rumbled on.

"All ready then, Matt?" Lieutenant Tad Cambury asked.

"I'm packed," Matt answered. "Ready? I hope so. That's a long trail down to the Nation."

Cambury himself was riding out. He and Fitzgerald were riding night patrols now. There had been some renegade problems on the western perimeter and Conway wanted to make sure the Indians saw blue day and night. Often that was enough to discourage them. So far there had been little real trouble; apparently it was only a few young bucks who had jumped the agency, trying to prove their manhood in the old way. A few cattle had been stolen, a barn burned, but the settlers were demanding patrols, and Conway was forced to oblige them.

Cambury stood at the window, staring off toward the outpost's main gate. Matt Kincaid had picked up his bedroll and his Springfield rifle.

"It doesn't roll in until six o'clock at the earliest," Matt said teasingly.

"I wasn't..." Cambury blushed. "I guess I'm a bit anxious."

"Who wouldn't be?" Matt rested a hand on the second lieutenant's shoulder. "I'm only sorry I won't be here for the ceremony."

"I wish you could be. I wanted you to be my best man, Matt. You've been terrific to me. All of you—the captain, Taylor, Fitzgerald. You've made it easy for me. And I know Pamela will love it out here, with all of you to make her feel welcome."

"She will be welcome, Tad, believe me. The captain's lady is looking forward to meeting her. Maggie Cohen has already planned some decorations for your new quarters."

Matt stuck out his hand and Cambury took it with both of his own. His open, ruddy face was thoughtful and happy at once.

"I'll be seeing you real soon, Tad. You'll have me to dinner?"

"The night you return. It's a promise," Tad Cambury said. He walked out onto the boardwalk, into the intense sunlight with Matt Kincaid, watching the flag that fluttered weakly on the pole at the center of the parade.

Corporal Wojensky had led Matt's horse over to them, and Cambury watched as Matt tied on his roll, slung his saddlebags over the bay's haunches, and swung up.

"Don't forgct," Matt said. "Dinner."

"It's a promise," Tad Cambury said with a grin. Then he watched as Matt Kincaid trailed out, leading his platoon eastward, toward Pine Ridge.

Cambury stood there a minute longer, watching the dust settle, listening to the sounds of the camp. She *would* like it. He had promised Pamela that, and he would see to it. What he had told Matt was true; having friends like Kincaid and Taylor would make it easy for Pamela to fall into the routine of army life.

He thought of her face, trying to picture it perfectly. Here eyes he could recall vividly, and those alive, incredible lips. The rest somehow faded in memory...no matter, she would be here tonight, tomorrow at the latest, and the chaplain would ride over from Regiment. She would be his wife and they would be happy out here.

He turned back toward the quarters, started to whistle dryly, and broke off, finding his lips dry, his throat tight.

Inside, Cambury began readying himself for the night patrol. He found himself worrying about nothing in particular. It's only a groom's nervousness, he told himself.

She *will* be happy here.